EDWARD MATHIS

LITTLE MAN BLUES

TOR

This is a work of fiction. All the characters and events portrayed in this book are fictional, and any resemblance to real people or incidents is purely coincidental.

LITTLE MAN BLUES

Copyright © 1987 by Edward Mathis

First printing: January 1988

A TOR Book

Published by Tom Doherty Associates, Inc.
49 West 24th Street
New York, NY 10010

ISBN: 0-312-93052-6

Library of Congress Catalog Card Number: 87-50876

Printed in the United States of America

10   9   8   7   6   5   4   3   2   1

This one is for Bonnie and Janet

Chapter One

It was raining in Merriweather, Texas. A cold persistent drizzle, clouds smothering the earth, dense and sullen above the subaqueous glow of Fort Worth smoldering ten miles to the west. Dampness invaded everything, the penumbral darkness itself laden with seeping moisture that slicked the skin and chilled to the bone. Oppressive, relentless, it sapped the spirit and stirred vague ancestral memories, bringing uneasiness to the strong, apprehension to the timid.

For three days the skies had been leaking, monotonously and dully, the kind of slow droning rain that farmers love and city dwellers find intolerable, a pervasive chilling wetness that disrupts quotidian existence, frays nerves, brings disproportionate anxiety to even the most insignificant conflict.

And, as a city dweller riddled with conflict, the man behind the wheel of the gray Ford van was no exception to the rule. Hunched miserably, dark eyes clouded with anxiety, a sheen of perspiration glistened on his brow and upper lip despite the cold wet November air streaming through the vented window. Conversely, his hands on the glazed surface of the wheel were cold and clammy, curled like talons, white-knuckled and cramped with the intensity of his grip. Without taking his eyes from the dark glistening highway, he leaned forward to adjust the rearview mirror, only vaguely aware of the muted, dissonant sounds coming from the radio.

"I don't know, Duke," he said huskily, moving the mirror until the tapered face was dimly reflected, thick eyebrows bunched and knotted in typical indecision, mouth curved downward in a petulant grimace. "I—I'm not sure I can go through with this by myself."

"Yes, you can!" The voice in his ear was low and warm and sibilant, somehow both reassuring and intimidating. "Of course you can. Opening-night jitters. Once you get into it, you'll see, everything will smooth out. Come on, Rocky, it's not like you were a rookie. So it's been a while. So what? It had been for me, too. I didn't have any trouble." Duke's voice swelled, thickened perceptibly. "Quite the contrary, as a matter of fact."

"If you liked it so damned much, why don't you handle this one? Why drag me into it?" Rocky turned the wipers up a notch against the steadily increasing drizzle, thumbing his red-rimmed eyes fitfully as the windshield smeared, appeared suddenly to fog.

"I explained that to you," Duke said patiently. "I only swing with women. You know I can't do what has to be done here. Besides, it's your ass as much as mine if Kerry gets caught. This Saltzman kid could link him to the Keller girl. If he goes down, he'll take me and you with him, you know."

"To hell with him," Rocky said viciously. He swung the van into the right lane as he saw the Gladman Road exit coming up. "Let him clean up his own damn messes."

"I agree. But that doesn't alter the fact that we have to protect him to protect ourselves. That's the way it is. If I've learned one thing in forty years, it's that the man in charge never walks close enough to his own shit to smell it. Not when he's got people like me and you to scrape it up and bury it for him."

"He's no damned better than we are."

"Absolutely. But the fact remains that he's still in charge. That's what counts."

Rocky eased the van around the corner onto Gladman Road, a narrow blacktop street arrowing wetly toward the distant glow of downtown Merriweather; wide-spaced, well-kept homes slipped by them in the darkness, slabs of yellow-gold light falling from their windows. He felt momentarily disoriented, febrile, vulnerable.

He drove in silence for a while, the only sounds the susurrus of tires on wet pavement, the dull thumping of the wipers at the ends of their arcs, the subdued drumbeat of the rock music. He felt a tightness across the muscles of his chest, a queasy hollowness in his stomach, his mind curiously empty, a deathly stillness inside that allowed him to hear the muffled echo of his heart, the rush of blood through constricted veins.

"It'll be all right, babe." Duke's voice was a low soft murmur, soothing. "You'll see. I was the same way with the girl. But once I started . . . once I was committed . . ." His voice broke, grew stronger, more vibrant. "It was such a . . . rush. Such a . . . Just like Houston . . . just like Chicago . . ." He trailed off into a throaty muffled sound that could have been a chuckle. "Almost . . . like . . . Oldfield."

"I don't know . . . I don't remember Oldfield," Rocky said through tight lips.

"Bullshit!" Duke began a derisive laugh, then cut it off abruptly. "All right, Rock. If you say so. We were pretty young then."

"I don't remember," Rocky repeated firmly. He fumbled in his jacket pocket for a cigarette, pushed in the dashboard lighter. He glanced defiantly at the face in the mirror.

"Do you have to smoke?"

"No, I don't have to, but I'm going to." He lit the cigarette, blew a puff of smoke over his shoulder. He stared into the spray of water attacking his headlights and hummed under his breath.

"Just don't smoke in there." Duke hesitated. "You sure you have everything?"

"You watched me pack it."

"The gun?"

"Yes."

"The bag, the blue bag with the drawstring?"

"Aw, shit, Duke."

"Do you have it?"

"Yes, dammit!"

"The plunger?"

"Yeah, but I think that's sick."

"The hairs. Don't forget the hairs. That's very important."

"Yeah, I have the damned things. I have *every* damned thing."

"I know you do," Duke said complacently. "I just wanted to remind you what to do . . . that everything was there for a purpose."

"I'm not stupid, brother," Rocky said coldly. "I know what you want done. I just don't see the reason for it, is all." He slowed for a curve and then slowed again as he saw the Merriweather city limits sign.

"The next lane on your right," Duke advised needlessly.

"I know where it is." He slowed even more, blinded by the bright lights of an oncoming car. "Son of a bitch!" He flicked the dimmer. The approaching car was almost even with them before its lights dropped to low beam. Rocky braked sharply and turned onto crushed white rock. He turned off the headlights. He took a last drag from the cigarette and started to toss it out the window.

"No," Duke said sharply. "From here on we leave nothing behind except what we want left behind. Put it in the ashtray."

Rocky made a disgusted hawking sound but did as he was instructed. "Are you sure he's going to be alone?" He wiped a film of fog from the inside of the window and stared at the dim outline of the house thirty yards from the street. "What if his family's there?" He lifted his foot off the brake and the van eased forward.

"They won't be. Tuesday nights they play bridge. They drop the girl off at her friend's house. Come hell or high water, every Tuesday night."

The house began to take shape through the rain, which had degenerated into a blowing mist. Large, dark, and imposing, a two-storied brick veneer with crisp clean lines, gleaming white trim, and two dormers embedded in a steeply pitched cedar shake

4

roof, the house was a quiet advertisement for comfortable middle-class affluence.

The crunch of rubber on gravel resounded loudly inside the van as it eased to a stop a few feet behind a small yellow sports car. A single light gleamed dully behind heavy draperies in an upstairs window. Rocky stared up at the rectangular slab of illumination in fascination, his mouth suddenly dry.

"Put on your gloves." Duke spoke barely above a whisper. "Better not take them off at all, but if you just *have* to touch him, be sure to wipe him down after. They have ways of picking up prints from almost anything nowadays."

Rocky jerked his head angrily. "Why would I have to touch him?"

Duke said nothing for a moment, then coughed lightly. "You know what I mean."

Rocky began an angry retort that broke off as the light in the upstairs window went out. The house suddenly looked larger, more ominous.

"Better go," Duke said. "He's going to bed." He paused. "Just do what I told you. Tell him it's an emergency. Have your ID ready. It always works like a charm. Get his hands secure first. Then the bag and the plunger. The hairs, don't forget the hairs. Don't use the gun unless you need it for control."

"Goddammit," Rocky hissed, "I know what to do." He worked his fingers into the skin-tight elastic gloves. He opened the van door and climbed out. He clicked the door shut quietly. He turned without a backward glance and walked quickly toward the big house, the briefcase gripped tightly in his left hand, his heart gently pounding, his throat dry, excitement pulsing through him with an intense steady beat. By the time he reached the door, he was humming softly under his breath.

Rocky leaped into the van. He threw the briefcase onto the motor cover and flipped the switch in one quick, jerky motion. The motor caught and seconds later crushed gravel peppered the underbelly of the van as he careened down the lane.

"Easy," Duke cautioned. "Not too fast. We don't want to attract attention."

"Jesus!" Rocky hunched forward, both hands on the wheel, his face a taut white mask. He swallowed convulsively, ran his tongue across his lips. "The girl was there! Sick in bed with the flu or something. I did . . . I did her, too."

At the end of the lane he slowed almost imperceptibly, then gunned the motor and lurched into Gladman Road. Too fast. The rear wheels lost traction, slipped sideways. Rocky cursed and fought the wheel, turning into the skid. The van rolled sickeningly, spewed a plume of rock and mud as the left rear wheel dropped off the pavement. The van fishtailed, sliding toward the ditch. He spun the wheel again, felt the jolting lurch as the power wheel caught the edge of the pavement, clawed back onto the glistening black surface.

"Damn! That's all we need, to get stuck in a ditch in front of the goddamned house!"

Rocky's raucous laugh carried a tinge of hysteria. "Not to worry, little brother, Rocky's got everything in hand." He punched the dash lighter and fumbled in his pocket for a cigarette. The elastic gloves gleamed starkly white, slick and formless and unearthly in the dim glow from the dashboard.

"Well?" Duke paused, then after a moment went on irritably. "You going to tell me about it or not?"

Rocky laughed again, sucked deeply on the cigarette. Words spewed from his mouth in a cloud of smoke. "Like I said, the girl was there. She stuck her head out of her room when we went down the hall. Like to scared the shit out of me. I grabbed her, made her go along to his room. I tied her up . . . made her watch me do him." His voice slowed, thickened. "Jesus . . . I'd forgotten . . . almost . . ."

"You should have called me up," Duke said, his tone betraying annoyance on the verge of anger. "Two of them like that. That was dangerous, Rock."

Rocky flipped his right hand in disdain. "No sweat, man. I handled it, didn't I? Besides, you said it was all mine. Don't go accusing me of being selfish. I asked you—"

"The girl? How did you do her?"

Rocky's head wagged gently from side to side. "I stripped her . . . tied her to a chair. After . . . after I finished him, I used the extra bag on her."

Duke laughed. "Right on, man. You brought everything out, the shorts, the rope, the gun?"

Rocky nodded and swung the van into the left-turn lane under the freeway overpass. He waited for several oncoming cars to pass, then drove into the on ramp. He took a last drag from the cigarette and threw the butt out the window. He rolled up the window and waited until they were on the freeway.

"You lied to me, Duke," he said calmly. "The boy didn't know the Keller girl. He didn't even know Kerry. You didn't do that girl for him, you did her for yourself."

"Yes. Are you mad?"

"You did it to get me back into it, didn't you?"

"Yes, but not entirely. The Keller bitch was pregnant and all set to blow the whistle on Kerry. I had to step in and take over, as usual. Are you mad?"

"No. At least, not right now. I may be later. Right now I'm too high to get mad at much of anything. You're a son of a bitch, though." He flipped the wipers to high, moving out and around a hurricane of swirling spray behind an eighteen-wheeler.

Duke laughed delightedly. "Granted. On a scale of one to ten, how was it?"

Rocky shrugged, fingers drumming the wheel. "Seven . . . maybe an eight."

7

"Christ! What do you want? You had two, one of each."

"I know, but it was too . . . quick . . . and dry."

"Okay," Duke said soberly. "The next one will be better—I promise. The next one we'll do together. Nothing real fancy, just something to blow their minds a little. The same, only a little something extra each time."

"What about Kerry? I think he was close to figuring things out in Chicago."

"He's a nerd. All he's got is money. He's a damned ostrich. He goes around with his head up his ass half the time. Don't worry about him. He's never come close to the truth before, he's not likely to start now." He made a liquid hawking sound of disgust. "If he did, he'd turn tail and run like a bunny."

"He's smart, though. Don't underestimate him, Duke. Ain't no telling what he might do. He can be a little crazy sometimes."

Duke was silent for a moment. "Naw. I'm not worried. He's got too much to lose himself. There's the kids . . . and that high-toned ex-wife of his. Not to mention his precious career." His voice tightened. "Remember how it used to be? In the beginning, right after we did the Red Witch and . . . and the others? We were all together then, man. All for one, one for all. But he got too big for us, too damn high and mighty and self-righteous. I saw it coming even if you didn't. I wasn't surprised, man. I watched him all the time. And you didn't. You didn't give a damn—" His voice choked off, faded into a sibilant sigh.

Rocky shrugged, his tone still reflecting doubt. "I hope you're right about him being too much of a coward."

"Sure I am." Duke made a smacking sound, a mercurial change in mood. "You still up?"

Rocky nodded languidly. "I'm coming down. Man, I feel loose . . . and free. . . . I can't believe it was like this before. I don't remember it feeling like this before." He grinned loosely and thumped his palm on the wheel. "Man, I *feel* good!" He wet his lips. "I—she reminded . . . she reminded me of the Red Witch. She had that same kind of copper-colored hair. You know, tight and curly—"

"I thought you didn't remember Oldfield," Duke said slyly.

"I don't . . . I mean, I do, but—" He broke off and clicked his tongue angrily. "I didn't do anything," he went on sullenly. "I just watched."

"Not me," Duke said gaily. "I was with him every step of the way. Without me, he couldn't have gone through with it."

Rocky hunched his shoulders and retreated into silence, the joyous feeling trying to slip away. He felt a sullen rush of anger at Duke's lack of understanding, his callous disregard for feelings. He punched savagely at the cigarette lighter on the dash, ignoring his waiting brother, shutting him out, fighting to recapture the exquisite moment of bliss when the Red Witch's eyes began to—no, no, the Saltzman girl's eyes—began to grow wide with terror, bulging at him through the shining transparency of the blue bag. . . .

Duke chuckled, breaching the growing hiatus with his usual insensitivity. "It's been a long time, babe. Too long. Too long without the power. . . . The power is the thing, man."

Rocky concentrated on the slapping wipers and tried to ignore the low soft voice, the seductive voice of reason.

"Just like being on smack, man. You may kick it, but you never lose the taste for it, never lose the craving. We've been too long between hits, babe, we've gotta make up for lost time."

"Sure. When?" Rocky gave up without a murmur, the crooning words bringing mind images that flooded his being with a wild, coursing joy.

"Four days. We have to give them a pattern, something they can figure out. Makes them feel good. Makes them think they're accomplishing something. They won't have shit. I got it all laid out, brother."

9

"Who? Do you know who yet?"

"One for each of us. Man and wife, nineteen and seventeen. Both students."

Rocky yawned. "Sounds good. I'll leave the planning to you. I'm an action man, myself."

Duke laughed. "You do that, babe, you just do that."

"Jesus, I'm hungry," Rocky said, and yawned again.

Chapter Two

❊❊❊❊❊❊❊❊❊

The wide-body jumbo jet ferrying Detective Sergeant Hamilton Pope home from his vacation in Los Angeles touched down at DFW Airport at exactly 6:08 PM, precisely two minutes ahead of schedule. Weak-kneed and loose-boweled, he picked his way impatiently through the crowd of fellow travelers and the artificial smiles of harried airline personnel. Luggage retrieval and waiting in line for a taxi consumed the better part of an hour, and it was almost eight o'clock by the time the blue and white cab deposited him in front of his small, three-bedroom frame in Merriweather, Texas.

He went up the walk listening to the ominous rumbling of his stomach, wondering how long it would take to recuperate from a ten-day barrage of all-American junk food.

Junk food and junk music, he thought glumly, no wonder we're becoming a nation of manic-depressives: replacing good, solid food with chemical additives on the one hand, substituting maniacal special effects, volume, and visual gymnastics for good, solid music on the other.

Inside, he hung his coat in the entry closet and carried the large battered suitcase into the bedroom. He began to unpack. Swiftly, methodically, the movements of a man who has long ago come to grips with his aloneness, with the knowledge that there is no longer anyone following behind to retrieve that which he carelessly misplaces.

Slightly taller than average height, thick in body, tightly

coordinated, he projected an impression of implacability, grim resolve, traits not at all unsuited to his profession. His face, touched lightly by his forty-five years, was broad and unlined with ruddy, close-grained skin. His nose was large and straight above a generous mouth that could curl in contemptuous disdain or curve in genuine empathy with equal facility. It was a formidable face, dignified and stern. But only if one avoided the eyes. The eyes betrayed him. Blue, the sky blue of a cloudless day, they twinkled, gleamed, and sparkled with an indomitable glee that had nothing to do with his state of mind. At times he found this ludicrous combination of a forbidding visage and guileless, benevolent eyes counterproductive and irritating, and as a result he had developed a habit of conducting the more serious aspects of his business with his eyes narrowed to tiny slits. The change was startling—and effective.

His hair was thick and black, deeply waved, striations of gray streaking the temples and the earlobe-length sideburns that were a grudging concession to the times.

He stowed the empty suitcase on the top shelf in the closet, then shuffled wearily back down the hallway. He was going through the door into the den when the phone began ringing.

He stared at it for a moment in indecision. It rang again, and again, each intrusive peal more imperiously demanding than the last.

Might be the kids, he thought, checking to see if I got home okay. He sighed and picked up the receiver.

"Hello."

"Hey!" The voice was startled. Then again, "Hey! I didn't expect to get an answer."

Pope grunted. "You spend a lot of time calling numbers you don't expect to answer?"

Merriweather Police Captain Roscoe Tanner laughed. "Well, I see your two-week vacation hasn't improved your disposition any."

"Ten days. I still have three days to go."

"What? Yeah, well, that's so, ain't it? How was your trip, by the way? Alice and the kids doing okay?"

"Fine. Everybody's fine." Pope searched his pockets for a cigarette and came up empty. He dropped wearily into the overstuffed chair by the phone.

"They must be . . . what? Fifteen, thirteen now?"

"Ted's seventeen and Becky's fourteen."

"Jesus, time sure slips away from you, don't it?"

"Not always," Pope said. "Not when you just got off a flying boxcar that scared the hell out of you for twelve hundred miles, not when you're tired and hungry and got diarrhea and your damn cigarettes are in your coat pocket in the closet."

Tanner laughed explosively. "Damn, it's good to have you back, Ham. I haven't been insulted for two weeks."

"Ten days. I still have three days to go." He leaned his head against the back of the chair and closed his eyes.

"Oh, yeah. Well, I guess you didn't have much time out there to be listening to the news or anything?"

"Not any more than I had to. Their news is even more depressing than ours, mostly a matter of body counts."

"Then I guess you don't know about the murders?"

"Murders? Or murder? The *L.A. Times* carried a piece about the girl last week . . . what was her name?"

"Keller. Emily Keller. Trinity High School senior. Seventeen years old. Raped and killed and dumped in a ditch out south of town."

"How killed? The paper didn't say."

"Asphyxiated. The scut used a plastic bag. Smothered her to death. Musta took a while. Bastard wanted to watch her face, I guess."

Pope frowned into the phone. "Watch her face? Not a garbage bag, then? They're opaque."

"Right. It was one of those bags you use with a portable toilet. It was tinted blue, but you can see through it. Enough, anyhow."

"Okay. You said murders?"

"Right. Two nights ago . . . Tuesday night. Donald Saltzman and his sister, Verna. He's twenty, she's nineteen . . . was. Killed in their own house. Both raped and asphyxiated."

"*Both* raped?"

"Right. Both. At least, that's what it looks like. They found semen in the boy's anus and in the girl's throat. We're assuming it wasn't voluntary sex since they were both tied up." He paused. "The killers—"

"Killers? More than one?"

"Looks like it. The techs came up with some wild hairs at the scene. One stuck to the boy's anus with the Vaseline they used, the other on the bed beside her. A blond and a redhead, looks like."

"Any physical evidence on the Keller girl?"

"No, no evidence of more than one man. I'd cast my vote for two, though. The M.O.'s the same . . . the same blue bag—" He broke off, then continued in a lower voice. "We have one other thing that pretty well cinches a repeater, but we're holding it back from the media, something to weed out the confessors."

"Had many so far?"

"Three on the Keller girl. One jerk came all the way up from Houston. One so far on the Saltzman killings, but it was just some nut from Dallas. The media're beginning to make noises about the possibility of a repeater."

"Who's working the case?"

"Well . . . well, Sheldon and Forbes caught the Keller girl, and they're working the Saltzmans also. Cal Stevens is helping out, and . . . well, I had to put Lew Quinn in charge—"

"Aw, hell, Roscoe!"

"Just technically," Tanner said hurriedly. "I've got him coordinating mostly. Hell, Ham, with you gone and Monroe retiring, I had no damned choice. I had to have a name with a little rank to feed to the media."

"A little rank, hell! He's the rankest asshole I know."

"Aw, Lew's all right. He's just a little—"

"He's *Traffic,* for Christ's sake! He wouldn't recognize homicide evidence if it leaped up and bit him on the nose."

Tanner laughed feebly, then cleared his throat. "Well, what do you say? You want to turn back the last day of your vacation, come on in in the morning?"

"I make it three."

"Two days is weekend. Okay, we'll compromise. You get two days' credit."

"Lew Quinn is out?"

"Okay. You're in charge."

"Who do I get?"

"Well . . . Sheldon or Forbes, either one, I reckon. I really need them in Robbery, but—"

"How about Sheldon *and* Forbes?"

"No can do. Take your pick. Maybe use the other one for backup, if necessary . . ."

"If necessary? Jesus! Okay, I'll take Bert Sheldon. Are you home or still at the shop?"

Tanner sighed. "I'm still downtown. Why, you coming down tonight?"

Pope barked a derisive laugh. "Not likely. I'm gonna run a hot tub and see if I can't soak out some of this California culture I picked up."

"How was it out there? Where'd you stay? Motel? Hotel?"

"I—uh—well, they had this guesthouse. I stayed there mostly."

"Guesthouse, huh? I take it Alice found her a live one."

"If you mean rich, yes."

"Kinda bad time to visit the kids, isn't it? Weren't they in school?"

"No, not really. The thing is . . . well, he's getting transferred to London. They're leaving next week. Maybe permanently. I

15

didn't think I could afford many trips to London on a cop's pay. Thought I'd better spend some time with them while I had the chance."

"I'm sorry, Ham," Tanner said awkwardly. "I know what . . . hell, I'm just sorry."

"Yeah. So am I. Maybe it's just as well. At least I won't have to feel guilty for not going to see them. And Alice promised they'd send them to spend the usual two weeks with me next summer."

"Hey, that's great."

"Not so great. We're strangers, Roscoe. Polite strangers who bore each other silly. Talk about generation gap, my kids and me have a canyon between us and no way to get across. I know, I just spent ten days trying. That's why I left early. It was either that or do something sad and desperate, like breaking down and blubbering. I'm just the guy they used to live with a long time ago—back when they were poor."

Tanner chuckled uneasily. "Kids. What can you do?"

Pope was suddenly aware of the other man's discomfort. "Yeah. Well, what the hell." He rubbed his hand across the back of his head and got to his feet. He wished he had a cigarette. "Roscoe. Do you have anything concrete at all yet?"

"The two hairs at the Saltzmans', a tire track across the road that may or may not be from the killer's car, the nylon cord used to tie the girl's hands, the bags, and the plungers."

"Plungers?"

"Plumber's Helper, I think they're called. Twelve inches long. The Keller girl and the Saltzman girl both had one inserted in their vaginas, the Saltzman boy had one in his anus. That's what we're holding back."

"Weird. Anything else?"

"Semen analysis from all three bodies gives us O positive blood."

"Great. That's a big help. That narrows it down to about eighty percent of the male population. No prints?"

"None. They wore some kind of rubber gloves, probably surgical type, according to the lab. The plungers were brand-spanking new, wiped clean. They found some smudges from the gloves on the suction cup, slick and smooth."

"Bags clean, I suppose."

"Slick as a whistle. Fisher loaned me a couple of men and Lew put them to checking the bags and plungers, but there are just too many damn outlets. Probably two hundred in Dallas alone, triple that in the entire Metroplex area."

"What it comes down to is we don't have anything, then?"

"Well, we've got the hairs."

"These hairs you're so proud of, do they have follicles?"

There was a moment of silence, and Pope could hear the big man breathing, a rasping smoker's wheeze at the end of each breath. "Well, you've gone to the heart of it. They were cut . . ."

"Then we don't have shit."

"Now, wait a minute. Willard thinks maybe these guys could have had a haircut lately, had loose hair still—"

"It's passing strange," Pope drawled, "that these two men left one hair each. And in such convenient places, too." He sat back down and pinched the bridge of his nose. His head ached and his eyes burned, and he fervently wished he hadn't answered the phone. The rumblings and hissings in his stomach had reached alarming proportions, and he wanted nothing more right then than to empty his bowels, take a hot bath, and go to bed. In that order.

"Yeah. Well, maybe it's a little too pat, at that."

"Okay, Roscoe. I'll be in in the morning. I have to go now. I think I brought back something besides smoggy lungs from L.A."

"What's that?"

"Montezuma's revenge. I think it's crossed the border."

"Well, I hope it ain't catching. See you tomorrow, Ham."

Pope got his cigarettes out of his coat and went into the bathroom. He sat on the commode and awaited developments, his head in his hands, a cigarette dangling from the corner of his mouth, his mind reluctantly reviewing what Roscoe Tanner had told him.

Murders—blue bags, plungers, sodomy, and rape. Craziness. Madness on the loose again. He shivered, feeling a swell of revulsion, a slow creeping chill of fear, a sinking feeling of helpless resignation.

He was no stranger to madness, to the perversions and incomprehensible twists the human mind could take when trapped in its unrelenting grip. He had lived with it throughout most of his childhood, accepting it as reality in much the same way a wolf cub accepts the harsh disciplines of its clan.

His father had died when he was three, replaced two years later by a man ten years older than his mother, a strict disciplinarian, a brutal, sadistic man who demanded instant obedience, the total subjugation of his small family, which was never quite enough to prevent the laying on of hands. A weekend drunkard, he enjoyed using his fists, occasionally the steel-capped toes of his logging boots.

Pope's mother had slowly withdrawn, escaping to her plaster saints with the sorrowful eyes and bleeding hearts, becoming, in her own subdued way, as fanatical as her husband, wielding the sword of eternal fire and damnation with Messianic fervor, constantly cataloguing the small boy's failings, eventually blaming him for the lunatic behavior of the man she had chosen as a mate. She often threatened suicide, threatened to kill them all with the purifying fire of God's avenging sword.

When he was twelve, he had watched his stepfather beat his mother to death in a drunken rage. Petrified with horror, unable to move, he had watched the demented man go about the methodical destruction of his mother and, somehow, in some bizarre way, had become aware that this strange man he had never understood was killing his own mother, the mother who had not wanted him, who had conceived him out of wedlock and left him to the tender mercies of institutional care. . . .

18

It was only when the mad, bloodshot eyes were raised to his that the spell had been broken, and he had fled into the pine forest behind the small clapboard house in East Texas, pursued by nothing more than his own imagined demons, spurred on by the flickering images of madness that chuckled and cavorted inside his head.

He had been taken in by his mother's brother and his wife, a middle-aged, childless couple who lived in Houston and exposed him for the first time in his life to the strange, wonderful world of normalcy, the give and take of caring relationships. They taught him how to feel good about himself, that he was not an inferior being forever destined for perdition. He began to understand the feelings he had had for his mother, his stepfather. He began to understand them, that his stepfather had been a psychotic, that his mother had eventually become a manic-depressive.

But it was years before he learned what his seven years of torment, his proximity to madness had taught him, given him.

A special talent, was what they had called it in Houston after the solution of the Call Girl Murders, a two-year string of eighteen prostitute killings, mutilations, and dismemberment, messages from the killer that made no sense, a plethora of physical evidence that led nowhere, meant nothing.

Pope had been assigned to the case at the beginning of its third year, a rookie detective with less than a year in Homicide, only one of more than a hundred detectives who had worked on the case. As the newest member, he had been given the job of keeping track of the paperwork, the tips that flooded the task force after each killing, the reports—lab, medical, investigators', forensic—and the letters from the killer that inevitably followed each slaying, the letters the other detectives found revolting and incomprehensible, the mutterings of a madman.

However revolting, they were not incomprehensible to Pope. Somewhere deep inside him they had stirred something long dormant, plucked a responsive chord, and he had gone back and read them all from the beginning, allowing the words to transcend their inherent incoherence, absorbing by some magic osmosis the torment of the killer, his obsessive need to destroy, his desire for death, recognizing in some inexplicable way the same savage compulsion he had seen in his stepfather as he killed his mother.

Ultimately, he knew beyond a doubt that the killer hated his mother with a deadly, consuming hatred, and thought it quite possible that he had already killed his mother in perhaps the same way he was killing the whores. He just *knew* it. He didn't know how.

With that in mind, he began poring over the long list of suspects, men who had been interrogated with inconclusive results, going from there to men whose mothers were dead, and again from there to men whose mothers had died under suspicious circumstances.

He narrowed the list of suspects to five.

Armed with new knowledge, a new direction, he had deserted his post at the paperwork desk and begun his own series of interviews.

He arrested the second man he talked to for the murders, a thin, pallid young man of twenty-five, the night manager of a pizza parlor located almost exactly in the geographical center of the various apartment buildings where the murders had taken place.

Afterward, he liked to think that the arrest had been the result of good detective work on his part; he'd played down in his own mind the electrifying, indisputable fact that he had *known* the instant he looked into the gold-flecked hazel eyes, refused to acknowledge the even more terrifying fact that the killer had *known* that he knew at that same instant and had made it almost embarrassingly easy for Pope to break through the young man's tissue of alibis.

His superiors had called it a special talent; some had called it a knack; some called it luck. Pope had no idea what to call it. It had gained him notoriety and promotion. It had also gained him assignment to every case that came along that had the slightest taint of madness about it. Eventually, he began to look upon it as a curse, useful but destructive.

Five years of that had been enough. Too much. He had left a sergeant's post in Houston and come north to Merriweather and started over. That had been fifteen years ago.

And now he was once again a sergeant in Homicide, once again faced with all the elements of madness loose in the land.

The thought followed him to bed, into his dreams, brought him wide awake at three o'clock in the morning to stare blindly into the darkness, shivering, feverish, in thrall to some terrible awareness that hovered menacingly at the edge of his perception.

Chapter Three

∞∞∞∞∞∞∞∞∞

Hamilton Pope added his four-year-old blue Dodge to the scattering of marked and unmarked police vehicles behind the Merriweather Police Station. Long, low, rectangular, the relatively new building of beige brick and dark mortar created an impression of no-nonsense functionality. Erected during the late energy-conscious seventies, it had few windows and the minimum number of entrances and exits required by law.

He angled across the green buffer zone between the parking lot and the building, only vaguely conscious of the residual queasiness in his stomach. Two rude awakenings in the night had rid him of whatever noxious substances he had smuggled back from California, and after a cautious, sparing breakfast of cornflakes and milk, he felt remarkably good.

Just inside the thick glass doors, in order to avoid passing Lieutenant Lew Quinn's glass-enclosed office, he turned left down a corridor that ran along the inside wall of the building and eventually led him to another glass-fronted office with a dangling overhead sign that read: Homicide.

Three desks, one of them without a chair, a coatrack, an electric typewriter, and two small filing cabinets. Not much. Particularly in view of the fact that two of the desks were never used except by an occasional visitor, a bored secretary, or a fellow detective seeking to dump a few unsolvable break-ins or robberies.

Located in the approximate center of the Dallas-Fort Worth Metroplex, the city of Merriweather was essentially a bedroom community. A university city with homes and apartments and very little industry, a modicum of gasoline stations and service facilities and an astonishing number of supermarkets and convenience stores. Not quite dry, it was possible to buy beer in the supermarkets and mixed drinks in the half dozen or so private clubs within the city limits.

There were few killings in Merriweather, fewer still that could be classified as murder by persons unknown and therefore require the expertise of the police department's Homicide Division —Sergeant Hamilton Pope. It had been a while, and Pope couldn't suppress a faint stir of anticipation as he entered his office. There was nothing like a sensational murder to boost the old ticker, he thought wryly, to get the adrenaline flowing—unless it was more than one sensational murder.

He hung up his suit coat, loosened his tie, and sat down at his desk. He lit his third cigarette of the day and studied the litter on top of his desk, trying to decide if anything had been moved. Satisfied that all was well, he leaned his chair to one side and picked up the phone. He put it down again when he heard the rapid clump of footsteps in the corridor. He laced his fingers behind his head, leaned back, and waited, the cigarette dangling from his mouth, smoke curling lazily past cerulean eyes.

Roscoe Tanner invaded the office. He filled the doorway with his bulk and seemed to shrink the entire room. Towering five inches above Pope's five feet, eleven inches, he was a solid forty pounds heavier. An overweight John Wayne with the same broad features and easy grin, he had deep-set gray eyes and a magnificent Roman nose. Acutely aware that he dwarfed everything and everyone around him, he rarely stood up during a conversation.

"Hey, Ham," he said cheerily. He hooked the extra chair over with his foot and sat down in front of the desk. "Glad to see you, man."

Pope nodded and sat forward in his chair, his eyes on the manila file folders in Tanner's big hand. "Hello, Roscoe. That them?"

Tanner took his cue from his subordinate's solemn face. "That's them, buddy. I just this minute took them away from Lew Quinn. Have to give him his due, everything seems to be up to date." He stopped and grinned. "He squealed some."

"Uh-huh." Pope took the two thin folders and immediately opened the thickest. Deliberately, methodically, he went through it, scanning each item thoroughly, pursing his lips in a soundless whistle when he came to the pictures. Tanner smoked and watched him quietly, marveling at the smaller man's total withdrawal, intense concentration.

The Saltzman folder took less time. Only two days old. A grim tapestry still unfolding. In a short time the two folders would be equal in size, undoubtedly equally frustrating. Pope barely glanced at the Saltzman crime scene photos; what he wanted, had to have, wouldn't be there. He closed the last file and laid them in the center of his desk. He lit a cigarette and stared at Tanner through the smoke.

"I'm coming in with a handicap, Roscoe. A cold trail. I hope you've still got the Saltzman scene sealed."

Tanner nodded. "I thought you might want to see it. They did a good job, Ham. Laid out a grid, vacuumed, brushed, dusted, used them linen booties . . ."

Ham moved his hand impatiently. "I don't doubt it. But how about the intangibles? The first men on the scene—what's their impression? Forbes and Sheldon, were they the first ones at the Saltzmans'?"

"Yeah. Except for the squad car. But they had sense enough to check vital signs and back out without touching anything. Sheldon and Forbes watched the entire operation from the doorway." He made a half-turn in the swivel chair and stubbed his cigarette. "As for impressions? Yeah, we've talked about it. They both lean toward random thrill killings." He scanned Pope's expressionless face. "So do I . . . for what it's worth."

24

"Nothing taken?"

"Nothing at all that the parents know about. The lab found traces of pot in the boy, but nowadays that don't mean a hell of a lot." He sighed and lit another cigarette. "We're checking their friends now—the ones their parents know. But they're both students. They're bound to know a hell of a lot of people their parents don't know about."

"The Keller girl?"

"Same deal. We've spent maybe two hundred man-hours on her so far and come up empty. She goes—went to the same high school as the Saltzman girl. Might be something there. And, by the way, we may be losing that case."

"Losing it? What do you mean, losing it?"

"County. The Chief got a call from Sheriff Bigalow this morning at home. He claims that Gladman Road, the east side anyhow, belongs to County. He may be damn well right. I know the line runs along Gladman for a couple of miles there. Depends on which side of the road we're talking about." He rolled thick shoulders in an expressive shrug. "One less for us to worry about, if it's true. I got the city engineer checking it for us." He rose and stamped his feet as if clearing his shoes of snow. He grinned down at Pope, exposing big white teeth. "Damn new shoes. Burning my feet."

"Where's the physical evidence?"

"I got it in the lockbox in my office. I don't want to trust the property room with this. They're too damn slipshod. You want to see it?"

Pope nodded. "I'll be down in a little while."

Tanner turned toward the door. "If I'm out, Nellie knows the combination."

"Hey," Pope said as the big man filled the doorway.

Tanner's eyebrows lifted quizzically.

"You thirsty a lot?"

25

"Yeah, some." He frowned. "Why?"

"Thirsty, burning feet—first signs of diabetes. Better get your blood sugar checked."

Tanner's brow cleared. "Yeah, Doc, I'll do that," he said, grinning. He disappeared from view, then stuck his broad face back around the jamb. "Hey, Doc, if you're gonna bill me, send it to the city, will you? I get my examinations free."

"Okay, smartass," Pope said mildly. "Don't come crying to me."

When he was alone again, Pope sat upright behind his desk. He placed both hands palms down on the Saltzman file folder. He closed his eyes and tried to clear his mind. He sat for a long time, face composed, motionless, hands pressing tightly downward.

It was an old, familiar routine, one he had tried many times before. It had never worked, and deep down inside him he knew it wasn't going to work this time, either. But he had to try. He had watched it work once, disbelieving, scoffing right up to the shallow gravesite of an eight-year-old murder victim, led there by a female psychic from New Orleans who held an article of the girl's clothing pressed tightly between her palms. He had become an instant believer, and thereafter he had always tried. But, sadly, it just wouldn't work for him. In twenty years, not even once. And again, later, he sat in Tanner's empty office and held the grisly implements of death and degradation in his hands, tried desperately to summon those unknown forces, to absorb by some inexplicable cosmic osmosis the essence of the monsters. And once again, as he had known he would, he failed.

"I'm Deputy Hackmore Wind."

The young man leaned indolently against the doorjamb, booted feet crossed at the ankles. He wore khaki, a sweat-stained cowboy hat, and an extra belt that supported a large-caliber revolver worn low on his right hip.

"Chief Durkin told me to see you about the purloined cadaver.

That is, if you're Hamilton Pope, head honcho here in Homicide."
He was smiling genially, a particularly handsome smile with white,
gleaming teeth under a thick black moustache.

Fully as tall as Roscoe Tanner, his body was spare rather than
beefy, running more to wide shoulders and small hips. Dark-
skinned, finely chiseled features, he wore his black hair a little too
long and was almost too pretty to be a man.

Or so thought Hamilton Pope. He dropped his eyes back to the
contents of the evidence bag, feeling an atavistic stir of dislike.
Any man that handsome had to be an egotistical shitheel.

He nodded curtly. "I'm Pope." He picked up the Emily Keller
file and dropped it on the far edge of his desk, laid the sealed
plastic bag containing the bag, rope, and plunger on top of it.
"Everything we have is here. She's in the morgue. You need any
help loading her in your pickup?"

Wind's brow creased. He blinked slowly, his dark eyes perplexed. "Pickup?"

Pope shrugged without looking up. "Anybody dresses like you
has got to drive a pickup."

Wind moved forward to the chair Tanner had recently vacated.
He laughed easily as he sat down. "Oh, I don't want her, Sarge."
He touched the folder and evidence bag with a tentative finger.
"Matter of fact, I don't want this either. I take it you haven't talked
to Chief Durkin in the last hour or so." He leaned back in the
chair and crossed his legs. He produced a cigar with a plastic tip
and removed the wrapper, dark eyes fixed on Pope, a half-smile
edging his lips.

Pope watched him unblinkingly, making no effort to hide his
annoyance. "I haven't talked to Chief Durkin in a month or so."

Wind nodded sagely. "Know what you mean. I stay away from
my brass, too." He scratched a kitchen match on his boot sole and
held it to the cigar. He continued talking through lusty puffs of
cigar smoke. "Matter of fact, in three years I've only seen Sheriff

Bigalow three, four times. I always manage to be out in the boonies when he makes one of his little inspection tours. Got caught short a couple of times, though. Once I was—"

"That's very interesting, Deputy Wind, but if you don't mind, I'm right in the middle of a murder investigation . . ." He let it trail off suggestively.

"Hey, no problem. You're right. I been sitting here running off at the mouth when we oughta be up and doing." His boots crashed to the tiled floor and he scooted closer to the desk. "What do we need to do first?" He propped his elbows on the desk, clasped his hands, and looked at Pope expectantly.

It was Pope's turn to blink and crease his brow in perplexity. "We?"

Wind snapped his fingers. "Oh, yeah, that's right. They haven't told you yet. Well, it seems our top brass got their heads together and figured this ought to be a mutual effort—you know, you from the city and me representing the county." He gazed at Pope through a column of pale blue cigar smoke, black eyes sparkling cheerfully. "What do you think?"

Hamilton Pope took a deep, shuddering breath. "I think," he said flatly, "they're out of their fucking minds!"

Wind drew up one corner of his mouth in a rueful grimace. "Yeah, that's what I thought at first, too. But, you know, it makes some sense at that. Same guy did both killings, looks like, so I kinda figured if we concentrated on your case and got him, it would automatically clear up mine."

"Look," Pope said evenly, "this has nothing to do with you personally, but I just happen to think—" He broke off, disconcerted by the penetrating eyes. "Look . . . well, just how much experience do you have in Homicide?"

"Not a bit," Wind admitted ruefully. "Like to learn, though. It's gotta be more interesting than setting up speed traps on county roads." He removed his hat and raked a long-fingered hand through thick black hair. "Hell, anything's gotta be more interesting than that." He grinned broadly, disarmingly. "You'd be the head honcho, of course."

Pope drummed his fingers and met the younger man's gaze head-on, half convinced he had detected a note of cynical derision beneath the good-old-boy facade. The dark eyes beamed back at him innocently.

Pope got up and went around the desk. He picked up the Emily Keller folder. "Why don't you look through this? I'll only be gone a minute. Physical evidence is here in this bag. Excuse me." He turned and stalked out of the room.

Hackmore Wind looked after him, grinning. He shook his head and puffed on the cigar. A stuffed-shirt prick, he thought wryly. I oughta tell him to kiss my ass. But everyone says he's good, and if you're ever gonna learn, Hack old buddy, might as well do it from the best. He straightened up in the chair and laid his cigar in the ashtray. He opened the Emily Keller folder.

He had finished Keller and was well into the Saltzman file when Pope returned. Except for a faint blush in his cheeks and a white line around his mouth, he looked the same. He sat down quietly and waited for Wind to finish.

"Okay," he said. "Looks like we're going to be working together." His voice was as noncommittal as his expression. "People generally call me Ham, when it isn't something worse."

Wind nodded and smiled. "Hack," he said.

Pope smiled grudgingly. "Ham and Hack. Sounds like a bad vaudeville act."

"Vaudeville?" Hack asked. "What's that?"

Chapter Four

Fred and Lorna Keller lived in a modest three-bedroom brick in a Merriweather subdivision named Oakwood Trails. Built before skyrocketing energy costs and prior to the time when a wooden roof became synonymous with "firetrap," the house sported an ailing cedar shingle roof and a plenitude of large, single-pane windows. Precision-cropped hedges lined the entire front wall of the home, and stately Italian cypresses stood guard at each corner. Native oaks, elms, and transplanted mulberries provided shade, and a thick spongy carpet of St. Augustine grass covered the front yard.

"Cutworms," said Hack, pointing to an irregular patch of dead grass the size of a small room. "Another one over there. He needs to spray. Shoulda done it back in August, September. May be too late now. Come spring, he'll have them little cutters all over the yard. Be able to roll it up like a rug."

Pope nodded absently and turned into the recessed entryway. He pressed the bell and stepped back to survey the yard.

"Could be a lot of things," he said. "Lack of water is one. None of it looks too good."

"Cutworms," Hack said emphatically, allowing no room for further argument. He folded his long arms and leaned a shoulder against the brick wall and eyed Pope complacently.

Pope's left cheek twitched. "You a horticulturist, are you?"

"Nope," Hack said with a half-smile. "Don't need to be to know cutworms when I see them." The smile escalated into a faintly superior grin.

"You don't see any cutworms," Pope said softly. "All you see is what I see. A patch of dead grass."

"It's the *kind* of dead grass," Hack said, his eyes gleaming. "Recognized it right off. It's all in the curl, the way the grass sorta curls up. The curl and the color."

Pope snorted. "*All* damned dead grass curls sooner or later. You don't know—" He broke off and turned as the door opened behind him. He smiled and took a step forward, and the door closed a fraction. He stepped back.

"I'm Detective Pope, Mrs. Keller. I called you a little while ago."

She nodded silently and stood watching them, a tall woman with meticulously coiffured hair, a lined, passive face. An angular face with a straight sharp nose, a small round mouth and dull brown eyes almost lost in deep dark passages. An attractive face once, Pope thought, perhaps not too long ago. But death and grief, or maybe just life, had taken its toll, left its indelible tracks.

"It would be better," Pope suggested gently, "if we could come inside."

"Yes. Yes, of course. Please come in." Her voice had the soft, liquid rhythms of the South, conjured up images of murky hollows and steep ridges, hardscrabble farms and rabbit stew.

She ushered them down a short hallway and into a large, bright room with paneled walls and overstuffed gold furniture with cushions a foot thick. She made a vague gesture toward an aluminum and leather wet bar almost hidden behind a bank of hanging plants in one corner of the room.

"Could I get you something to drink?"

"No, thank you, Mrs. Keller." Pope sat down on one of the bulbous cushions and felt himself slowly begin to sink. "This shouldn't take long at all. We have just a few questions." He wrestled a small notebook from his hip pocket and produced a pen.

31

"Now," he said, and cleared his throat. "Mrs. Keller. The last thing any of us want to do is cause you further pain, but since Detective Sheldon talked with you and your husband, we have discovered that your daughter was . . . well, are you aware that your daughter was taking drugs, Mrs. Keller?"

She nodded quietly. "Yes. We knew." She looked from him to Hack, then back again.

"You knew? Is there any reason you didn't tell that to Detective Sheldon?"

She gazed at him silently, as if she was considering it, then slowly shook her head. "No. I mean, there was no reason. She had been stopped for . . . at least three months. No, no reason. I suppose neither of us thought of it. I know I didn't."

"You say she had stopped? Are you sure?"

Mrs. Keller nodded slowly and clasped her hands in her lap. "As sure as . . . anyone can ever be. She was being treated. I talked to the doctor not a week before . . . and he was real pleased with her progress." Her eyes dropped to her hands in her lap, then came back to Pope's. "Why? Is there reason to believe she had started up again?"

"No, ma'am. We don't know that she did. It's just that whenever drugs are involved in a death, however remotely, we have to consider the possibility that the drugs somehow relate to that death."

"I see," she said, her voice revealing that she didn't see at all. "But my daughter didn't die of drugs, Mr. Pope."

"No, ma'am, she didn't." He made a few meaningless marks in the notebook to get away from her burning eyes. "You say she was being treated? Was that one of the drug rehabilitation centers or a private clinic?"

She shook her head. "It isn't—wasn't that kind of treatment. Not for the drug itself . . . that's a symptom. She was past that stage. Dr. Webster was treating Emily for the root cause of her . . . problems. Taking the drugs was just part of her . . . acting out, Dr. Webster called it."

"Dr. Webster. Is he here in Merriweather?"

"Yes. I don't know the street address, but he's on the corner of Pierre Boulevard and Pine."

"I know where it is." Hack spoke for the first time. "One of those old houses that was renovated?"

"Yes, that's the one. On the southeast corner, I believe."

"You said Emily was having problems, Mrs. Keller. What kind of problems?"

"The usual teenage problems. Insecurity, rebellion . . . she accused her father and me of not . . . loving her. She ran away for a short time when she was fifteen. I—we, her father and I, are not . . . overly demonstrative, I suppose, but Emily and her father, they were too much alike. Both of them stubborn, willful . . ." She allowed her voice to fade.

"Do you have any idea who might have been supplying your daughter with drugs?"

Her hands fluttered away from her lap, then came back together like small feeding birds momentarily disturbed. "No, no, of course not. I would have reported them to the police if I had known. No, she would never tell me. I assumed it was one of her classmates."

"How long was Emily on drugs, Mrs. Keller?"

"A year—maybe a little longer."

"Do you know what kind?"

"Pills, I think, and what they call speed. When she stopped she was on cocaine . . . and the other one."

"Heroin?"

"Yes, but that wasn't what she called it."

"How about boyfriends, Mrs. Keller?"

Her slim shoulders lifted eloquently. "Which one, Mr. Pope? Emily has had a number of boyfriends since she was fifteen."

"Anything serious?"

33

"Not if you're talking about being engaged. She was always going steady with one boy or another. That was another source of constant friction with her father. He has very definite and rather old-fashioned ideas about morality, I'm afraid."

"How about her current boyfriend?"

"I'm afraid we didn't discuss that subject too often. She was so touchy about her privacy. There was one, however, who called a few times when she was out."

"Do you know his name?"

"Rick. Or Ricky. He never gave his last name."

"Do you know what he looks like, what kind of car he drove?"

She shook her head. "No. He never picked her up here. At least, not when we were home."

Pope tried to lean forward but found himself defeated by the soft cushion. "You seem to be pretty lenient with your daughter, Mrs. Keller." Halfway through the sentence he realized he was using the wrong tense, but he decided not to amend it.

"Emily ran away once, Mr. Pope," she said quietly. "I didn't want to drive her away again." She glanced at Hack and attempted another smile. "There is someone who might know more about her friends. A girl she worked with at the Hamburger Box, Nancy Lessor. They were good friends."

Pope frowned. "I understood your daughter was still in high school."

"Oh, yes, she was. But she had a part-time job at the restaurant. Two evenings a week and weekends." She hesitated. "Emily was a very independent girl. She wanted to earn her own spending money."

Pope nodded and closed the notebook. He placed the pen in his jacket pocket and struggled to his feet. "You said before that Emily was on her way to keep a doctor's appointment that night. That was Dr. Webster?"

"Yes. I called him at home later that night when Emily didn't come home. She never got there . . ." Her voice faltered. "She was so eager to go. She was doing so well . . . 'bleeding bashes,' she called them." Her lips moved crookedly in an ineffectual attempt at a smile. Tears glistened at the corners of her eyes.

" 'Bleeding bashes'?"

"Group therapy. I don't understand it too well. The patients are encouraged to vent their anger and frustration and . . . pain. It sounds awful, but it seemed to be working for Emily."

"Regression therapy," said Hack Wind. "I read a book about it once. Everybody sits around and kinda does their own thing. Whole thing is based on early childhood and the way Mama and Papa—" He broke off abruptly, his dark skin suddenly a little darker. "Regression therapy," he repeated lamely. He studied Pope's frown for a moment. "Makes sense to me," he added, a quick gleam of defiance in his dark eyes.

Pope turned back to the woman. "Thank you, Mrs. Keller, for your help."

She shook her head and rose to her feet. "Not at all. I just wish I could do more, Mr. Pope . . . something that would help you catch this—this monster." She extended a slender, lifeless hand.

"We'll find him," Pope assured her. He grasped her cold hand and quickly relinquished it to Hack, who took it between both of his and pressed firmly.

"We will, Mrs. Keller. You can count on it." He gave her a bright, warm smile.

"Thank you," Mrs. Keller said almost shyly, visibly brightening in the glow of the young man's charm. Her free hand fluttered near her throat and she peeped up at him coquettishly. "I know you will," she said softly.

At the door, Pope snorted, then covered it up by coughing raggedly. A mistake. The fake cough stirred dormant smoker's phlegm and the attack became a real one. He was still coughing when the two men climbed into Hack Wind's black pickup.

"Sounds bad," Hack said. He backed the truck out of the driveway. "You oughta switch to cigars," he added fatuously.

Pope hawked and spat a gummy glob of something into his handkerchief. He closed his eyes so he wouldn't see it. He cleared his throat cautiously. Automatically he reached for a cigarette, then withdrew his empty hand. He looked up and saw Wind's smile and went back into his pocket again. He lit up and inhaled deeply, coughed, and took another deep drag.

"Like falling off a horse," he said hoarsely. "Gotta get right back on."

Hack laughed. He stopped the pickup at the corner and looked inquiringly at his companion. "Where to?"

Pope smoked thoughtfully for a moment. "I reckon we might as well talk to this Dr. Webster. Looks like nobody's been to see him. Maybe he can tell us what the girl's real problems were."

Hack turned right. "You didn't tell her that Emily was back on drugs?" It was more of a question than a statement.

"Don't know that she was. They found traces all right, but that don't mean she was back on them. Maybe she just fell off the wagon. It happens. Or maybe she got them from the killer. Maybe he gave them to her to make her easier to handle. Hell, who knows?" He leaned forward and deposited ash in the truck's ashtray. "Couldn't see no point in adding to her misery," he added morosely. "We find out she was lying, that she knew, we can always go back and lean on her a little."

"Yeah," Hack said dryly, "lean on her a little." He glanced at the square, stocky figure beside him, the grim threat of the aggressive features that was belied by the merry twinkle in the blue eyes. "I sure want to be there for that." He turned back to his driving a click ahead of Pope's slitted eyes and furrowed forehead.

"What does that mean?" Pope asked silkily.

"Nothing," Hack said quickly, deciding on discretion after all. "That's just the kind of thing I need to learn, is all. I never know what to do around women."

Pope stared at him for a second, then burst into derisive laughter. "I noticed."

It was Hack's turn to frown. "And just what the hell is *that* supposed to mean?"

"Nothing," Pope said, and laughed again.

They lapsed into silence. Hamilton Pope stubbed out his cigarette and watched the orderly rows of affluent brick homes gradually give way to not-so-neat rows of smaller frames as the pickup carried them swiftly into an older section of Merriweather. Building codes were not so stringent here, and a number of the small houses had been converted into business establishments over the years: small mom-and-pop grocery stores as well as various types of service-connected facilities.

But with the crossing of Ackermann Boulevard, the east-west dividing line, the commercial enterprises were left behind. Old homes here. Immense; gables and gingerbread and steeply sloping roofs, cupolas and spires and battered old weather vanes. Ramshackle for the most part, dilapidated and badly in need of repair. But here and there a few had been restored to their former splendor, proud and stately amidst giant pecans and towering elms. Antebellum South at its best, and worst.

One of several small farm-oriented towns between Dallas and Fort Worth in the early 1950s, with a population of fewer than six thousand, Merriweather had burgeoned without restraint during the intervening thirty-odd years, apartment buildings and single-family homes intermingling in seemingly haphazard patterns, swelling the population to 82,498 by actual count at the 1980 census.

The original downtown section along Highway 183 no longer existed as such. The ramshackle old buildings had been razed, replaced by flashy glass and brick fast-food restaurants, auto agencies, two neon-encrusted motels. A dozen shopping centers pocked the face of the city, bounded and buttressed by twin shopping malls bookending the eastern and western boundaries of the town. Fifteen minutes by freeway from downtown Fort Worth, twenty-five from Dallas, Merriweather was a place to come home to after a busy day at the aircraft plants in Fort Worth, a bruising day among the wheeler-dealers of Dallas. It was a place to live, not to work, a place to relax and enjoy the fruits of labor, the amenities of the good life in an atmosphere of coexistence and peace. The very old and the very new blending effortlessly in harmony.

Nobody ever killed anybody in Merriweather—well, hardly ever.

Hamilton Pope lit another cigarette and studied his companion's dark features. "Wind. Don't believe I've ever run into that name before. You a Texas boy?"

Hack's face remained expressionless while he considered the unsubtle question. He worked his way around a delivery van double-parked in his lane before answering.

"I reckon you could say that. Wind is short for Windinniquitta. If you haven't guessed, that's an Indian name. That makes me Indian. Part Indian. Actually, I'm a black Mexican Indian honky in about equal parts. My mother was half Irish and half Mexican. My old man was half black and half Indian. Windinniquitta is a little long for general conversation and my pappy decided to shorten it. But that's not the whole reason. With a name like Windinniquitta, everybody's gonna know right off that you ain't white."

Pope stared at the dark, solemn face. He felt a bubble of laughter in his chest, and opened his mouth and let it out in a loud braying peal. Mixed with equal parts of tobacco smoke, the air rushing out of his lungs started him coughing again.

He was still hacking and chuckling, chuckling and hacking when they pulled into the parking lot behind the gleaming yellow five-gabled building that housed the James K. Webster Therapy Center.

Five minutes later they were back on the street again, heading toward police headquarters.

"Doctors and bankers," Pope snorted. "We'll try his home when we get back to the shop."

38

Hack glanced at his watch. "Don't you quit at five?"

Pope pressed his hand against his diaphragm. "Don't make me laugh again, I'm too sore. In Homicide, you work until it gets done."

Hack shifted in the seat and rubbed his chin. "I kinda promised my wife I'd take her out to eat and a movie . . ." He let it trail away.

Pope gave him an amused glance. "I didn't say anything about you, did I?"

"Well," Hack said reasonably, "even you will have to eat and sleep sometime."

"Where is that written down?" Pope asked. "I'd like to see it."

"You can't just keep going," Hack argued. "I know we want to get the bastards as soon as possible, but it's not going to bring back the dead, and what's the sense?"

"The sense is," Pope said quietly, "that if they're repeaters, and everything points that way, then they're probably cyclic. That means they're establishing a pattern, a cycle, a rhythm that's in tune with something going on inside their goddamned heads. If that is true, then they're about due for a return engagement."

Hack's dark eyes locked with the merry, twinkling blue ones.

"Tomorrow night," he said.

"Tomorrow night," Pope agreed.

Chapter Five

Hamilton Pope was the first one to arrive at the conference room for the Saturday morning meeting. He carried a cup of steaming coffee to the head of the table, made sure there was an ashtray handy, and sat down. He was taking his first sip when Roscoe Tanner rumbled in, a cup of coffee in one ham fist, the evidence bags and folders in the other.

"Hey, Ham." He dropped the bags in the center of the table and slapped down the folders in front of Pope. "Everything's up to date again. Nellie did it before she left last night." He sat down at Pope's right and immediately fished out a cigarette.

"Anything?"

Tanner shook his head, busy with lighting up. He blew smoke across the top of his coffee, then sampled it. He made a face. "Tastes like hot piss."

Bert Sheldon came in, followed by Cal Stevens and Tom Forbes. Forbes said something halfway up the table that was lost in the chorus of greetings. He repeated it:

"Hey, Roscoe, we getting overtime for this Saturday shit?" He was tall, lanky, with an incipient paunch and freckled skin. Thin red hair poked from under a Little League baseball cap.

Tanner laughed. "Is Reagan helping the poor?"

"Shove it, then," Forbes said. He turned and strode toward the door. At the end of the table he made a sharp left turn and came back up the other side. He sat down across from Sheldon and grinned. "Scared the shit out of them that time."

"Hey, Ham, where's your county cowboy? You shag his ass home already?" Cal Stevens, blond, blue-eyed, the shortest man on the entire force, was almost as broad as Tanner.

"He shore did look purty," Bert Sheldon drawled. Another blond, Teutonic, he was a big, slow-moving, slow-talking man who accomplished more than any two other men in the Detective Bureau, with the possible exception of Pope. "And did you check out that great big hogleg he carries? My, my!"

Tanner grinned at Pope. "Is he coming?"

Pope smiled sheepishly. "I forgot to tell him."

"I'll bet you forgot," Stevens hooted. "You just want to keep him all to yourself. I sure hope you don't put him with me. I couldn't keep my hands off them sweet little buns."

"He just might shove that big gun up your ass, too, Cal." Forbes made a mock grab at Stevens's genitals under the table.

"Oooooh," crooned Stevens, "you think he might?"

"All right, you perverts, knock it off. We got serious business here this morning." Roscoe Tanner stubbed out his cigarette and picked up the two folders. "We have more than three hundred man-hours logged on these things, and we've got zilch." He lifted a placating hand. "I'm not being critical. I know you guys have been knocking your asses off on this." He looked around the table. "But the fact remains that we're beginning to get all kinds of heat—the media, the brass, the citizens. You might be surprised to know how many calls we've had from John Q. Citizen about these murders. This is not Houston, or Dallas, or Fort Worth. This is Merriweather. We don't have this kind of thing happen here." He cleared his throat and wet his lips. "But it *is* happening, and we're damn well stuck with it. And that's not the worst part. It might keep on happening—again and again. I think we all pretty well agree that all three of these murders were committed by the same men. They have all the earmarks of random thrill killings, and we all know from experience in other cities that that is the worst possible kind of killer to apprehend. There's usually no rhyme or reason or method in his madness. He almost always has to be caught in the act. And look how long that took in Atlanta."

He paused long enough to light another cigarette. "Motive. That's the key. We have no motive except what's in the killers' minds, and there's no way we can get at that without catching them first. And catching them without a motive is going to be a long walk barefooted in deep shit. I hope to God our theory is wrong. There's no doubt in my mind that the same persons did all three killings, but maybe this will be the end of it. Maybe it was some transient nuts. Maybe, but we can't count on it, and if we're right . . ." He stopped again and looked around the table. "If we're right, we'll probably know by tonight—tomorrow at the latest."

"You think there's a four-day pattern?" Sheldon asked quietly.

"Too early to tell yet for certain. If it happens again tonight . . . well, then we'll know."

"How about the FBI?" Forbes asked.

Tanner nodded. "After the Saltzmans were killed, we talked about it. They could probably come in on the Keller murder on the assumption she was kidnapped. But that's technically not our case any longer. County would have to request their assistance, but I see no real problem. How much they can help is another matter. They're not exactly overstaffed since the seventies austerity program."

"Bunch of publicity hounds anyhow," Stevens said.

Tanner turned cold, angry eyes on the short, rotund detective. "Get this straight. I don't care if the mothers are caught by the city dogcatcher, just as long as they're caught."

"Anything on the Keller girl's car yet?" Bert Sheldon, the peacemaker, leaped in.

"No," Tanner said shortly. He rubbed his square jaw and glared down at the table, already regretting his outburst.

"New information," Pope interjected smoothly. "Nancy Lessor. Anyone come across her yet?" He looked around the table at shaking heads. "Okay. She's a friend of the Keller girl, worked with her at the Hamburger Box. Probably knows who the Keller girl's current boyfriend was. By the way, who talked to Mrs. Keller?"

"I did." Bert Sheldon looked at him with cocked eyebrows. "Problem?"

"No problem, Bert. I just learned something else from her yesterday. Emily was supposed to have a doctor's appointment the night she was killed. Her mother says she never showed up there. I haven't been able to confirm it with the doctor yet."

Tanner, still belligerent, directed his attention to Sheldon. "How about it, Bert? How come you didn't find out about the girlfriend and the doctor's appointment?"

Sheldon's fair skin turned a dull pink. "She was in shock, Roscoe. I only had about two minutes with her before she came apart. I went back Monday, but she was in Dallas with her sister. They were still keeping her under sedation. I talked to the girl's father, but he couldn't tell me shit—or wouldn't. Cold-blooded bastard had to stop and think when her birthday was."

Pope nodded. "Lot of disharmony there. Papa and daughter didn't see eye to eye on much of anything, according to her mother."

"Maybe he trashed her," Forbes murmured. "Stranger things have happened."

"Yeah," said Stevens. "And maybe the asshole found out he liked it and decided to do it again."

"Wouldn't hurt to talk to him again," Pope conceded. "Bert?" He winked and grinned.

Sheldon nodded. "I'll drop around this afternoon." He smiled faintly.

"Okay," Tanner said, "here's where we stand. Bert, I'm assigning you to Pope full-time. The rest of you . . . well, unless they hit again, you'll go back to your regular assignments Monday. If they do hit again, we'll have to do some bobbing and weaving. I've got the promise of some patrol help from both Dallas and Fort Worth. That'll free up some of our troops if we need them. Same from Arlington on the south side. But not unless we have to go all-out effort. Let's hope we don't. Milly Singer will be in from sick leave Monday. That'll help some. Ham, I know this leaves you short, and we'll give you more help when you have to have it. But for now, Bert will have to be it."

"Don't forget the cowboy," Forbes snickered. "Ham, let him interr-oh-gate the ladies. He'll have them standing in line to bare their souls."

"Bare their asses, you mean," Stevens said dreamily. "Man, it must be great to be that pretty."

"Long as you don't have to squat to pee," Forbes amended. "Ham, you think he might be a little . . . dainty?"

"I wouldn't bet a busted jaw on it," Pope said. He stood up and put on his coat.

"Anyhow, it doesn't necessarily follow that just because a guy's handsome, he's queer," Sheldon drawled. "Look at me."

Forbes hooted derisively and the rest of them laughed. Tanner gathered up the evidence bags and gave them his usual parting shot: "Stay busy, you guys."

Sheldon looked across the table at Pope. "After I see Keller —what next?"

"You still have names on the Saltzmans' list—friends of the kids?"

Sheldon nodded. "A few we haven't been able to locate. Want me to get back on them?"

"Cal and me'll work on those if you don't have anything else for us." Forbes took a well-chewed cigar butt out of his coat pocket and put it in his mouth.

"Good. The Keller girl was into some kind of group therapy thing, and I have an idea we'll have a lot more names when I locate this Dr. Webster. I don't know how many people are at those meetings, but we're gonna have to check them all."

Forbes picked a bit of tobacco off his tongue. "We still gonna work the Keller case? Thought maybe County'd handle it."

"It's the same killers in both cases, Tom. We drop it, and we've wasted several hundred man-hours. Anyway, it's technically their case. That's the reason for the—for Wind."

"That's his name, huh? Wind?"

"That's right, Hackmore Wind."

"Ain't that the disease that horses get?" asked Stevens, grinning.

"Naw," said Forbes, "sounds more like a new brand of panty girdle."

"Or jock-itch powder," added Stevens.

"Or a new super feminine hygiene unit." Forbes looked at Stevens and giggled hoarsely.

Pope picked up the folders and walked toward the door. "I wouldn't jump to too many conclusions regarding Mr. Wind," he said a little stiffly. "Not just yet, at any rate."

Sheldon caught up with him in the hall. "Where can I reach you later, Ham? With any luck at all, I'll be through by two, three o'clock."

"I'm going from here to the Saltzmans'. After I leave there, I'll call in to the desk and leave word."

"Good enough." Sheldon punched the shorter man lightly on the shoulder. "Take care."

"See you later," Pope said vaguely, his mind already absorbed in preparations for the ordeal that lay immediately ahead of him.

Chapter Six

✕✕✕✕✕✕✕✕✕✕✕

Rocky drummed his fingers on the rim of the steering wheel and hummed along with the new tape by the Laughing Dead. Even above the thunderous beat of the rock music he could hear a high-pitched keening noise inside his head, the siren song that had begun only minutes after he had washed down the last upper with the warm remnants of his Schlitz. His head bobbed and weaved in more or less time with the music, and he watched with fascination as the car ahead of him disappeared into a long dark tunnel, only to miraculously appear again seconds later.

"Wow!" He snapped his fingers and rolled his torso to relieve the stricture of compacted muscles across his chest. The car ahead disappeared again. "Wow, man! *All* right!"

"Rocky." Duke's voice resonated in his head. "Hey, man, you sure you're up to this?"

Rocky giggled at the voice that now seemed to be drifting up from a deep well. He bobbed his head vehemently. "Oh, man, am I ever! I am hurting, man, *hurting*! I'm so backed up my pupils are white, man."

"It's the next exit, then. And don't you think you'd better turn down the music?"

Rocky waved his hand airily and snapped his fingers again. But he reached down and turned the dial on the tape deck. "Whatever you say, man. This is your show."

"Our show, Rock. We're going to do it together, remember."

"Right, man. And it's going to be . . . slow and wet!"

"Only a little, Rock. Remember, we only give them a little more each time. We gave them the plungers before, this time we give them the spikes, next time screwdrivers. See how it goes? Only the bags remain constant. Always the same, but different. We'll have them twirling in circles. They'll screw themselves right into the ground."

"Hell with them, man! I'm thinking about *me*. I wanna feel something wet and sticky."

"Easy, babe," Duke crooned soothingly. "I told you, a little wet. We'll take a little something with us this time. I'll show you —you'll like it, I promise."

Rocky guided the van down the off ramp and stopped at the corner a hundred yards farther on. He turned left and picked up speed. Sudden pain spiked his forearms, and he eased his death grip on the wheel.

"Not too fast, babe. We get stopped, we'd have to abort. I don't want that, do you?"

"Christ, no!" Rocky slowed the van and hunched forward over the wheel. The faint, tortuous beat of the Laughing Dead came at him from the floor, and he began to hum again.

They had long since ceased crying and pleading, the woman before the man. That she was the stronger of the two was obvious. She lay quietly, making no sound, while the man still hiccuped a sob occasionally, shuddering involuntarily. Once or twice she moved her hand minutely against his leg in an effort to sooth and calm him.

They were spread-eagled across the king-sized bed, facing in opposite directions, the woman on her back, the man on his stomach. Her left wrist was taped securely to his right ankle, her left ankle to his right wrist. Their remaining limbs were stretched wide and tightly affixed to the four corner posts of the bed. Helpless, open, totally vulnerable, they lay in stunned horror trying to understand the nightmare that had overwhelmed them, the madness that had come into their home and lives along with the rapacious monster now strutting around the room, hairy-chested and naked.

He had taken the woman first, the moment they were tied. Quietly, savagely. And when the husband protested, had paralyzed him into silence by squeezing his genitals.

Frozen with terror, her center cold and unfeeling, the woman closed her eyes tightly and tried not to think of what he had made her do while he was kissing her. But the images persisted and she gagged, tightened the muscles of her throat against a surge of vomit.

"What's the matter?" Duke asked suspiciously. "You're not going to be sick, are you, momma?" He moved up to stand beside the bed, his legs pressing in on each side of her head. He eased downward until his kneecaps were balanced on the edge of the bed.

"Open your eyes, baby," he said softly, "see what I've got for you. Maybe you'll like it better than my soul kisses." He placed his thumbs on her closed lids and pressed. She tried desperately to move, but he held her head tightly between his thighs.

"Oh, please . . . don't . . ."

"Then do like he says, goddammit! Open them eyes!"

A new voice, harsher, more shrill than the other, and her blood turned to ice. Oh, God, please, not another one! She tried to remember when he had come in, tried to move her eyes to see him, tried to find him in the dim glow of the light from the bathroom. She found nothing, saw nothing except the thick pendulous organ swinging a few inches above her face.

"Meet my brother, Rocky," Duke said, laughter in his voice. "Now we can really get going." He lowered himself until his member lay lengthwise down her face. "Rocky's bi," he said politely. His gloved fingers pinched her nipples, and he whimpered when she jerked. He pinched again, then straightened and moved away from her with a soft, shaky laugh.

48

"It's Rocky's turn," he said. "He wants the little man first."

The man was terrified; the woman could sense it, could feel the uncontrollable quiver of his arm against her ankle, could smell the fear and feel the panic that pulsed from his terror-stricken brain.

He lunged forward and choked off a scream as his body was invaded. The animal hunching and writhing on his back beat at his head and shoulders with plastic-covered fists.

"Shut up, little man!" Rocky dug his hands in the man's hair and pushed his face into the sheet.

"Shut up, goddamn you! Little man! Shut up!" Face bleached, empty eyes glassy and staring, Rocky dropped his head and began to convulse. He moaned a savage sound and bit into the man's shoulder. The woman flinched and the man screamed. Rocky gasped and laughed, his lips moving in cadence with the relentless rhythm of his plunging body, a singsong litany that barely reached the ears of the shivering woman:

"Little man . . . little man . . . little man . . . little man . . ."

Duke lay flat on the woman's body. He licked and sucked and nibbled at her mouth, crooning softly. The man lay dead beside them, his face mottled, swollen, empty eyes staring outward through the blue-tinted bag.

"The last time, sweet baby. The fun's about over. Aren't you sorry?" He squirmed and eased himself into her. "But only for you. The real fun's about to begin for me." He gazed tenderly into her still face, eased one hand under her hair and lifted. He had the bag over her head and the drawstring knotted before she was aware of what was happening.

"Got her!" Rocky giggled, the sound segueing into a guttural moan.

Her eyes flew open. She stared up through the tinted plastic, her nostrils flaring, eyes distended, the whites completely visible around the dark pupils. Her mouth opened and sucked at the precious oxygen; the bag, flimsy, flexible, whipped against the gaping orifice, then out again as she expelled air in a panic-stricken scream.

Another rasping, gasping breath, and then another, and her body began to squirm and flounder, buck and toss like a large beached fish.

"Red Witch is dying, Red Witch is dying . . ." Rocky chanted breathlessly.

Duke gripped her hips with his hands and rode her, writhing and twisting, whimpering when he felt the first faint throb deep in his loins.

Her movements slowed, became spasmodic, her head whipping and snapping as she tried to bite the plastic collapsed around her face.

Duke gazed lovingly into her dying eyes, his excitement mounting, his own body trembling, muscles limp and fluid, brain bursting with the intensity of his consuming joy.

Entranced, he watched her tongue slip from between her lips, moaned with pleasure as her teeth clenched and bit off the end.

Chapter Seven

Hamilton Pope knew instantly what was happening, knew the moment the shrill sound invaded his dream, was doubly sure when he swung his feet to the floor and flipped on the light and saw that it was 3 AM. He picked up the receiver on the third ring.

"Yeah."

"Sorry, Ham, but it's happened." Roscoe Tanner's voice was hollow and sonorous, an echo from a dark and empty cave.

"Yeah. Where?" He reached for his pants on the closet doorknob.

"Maple Avenue, just off Crestview. That row of new condominiums. Maybe you've seen—"

"I know the place. How bad?" He changed the receiver to his right ear and slipped his left arm into the shirt. He changed back and began buttoning the shirt with one hand.

"Two. Man and his wife. It's the same ones, all right. They used the bags."

"Is it sealed?" He gave up trying to put on a sock with one hand and lit a cigarette. His head throbbed gently, a slow pulsing beat in tune with his heart. His stomach rolled, began to seethe.

"Tight as a dead gnat's ass. The radio cop tiptoed in and out again. They're stone cold. Dead about two hours, he thinks."

"All right. I'm on my way."

"Yeah," said Roscoe, "so am I."

* * *

51

He was there before Roscoe Tanner. He threw away his cigarette as he approached the small knot of men at the entrance.

"Where?"

A young patrolman opened the door and pointed. "To your right, sir. At the top of the stairs. The bedroom on the end."

"You're the only one who's been in there?"

"Yes, sir. The door was open—"

Pope nodded and brushed past him. Time for that later.

Just inside the door, he stopped and kicked off his shoes. He slipped a pair of white linen fit-alls over his socks. He shrugged out of his coat and hung it on the inside doorknob. He climbed the single flight of stairs, only dimly aware that the tempo of his heartbeat had almost doubled, that the distant drumbeat he heard came from inside his own body.

He stood in the doorway for a full minute, scanning the portion of the room he could see beyond the edge of the half-open door: a pair of narrow windows with shades and frilly lace curtains, a small padded chair against the wall, a television set on a stand in one corner, picture on, sound off, grainy black and white images flickering on the screen with the staccato rhythms of the early talkies. A western; William S. Hart, Buck Jones, one of them, he thought distractedly, postponing the apocalypse, dreading the inevitable.

He stepped inside the room. Past the edge of the door. Still not looking at the bed for a time, imprinting the rest of the room, turning to the frozen bodies only when there was no longer a plausible reason not to do so, only when he could no longer endure their silent shouting voices, their mute pleas for recognition of the horror perpetrated against them, the sorry way their lives had ended. He had seen it in many forms and shapes and fashions: death. But the violent, senseless ones never failed to stir his emotions, to bring blind, unreasoning rage, a swift consuming burst of anger that lasted only a short time but held him helpless in its thrust. That was why he preferred to be alone with it.

He took a deep breath, held it, expelled it with a sharp explosive sound, then took another, and another, each new supply of oxygen bringing a measure of equilibrium.

Gradually his heart steadied, the pounding diminished. His head began to clear, and the chilling realization of the atrocity before him seeped into his consciousness. And with that awareness came a measure of calm, a cold, calculating determination.

He scanned the bodies slowly, minutely, standing first at the man's head, then finally circling the bed to stand by the woman's, her face swollen and discolored, seized with a look of unthinkable horror, clearly visible through the blue-tinted plastic. She had bitten through the end of her tongue; the tip dangled against one puffy cheek.

He leaned forward, examining closely the oval patches of raw red meat where the skin had been sliced from her body. He counted eight. He straightened, a perplexed frown on his broad forehead.

Egg-sized patches, four on her breasts, the other four scattered about her shoulders. Very little blood, an indication that she had been dead when the mutilations occurred.

His forehead creased again. But why? Where were the patches of skin? Did they eat them? Carry them away? His stomach churned briefly in revulsion. He turned his attention to the man.

Similar patches, but here there were copious amounts of blood. Thick brown trails. Large stains beside and underneath his diaphragm and again beneath his hips. He had numerous slices missing from both his shoulders and his buttocks. And something else. Something that glinted briefly in the overhead light. Pope bent and gently pried apart the cleft between the man's buttocks.

Until that moment he had forgotten about the plungers, and he felt a thudding shock as he saw the flat shiny head of the spike. He moved swiftly to the woman, found its mate embedded in her vagina, the head hidden by the soft cold labia.

He straightened and breathed deeply again, quelling nausea

53

before it could find a firm foothold, summoning equilibrium, forcing out rage.

He began to look for the hairs. As he had expected, he found them. One coiled innocently near the tip of the woman's shoulder: blond. The red one was glued to the man's rib cage by dried blood.

He straightened once more and allowed a tight, wolfish smile to crack his precarious control, pale eyes shining like splinters of ice.

"You son of a bitch." He breathed the words aloud into the thick smell of death. "Not this time, bastard! There's only one of you! And you're neither a blond nor a redhead." He closed his eyes and grinned a death's-head grin into the darkness inside his mind. "You're smart! You're oh, so goddamned clever. And you may or not be a madman. But either way, bastard, I promise, I'll get you!" He swayed, fists knotted, riven by emotions out of control.

It was then, peering into the stygian gloom inside his own skull, that he felt the almost imperceptible shift in the atmosphere, became aware of pain in his head and that he was panting. He opened his eyes and wet his lips and swallowed, suddenly shaking, abruptly conscious of a paralyzing chill that went to the marrow of his bones.

He hunched his shoulders and shivered, wondering with a thrill of horror if the overwhelming acrid odor, the sulphurous smell that burned his nose and clotted his throat, could be the residual essence of the incredible evil that had been present in the room.

He backed cautiously away from the bed—baby steps when he had an overpowering urge to run, a keening whimper locked in his throat when he had an overwhelming desire to scream.

The thick, cloying odor seemed to follow him; a noxious mist, swirling and forming before his incredulous eyes the blurred, indeterminate outlines of a human form, obscene and featureless, gesticulating with amorphous arms, propelling itself through empty space with sinewy transparent legs, a faceless grotesque head with hollow, burning eyes—the essence of evil, a jeering, menac-

54

ing presence, enveloping, touching his feverish cheeks with the endless chill of death—

He blinked and stumbled backward, throttling an impulse to add his own fearful sounds to the silent room already besmirched with the terror-stricken noises of the tortured dead; he had an irrational desire to turn and run.

He blinked again—and it was gone.

Nothing there except the room and the bed, the silent contorted forms, the coppery smell of blood, the rancid stink of his own fear. He shivered and snorted to clear his nostrils, chuckling shakily at this adolescent fear of the unknown that he had never been quite able to rationalize, the tasteless flights of fantasy his imagination subjected him to when confronted with the bizarre, the obscene, the hideous extremes of human madness.

He snorted again and backed slowly toward the door, shaking his head in denial, trying to repress what could not be repressed, block what would not be blocked.

For one fleeting, paralyzing moment he had felt an incoherent jumble of madness inside his mind, the savage rage and soaring joy the killer must have felt at the zenith of his frenzy.

He hunched his shoulders at the doorway and grimaced, his mind gathering stability, coherence, rushing to protect sanity.

"Damned imagination," he intoned hollowly. "That's what comes of being an only child, living in a goddamned fantasy world."

He straightened, squaring bulky shoulders, consciously erasing the fear from his face, if not from his mind, and stumped solidly down the stairs.

"Here comes your friend," Roscoe said. He looked past Pope toward the black pickup pulling up to the curb across the street.

"I know," Pope said, "I called him."

55

They were standing near the sidewalk, smoking. Bert Sheldon leaned against a nearby squad car talking to Forbes. Occasionally one or the other of the men would look toward the second-story bedroom, the squares of light that spilled out of the windows and faintly illuminated their features. Intermittently, shadows and bright flashes of light appeared in the openings as the technicians went about their tedious business.

Hackmore Wind came up beside Pope. He nodded at Tanner and Sheldon. "Thanks for calling," he said quietly.

Pope nodded and turned back to Tanner. He picked up the thread of their conversation. "He's trying to jack us around. He's all by himself and he's got black hair or maybe brown. Anything but blond or red. He probably picked that hair up somewhere in a barbershop."

Tanner puffed furiously on his cigar and looked off into the clear, cold Texas night. "Damn, Ham, I don't know. This guy figures to be a maniac. A maniac is a nut. A fucking nut wouldn't plan that far ahead, I don't think."

"This one does."

"I don't know," Tanner said stubbornly. "Willard could still be right. If they don't comb or brush their hair or wash it very often, they could still have loose hairs from their last haircuts."

"He's playing with us," Pope said calmly. "And he knows a lot, or thinks he does, about forensics. Why would he be so super-careful as to wear latex gloves to handle their bodies, and go so far as to cut off his bite marks?"

Tanner's head snapped around. "Bite marks? You think that's what those cuts are?" He had stuck his head inside the door for a swift look before the techs began.

"Were," said Pope. "He's afraid of what we can do with teeth marks. Probably a lot more than he needs to be." He lit a cigarette and explained the bits of missing skin to Wind.

"It's either that," Pope concluded, "or he's taking them for souvenirs—and I don't much buy that since he hasn't done it

56

before—or he ate them, and I don't much buy that, either. Too many." He felt that curious chill again, and shuddered.

"If he's a biter," Hack asked, "why do you think he hasn't done it before?"

Pope shook his head. "I'm not sure. Maybe it's an orderly progression of some sort—a little worse each time. Maybe the frenzy, or whatever it is that's causing him to do it, is getting worse. He's changing the game plan, that's a cinch. From Plumber's Helpers to spikes to—what? Could be anything that would fit. Maybe these things have some symbolic meaning to him—but maybe not, either. Maybe he's not a psycho in the ordinary sense. Maybe he just *likes* to do it. Maybe this is the only way he can get it up." He shrugged and smiled faintly. "A lot of maybes."

"Or maybe he just ran out of Plumber's Helpers and had some spikes handy." Bert Sheldon's cigarette described an arc in the night and landed in a blaze of sparks.

"It's possible," Pope admitted.

Sheldon and Forbes walked over to join the little group. "Did I hear you tell Roscoe the man was alive when he sliced on him?"

"I'd say so, judging from the amount of blood."

Sheldon nodded. "That could account for the screams Mrs. Marcus heard at about two-thirty AM." He turned and pointed toward a house across the street with its lights ablaze. A small knot of people huddled on the front porch, watching. "She was the one made the call."

"You take her statement?"

"Right. She got up to let the dog out about two-fifteen. When he didn't come back right away, she came out to look for him. Usual deal. She heard screams, but she thought at first it was the TV over here. Then after she thought it over awhile, she decided to call."

"How long a while?"

He shrugged. "She says fifteen minutes, but I'd bet more than that. She looked too guilty."

"Anything else?"

He flipped a page in his notebook. "She thinks there was a light-colored van in the condo parking lot when she went out after the dog. It isn't there now. Could be the one. She says it was kinda behind that dumpster there. She couldn't see it very well from her yard. Couldn't give me the make or model."

Pope turned to Tanner. "I'm going to need a lot of help, Roscoe. Who do I get?"

Tanner looked thoughtful. "Okay, you got Sheldon and Wind here." He glanced at Wind. "You in for the duration?"

Wind nodded. "I'd like to have a small piece of him."

Tanner counted on his massive fingers. "Okay, that makes three of you. I can give you Forbes here, or Stevens—and Milly," he added hastily as he glanced at Pope's face. "She'll be back tomorrow."

"That's fine," Pope said evenly, "as far as it goes. But I need people now, today, to canvass this neighborhood."

"Okay," Tanner said quickly. "I'll bring in some troops on overtime to help with that. That'll leave your team to handle the nitty-gritty stuff. Okay?"

"Only if you get Milly over here this morning."

"Shit, Ham, she's on sick leave."

"If she's gonna be well tomorrow, she's well today."

"Okay, I'll call and feel her out."

"Feel her up, you mean." Forbes spat a stream of amber juice and grinned at Tanner.

"Don't he wish." Sheldon's teeth flashed whitely in the gloom.

"Wouldn't mind that either," Tanner said equably. "Guy could do a lot worse. I'll bet she's pure unadulterated hell in bed."

"Is she, Ham?" Sheldon asked innocently.

"If I knew, which I don't, I sure as hell wouldn't tell you loose-lipped bastards."

"Milly's got eyes for Ham," Forbes explained to Wind. "She told me she likes fierce-looking, massive old men."

"Hell, they don't come any more massiver than me," Tanner said. He grinned. "Maybe I ain't old enough."

"With you, I don't think it's the age. I think it's the body odor."

Everyone laughed except Tanner.

"I don't think that's funny. I can't help it if I've got large sweat glands."

"That's the only large gland you've got, if we can believe your wife Bunny," Pope backed away a step. Tanner had been known to retaliate physically when he ran out of appropriate repartee. Like most really big men, he seemed not to realize his own strength, and over the years had playfully cracked a few ribs and dislocated a shoulder or two. Verbal jousting with him had been compared to playing touch football with a wild but friendly bear.

Surprisingly enough, he led the laughter. But the gleam in his eye and the thrust of his jaw told Pope it would be wiser to change the subject.

"Anybody know which M.E. has the duty?" He lit his last cigarette and crumpled the pack.

Sheldon nodded. "Paris is on call this weekend."

"He's okay," Tanner said. "But I'd rather have Miller. We'll be lucky to get a reading by Tuesday."

"I don't think there's too much doubt about the cause of death," Pope said dryly. "All I need from him is the time."

Tanner snorted. "He'll tack an hour and a half on each end. It's called covering your ass."

Pope stamped his cold feet and moved in a restless half-circle. His eyes drifted along the row of condominiums. "Anybody know how many of these things are occupied?"

"I took a walk while you were upstairs," Forbes said. "Looks like only four out of the dozen. One down about the middle and two more on the other end. They had plenty of privacy."

"Maybe that's one of the reasons they were selected," Hack said. "Do we know who they are yet?"

Tanner nodded. "Peter and Rochelle Jackson. Only moved in two weeks ago. The realtor said it was touch and go for a while as to whether they'd make their down payment. Can you believe they're gettin' eighty thousand for these cracker-boxes?"

Hack cleared his throat. "I'd like to go up . . . okay?"

"Sure. Just ask somebody before you touch anything. They should be about finished." Pope turned to Tanner. "You sure somebody called Paris? He should be here by now."

"He's supposed to be on his way."

Pope tugged at the edges of his coat. "I'm going. I'll check in later." He turned to Sheldon. "I'll be back sometime around noon. If you hit a hot spot, get word to Roscoe." He shifted back to Tanner. "You got anybody coming in to work the lab?"

"Penrod'll be in about eight. Where'll you be?"

"To see a girl about a hamburger, then a visit to a doctor."

Tanner's brow wrinkled. "A hamburger? At this time of day?"

"A friend of Emily Keller, and then her doctor. If I can locate him."

Tanner's frown deepened. "The Keller case? Shouldn't we be concentrating on the more recent ones?"

"We are, as hard as we can go. But the only leads we have with any continuity are on Keller. We solve one, we solve them all, Roscoe."

"Maybe. But the Keller case is county jurisdiction—"

"There's a fine line there. She lived in Merriweather. Also, she is the only one who doesn't fit the pattern. She was killed somewhere else and dumped. She had a boyfriend I need to locate, and she was having a lot of problems at home. These are outside influences we don't have—at least, don't know about yet—with the Saltzmans and these two here."

"Well, maybe," Tanner said, unconvinced.

"I'll see you," Pope said, and turned away.

Tanner followed him to his car. "You'd better go east out of here if you want to avoid the reporters," he said. "We're holding them up at the corner." He paused. "Unless you'd like to talk . . ."

Pope laughed derisively. "Not likely. That's your end of the stick." He closed the door and switched on the motor. "I thought this was a dead-end street."

"Little dirt road across that field down there. Leads over to Auburn Avenue. You'll have to jump the curb is all."

Pope nodded and fished in the glove compartment for a fresh pack of cigarettes. He lit up, waggled his fingers at Tanner through the window, and drove off down the winding street.

As soon as Tanner's bulky figure and the blazing lights of the condo fell away behind him, Pope delved into his tightly compartmented mind for something to think about that had nothing to do with murder and human atrocities. He had discovered long ago that self-preservation demanded separation and isolation of thought, demanded effective partitioning, strong resilient walls between what he perceived to be good and reasonably decent behavior and the antisocial, aberrant acts he encountered in his daily life.

He had no way of knowing that this was a unique ability as well as a useful one, but as a result, by the time he traversed the rutted dirt road and bumped onto Auburn Avenue, he had wiped all thoughts of murder from his mind and was thinking about football.

Specifically varsity football at Houston's Alamo High School. Even more specifically, a blazing September sun, a dusty field, and high anxiety while he waited for his shot at the glory job: quarterback.

Only an inch away from his final height of five feet eleven inches, a long, hot summer of incessant practice behind him, out until dark every day with Mike Dunney, an aspiring fullback who had visions of legendary catches before adoring fans, he felt efficient and assured, confident that he would dazzle the beer-bellied coach—or if not dazzle, then at least make an indelible impression.

At the first scrimmage, the center slammed the ball into his sweaty hands; he had a fleeting impression of rough-textured leather, felt his hands snap together as the ball squirted out between his fingers, bounced crisply off the toe of his right foot, and wobbled uncertainly until it was smothered beneath a sea of white jerseys.

The second time around went better: he got the ball away. A snappy bullet pass to Mitch Farleigh, dancing backward fifteen yards away, poised and waiting. A blur of intercepting white, a derisive yell, and twenty boys went shuffling back to the line of scrimmage while Pope and Farleigh stood looking vacantly at each other.

All right, dammit, Pope thought. You got two bad breaks in a row. Saddle up and settle down and show these bastards your running game.

He executed flawlessly, concentrating on form, fading two quick strides and slamming the ball into the set of numbers on the green jersey gliding by. The wrong set of numbers. He watched in helpless horror as the ball dribbled to the turf.

Stung with despair and humiliation, he tried one more time, a passing play, lofting the ball in a perfect arc to thunk with a muted, beautiful sound against the chest of Mitch Farleigh. A touchdown play in any man's game, and he had looked toward the sidelines to find the beer-bellied coach deep in conversation with his assistant, his back to the field.

Pope had yanked off the headgear, drop-kicked it into the bleachers, and walked off the field. He never played football again.

Waiting at a red light, Pope shrugged ruefully at the memory, lit another cigarette, and dug around in his mind for something else to think about.

Rocky sat hunched deep into the leather chair, his head in his hands. He pressed his forefingers against his eyes and breathed slowly, deeply into his cupped fingers. He was exhausted, totally enervated, his body loose and flaccid, a deep numbness in his groin, a fluttering, tingling sensation in his vitals, a terrifying emptiness in his mind.

"Duke." Thin, querulous, demanding, his voice sounded unnaturally loud in the still room. "Duke, goddammit, answer me!"

"Yeah, babe." It was a tired, quiet sigh, very nearly a groan.

"I'm scared, Duke. This—this what we're doing . . . isn't it . . . isn't it wrong, Duke?"

"No, Rock, it's not wrong. It's bad, maybe. But people do bad things all the time. They've always done bad things. Now it's just our turn, that's all."

"But . . . but I'm afraid he'll find out . . . that they'll find out. What'll they do to us, Duke?"

"They won't," Duke said firmly. "Haven't I always protected you? Remember when we were kids? I protected you then, didn't I? And Chicago and Houston. I didn't let them get us then, did I? Well. They won't get us this time either."

"I don't understand about the hairs, Duke. Why are you letting them know there's two of us?"

Duke sighed. "I explained . . . Okay, Rock, one more time. The hairs are not going to fool them for very long. Maybe they know already. They'll know they're planted to make it look like two men. So they'll jump to the opposite conclusion, that there is only one of us. They'll be looking for one man—and definitely not a blond or a redhead. Understand?"

Rocky lifted his head and nodded vaguely. "Yeah, I guess I do."

"Okay, babe." Duke chuckled and groaned. "Jesus, I'm pooped. Let's get some sleep, okay?"

"All right, Duke," Rocky said obediently.

Chapter Eight

✕✕✕✕✕✕✕✕✕✕✕✕

The Hamburger Box was tucked among thirty-odd other eating establishments on Restaurant Row in East Merriweather, less than half a mile from Dallas city limits.

Pope had located the manager and learned that the fast-food restaurant opened at eight o'clock on Sundays and that it was Nancy Lessor's turn in the barrel. Pope pulled into the parking lot at eight-ten and parked his Dodge under the overhang that dated from the time the restaurant had been a drive-in complete with carhops, big foaming mugs of root beer, and hamburgers made from genuine meat. A noisy, festive gathering place for the younger set, hot rods and ducktails and leather jackets. A social phenomenon that had disappeared with the arrival of the expansive, air-conditioned malls.

There were two other people inside the square boxy restaurant besides the saucy, petite blonde whom Pope recognized instantly from the manager's description: a chubby young man in a white apron and a baseball cap scraping down the grill, and a tall, lanky brunette swiping desultorily at tables in the rear.

Nancy Lessor stopped whatever she was doing behind the counter and watched him approach. She had large, round eyes almost as blue as his own, a small nose that crinkled above a cheery grin.

She made her fist into a pistol and pointed it at him. "I'll bet you're the cop Louie just called about." Her voice was soft and surprisingly resonant. "Am I right?"

"That's a fact, ma'am," Pope said, doing a bad Joe Friday, feeling a little silly at his instant response to her bright-eyed exuberance. "Hamilton Pope. Detective Sergeant Hamilton Pope," he added, feeling foolish again. "And you're Nancy."

"Well, Detective Sergeant Hamilton Pope, why don't we sit down at a table? Lord knows, I'll be on my feet enough today." She was small and round, five-two, he guessed, twenty-five at the outside. An oval face with small, plump lips and pale freckled skin with little or no makeup. "You just go on over there and sit in that end booth, and I'll get us some coffee. You take it black, I'll bet."

Pope nodded and smiled and did as he was directed. He sat down and lit a cigarette. He looked out at the thin Sunday-morning traffic, and couldn't help wondering how she would be in bed. It had been a while, he reflected. He tried to remember the last time. Milly, of course. Since the divorce he had turned into something of a loner and, like most loners, never gave much thought to women until the need became overpowering.

A divorcée herself, Milly was adept at reading the signs, at cycling her needs to mesh with his. She would put up with his surly grumpiness as long as she could take it, then throw up her hands, make him take her out to dinner, then allow him to seduce her. A good relationship, he would tell himself when he chanced to think about it. He knew she dated other men, undoubtedly slept with some of them. But that was okay. He made no demands, expected none in return. Platonic ninety percent of the time, their relationship was primarily that of good friends, and that enabled them to work together.

"Well, Detective Pope." Nancy Lessor placed a napkin and a paper cup of coffee in front of him. He watched her seat herself across from him and caught a faint whiff of lilacs.

"It's about Emily, isn't it?" She stirred her coffee slowly until it was a pale gray color, her eyes never leaving his face. "That was really a goddamned shame, wasn't it?"

He tried not to look shocked, not to change expression, realized ruefully he was accomplishing neither when he felt heat stealing into his face. He tasted his coffee, blew on it, tasted it again, coughed gently, and returned to her eyes.

"Yes," he said finally. "It was a terrible thing."

"They ought to cut that mother's balls off when they catch him," she said matter-of-factly, shaking her head and pursing her lips grimly. "I can maybe see a man taking it by force if he's teased a little too much. But killing . . ." She shuddered delicately. "Why, that's a sin!" Her wide eyes sought his for corroboration.

"Yes . . . it is," Pope said blankly, the incongruity of the soft, sweet voice and the gutter language shaking him to the core.

"Well, Detective Pope, what do you want to know about Emily? I was about her best friend in the whole world, I guess." She cupped small, plump hands around her cup and waited expectantly, tiny white teeth gleaming through parted lips.

He dug out his notebook and found a pen. "Well . . . well, first of all, her mother said she had a boyfriend named Rick, or Ricky. What do you—"

She waved a disparaging hand and shook her head impatiently. "Ricky Chalmers. That creep. He was Emily's boyfriend—for a little while. He used to work here. He was the cook before they hired Tubbo back there. He was a real weirdo. I could never see what Emily saw in him. I think she just felt sorry for him, if you know what I mean."

"Just a minute. You say he used to work here. When did he quit?"

"About a week before—before Emily was killed. And he didn't quit. Louie fired him."

"Fired him? Do you know why?"

"Sure, he caught him spitting on a hamburger."

"Spitting . . . ?"

"You know, a guy came in late and that pissed him off. He used to do worse things than that, smear other stuff on them, if you get my drift."

I don't think I want to know, Pope thought. "And you don't think he and Emily went out together after that?"

"No. They'd already broken up. He came around once when Louie wasn't here, but Emily wouldn't talk to him. That sicko."

"Why a sicko?"

"Strange, you know. Always trying to brush against you, sneak a look, things like that. Always had a hard-on, and I mean always. Then he'd sneak off into the can . . ."

"Why would Emily go out with him if he was so creepy?"

"She felt sorry for him. He had this birthmark on the side of his face, big as a lemon, real rough and scaly." She paused, reflecting. "But he could be nice sometimes. It's just that he had spells when he was a real grunch. And he'd do weird things. Like putting those two kittens in a garbage bag and throwing them into the garbage truck. Things like that."

"Whose kittens were they?"

"Just two strays. They hung around here a couple of days. He ran them off, but they kept coming back. That asshole." She smiled prettily.

"Would you have his address here at the restaurant?"

"I guess we do, but I can tell you where he lives. You know that trailer park out on Teagarden Road? He lives in the second trailer on the right side as you go in the front."

Pope wrote it down, wondering vaguely how she knew.

She read his mind. "The reason I know is I live out that way myself in the Cedarwood Apartments. I see his van every time I pass—"

"Van? His cheeks were suddenly hot and he felt something tighten in his chest. "What color?"

"Kinda sandy color, tan, I guess."

"Do you know what make it is?"

She wrinkled her brow. "Ford, I think. I don't know much about makes of cars."

"But he had it when he worked here?"

"Oh, yes."

"Did you see it there this morning, by any chance?"

Her brow furrowed again. "No, as a matter of fact, I didn't. Come to think of it, I don't believe I've seen it for several days. Is that important?"

"Probably not," he said. He closed the notebook and got to his feet.

"You have beautiful eyes," she said. "They're bluer than mine, prettier, too."

"Thank you," he said, "but that isn't true. Your eyes are much prettier than mine." He returned her smile. "Do you have a phone I could use?"

"Sure. Just go in that little office there. The door isn't locked." She bounced to her feet. "Come on, I'll show you."

She led him to an office the size of a footlocker and pointed unnecessarily to the phone on one corner of a small desk. He thanked her and waited until she left, then dialed police headquarters and asked for Roscoe Tanner.

"Roscoe, I need a pickup on one Rick or Ricky Chalmers. Lives at the trailer park on Teagarden. . . . Dammit, there's only one. We need him now. He was the Keller girl's boyfriend, and he has a tan-colored van. Described as a weirdo, a sicko, to be exact. I'm on my way in. . . . What? No, I didn't get a description. How many Ricky Chalmerses can there be at that damn trailer park with birthmarks on their faces? . . . Okay. Better send two units. If he's our man . . . make it suspicion of burglary. Might throw him off guard. Not likely, but it might. . . . Okay, see you in a few minutes." He hung up the phone and stared at the littered desk. Too damn easy, he thought. This is not the way it happens—not in a million years. Fry cooks with birthmarks didn't kill people, not the kind who killed kittens, jacked off in the can, and spit on hamburgers out of spite. In a murderous rage, perhaps, but not with cold, calculating precision, well planned in advance and executed flawlessly.

He shook his shaggy head and fumbled in his coat for a cigarette. No way. He lit up and went to find Nancy and the description of Ricky Chalmers, sicko. It never hurt to check.

She was waiting by the drinking fountain. "Make your call?" she asked brightly, giving him a wickedly sweet smile that he found somehow disquieting. "Your wife?"

He shook his head soberly. "Business." And then added for no logical reason that he could think of, "I'm divorced."

She laughed her mellow laugh. "Aren't we all?" Her expression stopped just short of being coquettish.

He took out his notebook. "Could you describe Chalmers for me?"

She cupped her chin in one hand and wrinkled her nose. "Well, he's about your height, slender, dark brown hair, not really bad-looking if it wasn't for the birthmark."

"Hair short or long?"

"Medium. About to his earlobes, I guess." She arched her eyebrows shrewdly. "You think he might have killed her?"

"Not likely. But we'd like to talk to him nevertheless."

"Maybe it was her new boyfriend."

"New boyfriend?" Pope looked up from the notebook, his eyes narrowed. Nancy took an involuntary half-step backward.

"Hey, don't look so mean!"

"I'm sorry. What about this new boyfriend?"

"Well, not really new, I don't think. She wouldn't talk about him much, but I got the feeling it had been going on for some time in an on-again, off-again kind of way."

"Any idea how long?"

"Not really." She shook her head vigorously, and a twig of blond hair that had come loose from her upsweep bounced at her temple like a coiled spring. "Like I said, she wouldn't talk much about him. He was older, I gathered that much. But I don't know how much older." She hesitated and poked the stray hair back into place. "Did they find out if she was pregnant or not?"

"No. The autopsy didn't mention it."

She nodded. "She thought she might be. She missed a period. I know she was worried about it. I told her to buy one of those do-it-yourself kits. I don't know if she did or not."

"Do you think she was sleeping with Chalmers?"

She nodded slowly, her eyes wide. "Yes, she did—once or twice, anyway. She said he was . . . not bad." She shivered. "I couldn't. Skinny runt." She paused and flicked a glance at him from under lowered lids. "I like big men. Big, massive men."

There was nothing he could say to that, so he turned back to his notebook, made a meaningless mark. He flipped it shut and put it and the pen away.

"Maybe that's because I'm so little," she murmured, her eyes waiting for his to return, a small, mocking smile on pouting lips. She smoothed and tugged at the starched cotton material that covered her high, round breasts.

"Maybe," he said seriously, feeling suddenly very old and fragile. Too tired and vulnerable to respond to the obvious mating call of a sweet little dream twenty years his junior. No matter how tempting. No matter how available. No matter—

"Emily and I had one thing in common," she was saying softly. "We both like older men. The young ones, they want to own you body and soul. And all that macho shit—you're supposed to swoon when they touch you, blow your mind every time they ball you, be everlastingly grateful . . ." She made a small derisive sound. "Being in there is all they consider necessary." Her eyes gripped his with mesmerizing force. "But we know differently . . . don't we? You have to work at it." She stopped and wrinkled her nose. "I can't make it much plainer, unless I feel you up."

She had somehow come closer, stood looking up at him with rounded eyes, lips parted in an enigmatic smile that changed slowly into a rueful grimace as he stared at her dumbly, dimly aware that he should be saying something light and witty, something sophisticated and charming, something—

70

She expelled her breath in a small, gusty sigh. "Too bad, big man. Blue eyes make me wild, pretty blue eyes like yours make me crazy." She raised her eyebrows in a mocking salute and marched around the end of the counter.

He heard water splashing and glasses clinking and, after a while, when she didn't look up, he left.

Chapter Nine

~~~~~~~~~~~~~~~

Cal Stevens and Roscoe Tanner were interrogating Ricky Chalmers when he got back to headquarters. Hackmore Wind straddled a straight chair in a corner, dark eyes intent and watchful, a dead cigar between his lips.

Pope motioned for them to continue and leaned against the wall by the door. After ten minutes he shook his head at Roscoe and left the room. Tanner caught up with him in the hall.

"What do you think, Ham?"

Pope shook his head wearily. "He's not the one."

Tanner nodded soberly. "Looks like it. His van's been in the shop since last Friday. Transmission's tore down. I'll hold him anyhow until we can check his poker-playing buddies Saturday night."

"More damn names," Pope said sourly. "The harder we try, the behinder we get, Roscoe." He stopped at the coffee machine. "I didn't read the Keller autopsy report as well as I should have. Was there anything in there about her being pregnant?"

Tanner shook his head. "No, not that I remember. Was she?"

"Don't know. She thought she might be. She already been released?"

"Friday. They're burying her tomorrow."

"We still have time to check, then. Be better to do it today, in fact. She told her girlfriend she thought she might be."

Tanner frowned. "I don't see that it makes a hell of a lot of difference. If her boyfriend's clean—"

"She had another one. One that maybe precedes Chalmers, maybe comes after him, too." He watched the paper cup fill with mud-colored coffee.

"I still don't see what difference it makes," Tanner grumbled. "We know the guy's a psycho—or guys—and I'm sure they didn't pick her 'cause she was pregnant."

Pope shrugged. "You never know. I want it done, Roscoe—if you don't mind." Their eyes locked briefly, held.

Finally Tanner smiled faintly. "Okay, you got it, Ham. You're the boss."

Pope smiled, too, and punched the big man lightly. "And don't you forget it, Captain." He sampled the coffee and made a face. "Anything from the lab yet?"

Straight-faced, Tanner replied succinctly, "Hairs. Same as before."

Pope nodded. "Anything else?"

"Catshit."

"Catshit?"

"Catshit. They found a small wedge of the stuff near the bed. Dried. Triangular shape, like maybe it came from somebody's shoe where the sole meets the heel. They've checked all the shoes in the Jacksons' residence. You didn't have catshit on your shoes, did you, Ham?"

Pope gave him a disgusted look. "I wore fit-alls."

Tanner grinned. "Musta been spooky in there. Did you get any kind of . . . feeling for it?"

"No," Pope said shortly. He tried another sip of the coffee, then dumped it into the machine's drip tray. He threw the cup into a nearby trash can. He lit a cigarette and studied his superior through a cloud of smoke.

"We need somebody, Roscoe. Somebody like Rossacher from Houston—a forensic pathologist, a *good* forensic pathologist. I'm just a goddamn detective. I can only use what I can find, what I can see. Our technicians are good, maybe, but they're still just detectives like me. We need somebody." He stepped closer to the big man and tapped a finger on his chest. "Nobody, I repeat, nobody, can be in a room as long as that son of a bitch was and not leave something behind, some trace of himself—and if you mention those goddamned hairs again, I'll hit you!"

Tanner backed away in mock fright, almost bumped into Hackmore Wind coming up behind him. He turned and grabbed Hack's arm, cowering. "Save me, old bastard's getting mean!"

"Well, what about it?" Pope said.

"What about what?" Tanner asked innocently.

"Rossacher."

"He's kinda expensive, ain't he?"

"Couple hundred a day, probably, plus expenses. That's nothing."

"Have to clear it with Clinton."

"What the hell has the city manager got to do with it?"

"Jesus Christ!" Tanner threw up his hands. "Where do you think we get our money?"

"You've got a damn budget. Take it out of that."

"Yeah," Tanner sneered. "We've got a budget. And it's about gone, and we're scraping bottom with a month or more to go until the next—"

"We need him," Pope said stubbornly. "Or somebody like him. Roebeck in Memphis—"

"All right, all right!" Tanner bellowed. "I'll see what I can do." He stomped away down the corridor, head erect, shoulders squared, fists doubled.

Wind's dark face split in a grin. "You got more guts than I have. I wouldn't argue much with that big sucker."

"He's a pussycat," Pope said. "You've just got to outlast him. Arguing makes him nervous. He believes everybody thinks he's a bully because he's so damn big. He tends to overcompensate, gives in too easy." He grinned. "I feel downright guilty sometimes."

"I'll bet," Hack said dryly.

Pope turned down the corridor toward the exit. "Let's take a drive."

"You bet. Where we going?"

"Dr. Webster. He'll be in his office in about twenty minutes."

Outside, he turned to the younger man. "County buying your gas?"

"Sure."

"Good. We'll take your pickup. You heard Roscoe, our budget's running low."

Dr. James K. Webster was a soft-spoken, medium-sized man with dark, friendly eyes and a totally bald head. Somewhere in his late thirties, early forties, there was an air of quiet intelligence about him, an aura of sympathetic understanding, empathy, that many doctors aspire to but never acquire. Despite his self-effacing manner, his grip was firm, and Pope felt drawn to him immediately. Like most professional men with a mediocre education, he felt a grudging respect for those who possessed it, and framed degrees and certificates of one kind or another lined the walls behind the doctor's desk, ample proof that he was indeed well versed in his chosen profession.

"You realize, gentlemen, that there may be a question of doctor-patient confidentiality here?" Dr. Webster blinked, then clenched his eyes tightly for a second as if they pained him.

"Not at all," Pope said quickly. "In the state of Texas that applies only in certain circumstances. In this case, the patient is dead—murdered. That releases you of any and all obligations you may have to your patient."

Dr. Webster smiled faintly. "You may be entirely correct, Sergeant Pope. I have never had occasion to question that particular ruling. It just never came up before." He folded slender hands on the desktop. "Very well, I'll take your word for it. What may I help you with?"

"Emily Keller was a patient of yours. Why were you treating her, Dr. Webster?"

"Depression," he said promptly. "Feelings of rejection, tension . . . the inability to feel."

"You mean numbness?" Pope asked, ignoring a small, knowing sound from Hack Wind.

"Not at all—although a logical progression could ultimately lead to that. No. The ability to feel emotions. Love, hate, anger, even normal fear. I say normal fear, since there is a profound difference between the quotidian fears we all have and the abnormal, inexplicable fears of a neurotic such as Emily."

"Neurotic. Isn't that pretty much a catchall term that covers a wide variety of sins?"

Webster nodded. "Neurotic behavior, simply, is symbolic acting out by an individual to relieve tensions created by repressed feelings of one kind or other. Or to be perhaps more specific, unfulfilled needs. Because unrequited needs can often cause extreme discomfort and in some cases pain, these needs have been hidden, suppressed in the consciousness, and as a result, intolerable pressures to seek some sort of substitute gratification are inevitably created. This results in symbolic acting out, symbolic behavior of one kind or another."

"Interesting," Pope said, skepticism reflected in his laconic tone. "What form did Emily's 'acting out' take?"

Webster tugged at his chin reflectively, a hint of amusement in his bloodshot eyes. "Rebellion, low self-esteem, and, as an inevitable result of that, sexual promiscuity. She was willful and something of a manipulator. Her sexual orientation contained rather strong masochistic overtones."

"Did she mention being pregnant to you?"

Webster's eyebrows knitted, a single furrow arrowing across his smooth brow. "No, not to me. Possibly to Dr. Burdock . . . although I've heard all the tapes, both one-on-one and the therapy sessions, and I don't recall any mention of it."

"A week ago last Friday night. The night she was killed. She had an appointment with you—"

He shook his head. "Not an appointment with me. She was scheduled to attend a therapy session here in the building."

"Group therapy?"

"Yes. She normally came two evenings a week, Tuesday and Thursday. But since Thursday was Thanksgiving, the meeting was scheduled on Friday."

"How many people are in one of these groups, Doc?"

"It varies somewhat depending on circumstances. Let's see, I believe there were ten—no, eleven that night, not counting Emily."

"Plus you."

"Yes. And in addition, Dr. Burdock was in attendance, I believe."

"There were two of you doctors, then?"

"Yes, Dr. Burdock is my associate. Twelve is rather a large number for one therapist at one time, since the patients often get rather involved in their regressions."

"Was anyone else absent from the group? Or came late? Or left early?"

"No to all three questions."

"How can you be so certain?" Hack asked suddenly. "Do you remember all your sessions this well? And you seem to have total recall about Emily."

Webster's face lit up and he grinned, a boyish, good-natured grin that brought a bright sheen to his dark, expressive eyes. "I'm afraid you've found me out. I cheated a little. After Detective Pope called, I reviewed Emily's file. I also suspected you might be interested in that last session." He opened his middle desk drawer and held up a thin manila folder.

Pope threw Hack a smiling glance. "Good question, though."

Webster bobbed his head. "Yes, indeed. Very perceptive."

Hack nodded and shrugged as if perceptive questions were his most insignificant talent.

"To your knowledge, Dr. Webster, was there anyone in the group who showed an interest in Emily? From her pictures I'd say she was a very lovely young girl. Did anyone show any undue interest in her—as a woman, I mean?"

He passed a hand slowly over his bald pate, then shook his head. "Not that I noticed. But that doesn't mean a lot. I'm usually very busy during the sessions with one patient or another." He paused. "She did mention her boyfriends occasionally during the one-on-one sessions, however. She once mentioned a man named Ricky, as I recall."

"We know about him."

"Then there was another . . . oh, perhaps a month ago during a therapy session conducted by Dr. Burdock. I heard it on the session tape later."

"Did she mention his name?"

"No. She never went beyond a casual reference or two. Usually during the presession warm-up. We encourage the patients to talk about anything on their minds."

"Was there anything else about this guy?"

"Well . . . yes, as a matter of fact. I seem to remember that she mentioned something about a twin brother. I don't recall her frame of reference." He squeezed the bridge of his nose and gently rubbed his eyes, blinking slowly as if they weren't working properly.

"Maybe she was talking about Ricky. Maybe he has a twin."

Webster slowly shook his head again. "No, I don't believe so. I had the distinct impression that this man was older—quite a bit older than Emily, at least. And . . ." He stopped for a moment, his face puckered, his eyes squinted and glassy with thought, riveted on the green blotter on the desk. "Oldfield. Yes, that was it. Oldfield, Texas. It was during the time of the oil-field fire there a month or so ago. The subject came up in one of the group sessions and Emily mentioned that her boyfriend once lived there." He shrugged disparagingly. "I don't know of what value that might be."

Pope nodded cheerfully. "Never know, Doc. Can't have too much information. Well, if you'll give me the names of the other members of the group, that'll about wind it up for this time."

Webster frowned. "I'm afraid I can't do that."

"Sure you can," Pope said confidently. "I'm not asking you to give me any of their deep, dark secrets—just their names." He stopped, seeing the stubborn set of Webster's jaw. "Look, Dr. Webster, time is important. We have two days to catch this bastard before he does it again. The chance that it's one of your patients is practically nil. But what if it is? We need to scratch them off the list, get them out of the way. That's the only way murders are solved. You eliminate the ones who are innocent and that leaves you with the one who's guilty. Let's not waste any more time, Doc, please. I can get a court order if I have to."

Webster nodded. "Okay. I'll get them for you."

"You have some kind of attendance record for the group sessions? I'll need a copy of that also."

"All right." He got up from the desk. "I'll be just a minute." He crossed to a door behind the two men and went out.

"Well, what do you think?" Hack asked. "About her other boyfriend, I mean?"

Pope shrugged. "No way to tell anything yet."

"Well, there are *two* of them."

Pope swiveled his head to look at him pityingly. "Don't tell me Roscoe's sold you on his precious hairs. Anyhow, twins usually have the same color hair."

"Not always. If they're fraternal twins, they could be blond and redhead. And there's the semen."

Pope lifted his brows inquiringly, blue eyes twinkling merrily.

"The autopsy report on Keller said there was an unusual amount of semen, more than the average man would normally ejaculate."

Pope shook his head in disgust. "Maybe he did her twice, or even three times. We don't know how long he had her before he killed her. They give eight to ten as probable time of death. She

79

left home a little after six—by the way, we don't want to forget to ask Webster what time these shindigs start. Anyway, I would think the amount would vary from man to man."

"I'm only telling you what it said."

"I know what it said. You're a young, healthy male. How many times could you make it in three to four hours with a brand-new, sexually stimulating girl? Be honest, now."

Hack sighed. "I get your point."

"They also said," Pope said gently, "there was only one blood type involved. That may not mean anything. But if they had found two blood types—"

"Okay, okay," Hack said irritably. "But probably twins would have the same type blood, wouldn't they? And that's my last word on the subject."

Pope laughed. He was prevented from replying by the doctor coming back into the room. Webster handed Pope a single sheet of paper.

"This is the log for the Friday night meeting. The times they arrived are on there. Everyone was here when we started at seven—except, of course, Emily Keller. We broke up at ten."

"Could anyone have left undetected? I mean, if there was a lot of confusion, say . . ."

Webster shook his head. "Not likely. Everyone signs in and signs out. Of course, people do leave to go to the bathroom down the hall, but if anyone left for any amount of time, they would definitely be missed. A group that large we divide up into two smaller groups, so actually we have only six patients each. In this case, six and five."

Pope folded the paper and slipped it into his pocket. "What do you think of our killer, Doctor?"

Before answering, Webster removed a folded handkerchief from his pants pocket and gingerly blotted his eyes. The edges of the lids were an angry red and slightly puffy, the sclera crisscrossed with a spiderweb of lines. Hangover or allergy? Pope wondered. Or maybe just a late dose of hay fever?

Finally Webster shook his head. "I'm afraid I don't know much about it, Sergeant Pope. I rarely read the newspapers and seldom have time for television. I did happen to read Dirk Bogard's article in today's paper, however." He walked to the desk and picked up a single sheet of folded newsprint. "I was reading it before you came in." He unfolded the newspaper. "As a psychologist, our friend Mr. Bogard makes a good reporter. Listen to this." He read a long, involved paragraph of esoteric psychiatric jargon that meant exactly nothing to the two detectives. He finished and tossed the paper back on his desk with a low laugh. "Not a particularly enlightened treatise, I'm afraid. Psychopathic personality. Human beings cannot be so easily compartmented."

"What's your opinion?"

"The only thing I can say with any certainty, Sergeant Pope, is that he is in a great deal of turmoil, so much that he is being driven to sociopathic behavior. That type of turmoil indicates a great deal of underlying pain."

"Pain? Not rage? Isn't rape an expression of rage?" Hack Wind looked down on the doctor from his towering height, his black eyes alert, nostrils quivering.

"It is sometimes. Not always, by any means, although that could be a part of your killer's motivation. But based on what little I know about him, I would say he is suffering from repressed pain. Tension that has been festering inside him for a long time and has finally reached intolerable limits, forcing him to strike out for some sort of substitute gratification of the unfulfilled needs that caused the tension in the first place." He shook his head again, his face clouded. "Such a terrible compulsion it must be to cause him to do this. And if the newspaper article is correct, he is beginning mutilations. It may well grow worse. If the gratification is as intense as I suspect it must be, the more often he will seek it, the more transitory the effects, and the greater will be his frenzy each time to increase and perpetuate the feelings of relief, the feelings of joy."

"Then you think he's just sick," Pope asked, the skepticism back in his voice, numbness growing in his chest. Sickness equated to madness.

"Not just sick, my friend. Terribly sick."

"But if he's that sick, wouldn't he show it? Wouldn't people notice?" Hack peeled the cellophane from a plastic-tipped cigar, his gaze locked on the doctor's seeping eyes.

"Not necessarily. A trained observer . . . possibly. He undoubtedly has other symbolic substitutions he uses in his daily life. Overt physical manifestations, perhaps unique character and personality traits—there are many possibilities. These things help him to survive and exist in the normal world. It is when the internal pot boils over, exerts too much pressure, that your killer must react."

"You think something happened to him when he was a kid?"

"Not just *a* something. A *lot* of somethings, in all likelihood. Possibly a series of somethings with each incident adding incrementally to the cumulative burden, until it became unbearable and his mind shut down and ultimately created an acceptable substitute for the release of tension. Rejection, lack of parental affection and care, continuing physical abuse are some of the most common causes. The human needs remain, however. He still wants acceptance, requires Mama and Daddy's love, and needs not to be abused." He shrugged. "Without knowing more about him, it's difficult to be specific, and you must understand, Mr. Pope, that what I have said is theoretical. There are those who would disagree."

"And he just goes out and abuses and kills people." Pope shuffled his feet restlessly, moved toward the door. It all had a familiar ring, words he had never wanted to hear again.

"Sadly, yes. That's rather an extreme reaction, thank goodness."

"You think a man like this could be cured?"

"He can be helped."

"That isn't my question, Doctor. Is it possible he could be cured?" He damn well knew the answer to that one, but he wanted another opinion.

"That would depend on a lot of things—variables. The causative factors of his psychosis, how deeply ingrained it is in his psyche, possibly his age . . ."

"You don't think he could be cured, then?" Pope repeated stubbornly as the doctor came out from behind his desk, blinking his eyes.

"I doubt it. He has undoubtedly passed from the neurotic to the psychotic long ago." He scanned Pope's somber features. "That is not to say he shouldn't be treated," he added firmly.

"Do you think he'd be certifiably insane?"

"That's an ugly, useless label, but, yes, I believe he is not responsible at the time." He frowned, his face tightening. "No more than a small child is responsible for soiling his diapers."

Pope nodded and walked toward the door. "Thank you, Doctor. I appreciate you giving up part of your Sunday this way."

"Not at all. Glad to be of what help I can."

"I was wondering, Dr. Webster," Hack said, "if your type of therapy ever . . . well, if it worked on physical ailments?"

"Only if they are psychosomatic in origin."

"How about migraine? This buddy of mine has a wife who has migraine pretty bad."

"We know very little about migraine, actually, but it has proven to be responsive to regression therapy in a great number of cases."

"Maybe I'll tell him to give you a call."

Webster opened the door and shook their hands, then gave them his boyish grin again. "Fine. We can always use new patients.

If your wife's problem isn't physiological in nature, I'm sure we can help her."

Hack grinned sheepishly. "How did you know?"

"Just a lucky guess. Why don't you have her come in for a physical? We'll see what we can do."

"How do you think he knew?" Hack asked when they were back in the pickup.

"Well, you're so dark it's hard to tell, but you looked like you were blushing. You're not a very good liar, Hack."

"Yeah." Hack started the engine and drove off the lot. "That's the damn honky in me," he said morosely.

Chapter Ten

Hackmore Wind finished toweling his lanky body and dropped the cloth into the bathroom clothes hamper. He raked long fingers through his damp, tousled hair and stepped back into the bedroom naked. He found neatly folded pajama bottoms in the second drawer of the dresser and slipped into them. He straightened and raked his hands across his hair again, the cool air in the room chilly against his bare chest.

Only then did he look toward the big bed. She lay curled into a fetal ball and, except for slim fingers pressed against her temples, in almost the same position he had left her.

His eyes clouded. He walked to the night table on her side of the bed and lit one of her cigarettes. He sucked perfumed smoke deep into unaccustomed lungs and coughed. He sat down on the edge of the bed. He laid a hand on her thigh and stroked the soft skin lightly.

"Is it bad yet? Do you want a pill now?"

She shook her head minutely. "Not yet. I'll wait, maybe it will stop."

He smoked silently; the cigarette tasted great now that his lungs were over the initial shock. Maybe I'll start again, he thought. What the hell, you only live once. Cigars were too strong to inhale and they only partially stilled the craving. He missed the soothing ritual, the comfort of busy hands and nicotine rush.

"Wendy. I talked to a doctor today. He thinks—he's almost sure he can help you."

Her head moved again. "Please, Hack, no more doctors. Please."

"This one is different, hon. He's kind and gentle and . . . and compassionate. He's had really good luck treating migraines. He's had nearly . . . seventy percent cures, he said." He was certain Dr. Webster would forgive him the small lie. "I really think you ought to go talk to him, at least."

He glanced downward and found her gray eyes regarding him steadily, soberly. "How many times have we heard that before?" A single thin line marred the smooth perfection of her brow, a sure indication that she was hurting.

"He's not like the others, Wen. You should see his office wall. He's got it papered with degrees and certificates. I was impressed with him, hon."

He stubbed the cigarette. "I really would like for you to go see him, Wen," he said quietly. He leaned forward suddenly and kissed the groove in her forehead. "Look, what do you have to lose except a little time?" He trailed his hand along the slim leg, marveling as always at the contrast between his dark skin and the satiny whiteness. "I would really like for you to go, Wendy," he repeated. "I believe he can help you."

"None of them have so far." Her voice had a hushed, breathless quality, as if she were trying not to awaken the restless demon in her head.

He lit another of her cigarettes. If I keep this up, he thought gloomily, I won't have to worry about starting up again. He rolled the long cigarette between thumb and forefinger, wondering how best to say what had to be said.

"You know," he began gently, "that most of your headaches —your worst ones, anyhow—begin . . ." He stopped, seeing the widening of her eyes, knowing that she knew what he was going to say. He went on doggedly, "Begin when we have sex."

"Hack!"

"We both know it's true—no, no, let me finish. I'm not filled with self-pity and I don't mean to sound like I'm whining . . . but do you have any idea how that makes me feel? Apart from the fact that it tears me up to see you suffer like you do, the fact that I feel responsible for a good part, or maybe all of it, is tearing me up inside." He shook his head and placed a finger over her lips. "I feel," he said, his voice suddenly thick and hoarse, "I feel like sometimes . . . maybe . . . maybe you . . . deep down you regret that you've hooked up with a black Mexican Indian honky—"

"Oh, Hack! That isn't true! You know it isn't true! I love you! Oh, God, how I love you!" She threw herself up from the bed, clung sobbing to his neck.

"Hey, hey, come on, baby. You'll just make your head hurt worse. Come on, now." He cradled her in his arms, crooning softly. He kissed her wet cheeks and spanned her forehead with his big hand, wishing desperately that he could draw the pain into his own body, feel and understand the helpless terror he often saw in her eyes.

Gradually the sobbing subsided to a gulping sigh, an inarticulate mutter. She was quiet for so long he thought she had fallen asleep. But then her voice came, hushed and oddly frightened:

"I'll go see the doctor, Hack. Whenever you say."

Chief of Police Leo Durkin glared down the length of the table, cold green eyes indiscriminately spewing malevolence among the people seated before him. He leaned forward on the knuckles of thin bony hands, his body, lean and natty in blue and white and polished brass, coiled and compressed, ready to spring at the slightest provocation. He lifted one hand long enough to slam it on the scuffed mahogany.

"Nothing!" he roared. "Not one damned thing we can get our teeth into! Four of our citizens brutally murdered, raped, mutilated . . ." He paused for effect. "And we don't have a fucking thing!" His eyes flicked to Milly Singer, then away again. Hell with her! She wanted to be a goddamned cop, didn't she? She could bite the nut along with the rest of them.

"Not exactly nothing, Chief," Tanner said mildly. "We got them hairs and there's the saliva they found around the cuts, plus that piece of cat . . . dung."

"Bullshit!" Durkin snarled. "People are being murdered, and you give me hair and spit and catshit!" His outraged eyes swept down one side and up the other. "And you can't even agree on how many of them there are!"

"That's just a difference of opinion," Pope said. "When we catch him—or them—it won't make much difference—"

"*If* you catch them," Chief Durkin said, his tone considerably lower since he was talking directly to Pope. He was never sure how to treat the stolid, humorless man. He looked mean enough to bite and strong enough to hold on. Durkin had often balanced that against the fact that he himself was the superior, but the scales had always tipped in favor of discretion.

"Ham, dammit, we have to do something. The bloody media are eating my lunch. There's a gaggle of reporters outside right this minute and I haven't given them anything new in two days. Give me something, man, anything." There was an unaccustomed note of pleading in Durkin's harsh voice that nobody missed.

"Well," Pope said, cutting his eyes at Tanner, "in addition to the usual ongoing investigation crap, you might tell them we're bringing in a specialist, a forensic pathologist—"

"Hey," said Tanner, alarmed. "We don't have a reading on that yet, Ham."

"And you might tell them there's a strong lead in the Keller case, a mysterious boyfriend—"

"Keller case! Dammit, Ham, that's not even our case. That belongs to County." Chief Durkin's red face swung back and forth between Tanner and Pope. "We've got our own cases to worry about."

"Nope. We agreed—you, in fact, agreed to a unified effort, as I remember."

"Yes, but that was before all these other murders."

"Don't make a damn," Pope said stubbornly. "It's the only case we have anything concrete on. She wasn't killed in her home like the rest of them. Why? And not from lack of opportunity. Her parents were gone to one function or another two or three times a week. She was home alone a lot of the time. So why did he kill her somewhere else and dump her in a ditch? Maybe he took her home with him and killed her there. If he did, there'll be evidence. We know now that she was pregnant. Does that have a bearing? Could be. That's what we have to find out. The rest have all the earmarks of random selection, however carefully planned and executed. Random selection with a certain continuity, certain criteria known only to the perpetrator. The Keller girl was promiscuous, had a lot of men friends. We've more or less cleared one of her recent boyfriends, but there's another one in the background who has been around her for some time. A married man? That could be, too. That's the lead we have, the *only* lead we have right now." He paused, his throat dry. "And the only one we're likely to have, unless we just get lucky and some patrol car picks up on him, or he gets careless." He paused again, beamed in on the irate eyes of the Chief. "Or unless we get someone into the crime scene who can microscopically fine-comb the area and give us something to work with besides some stray hair off a barbershop floor."

"Who do you want?" Durkin asked tersely.

"Rudolph Rossacher from the Rossacher Institute in Houston. Or—"

"You got him," Durkin said. He pointed a finger at Tanner. "Get him!" He picked up his hat, placed it squarely on his narrow head, and nodded vaguely. "Carry on, lady and gentlemen," he said crisply as he left, erect and dignified, mind already busy with the upcoming press conference.

"Shit," Tanner said fervently. "Clinton already said we couldn't afford him."

Pope smiled thinly. "Looks like you got a problem."

"Thanks for soothing the savage beast," Milly Singer said from across the table. A comfortably plump woman, she had a beguiling smile and an extraordinarily smooth complexion for an outdoor Texas woman of thirty-two. A profuse mane of brown hair beginning to streak with gray tumbled around her face. She bunched her eyebrows and crinkled her nose at Pope, one of her signals that she might be responsive to a direct proposition.

"Don't mention it," Pope said, grinning, feeling a slow warmth spreading in his loins. What with her sick leave and his vacation, it had been a while. Unaccountably, his mind flashed to a petite blonde with a round face and saucy, pouting lips.

"You look tired," Milly said. "How long since you've had any sleep to speak of?"

"My, my," Stevens smirked. "Are we working the little fella too hard? Why don't you let Milly take you home and tuck you into bed?"

Pope gazed at him coldly. "Sometimes, Cal, you're pretty hard to take, you know that?"

Stevens's face reddened. "Come on, Ham, I was just kidding. But if you don't like it—"

"Hey, Ham," Tanner put in quickly, "what was all this crap about another boyfriend for the Keller girl?"

"That's right," Pope said evenly, the blip of anger draining away as quickly as it had come. "The Lessor girl at the Hamburger Box mentioned it, and Dr. Webster more or less corroborated it."

"No name?"

He shook his head. "Not yet." This thing is getting to me, he thought. Maybe Stevens is right. Maybe a long night with Milly is just what I need. But somehow the thought wasn't as appealing as it should have been.

After a few more minutes of desultory talk about nothing, the meeting broke up. He avoided looking at Milly on the way out.

The new night was cold and still and clear. He lit a cigarette and drove home, the horizon ahead of him aglow with the golden reflection of Dallas burning.

Later, when he had time to think about it, he decided that she must have been parked somewhere nearby. Either that, or she'd followed him from the police station. The timing was just too precise for it to have been a coincidence.

He had barely walked the length of his house to the kitchen and popped the pull tab on a can of beer when the doorbell rang. Feeling sheepish, annoyed, and a little defensive since he was almost certain it was Milly, he yanked open the door, the beginnings of a rueful smile tugging his lips upward at the edges.

"Hi," she said brightly, blue eyes peeking at him with uncertain belligerence, her flushed face almost hidden by a thick mass of blond hair that now fell free, bunching in a jumbled tangle on the shoulders of her brushed-leather coat. "Remember me?"

"Yes, yes, of course." He shifted from one foot to the other, shock reaction adding a ludicrous twist to the incipient smile, rendering him mute.

She made a low, chuckling sound. "Well, aren't you going to ask me in? It's not like I'm a total stranger or something."

"Oh, yes, sure, of course, come in." He stepped back two paces farther than was necessary, suddenly acutely aware that her twinkling eyes had been fixed on his since he opened the door, assessing his reaction to this unheralded invasion of his privacy and his home. He rearranged the smile, making it friendly.

She stepped inside and closed the door. He stood woodenly, at attention, while she undid the two large wooden buttons on the coat and shrugged out of it, avoiding eye contact, looking around and smiling faintly when he made no move to take it from her.

91

Inexplicably tongue-tied, he watched her move toward the hall closet.

She wore a pale green sweater and tight black pants that could have been designed with her in mind, and a narrow red ribbon tied in a bow at her slender throat.

Without asking, she hung the coat inside the entry closet and closed the door. She smoothed the satiny fabric across her hips, her plump hands startlingly white against the dark material. Her small white teeth gleamed through slightly parted lips, not quite a working smile, but edging in that direction.

Pope finally found his tongue. "Well, Ms. Lessor, to what do I owe the pleasure of this—" He broke off, realizing how stuffy he sounded, how really dumb the question was in view of her parting remarks earlier in the day, in view of the gleaming blue eyes that watched him with heavy-lidded seductiveness. Without warning, his heart began to pound, a warm hand moving gently in his stomach.

"I have something for you," she said. "Something I purposely didn't tell you earlier today." She wet her lips. "I can tell you right now and go . . . or I can tell you later . . . after."

He was totally disoriented, flabbergasted. Nothing remotely resembling what was happening had ever happened to him before, and he had no clear idea what to do about it. Even with Milly, he had agonized through a half dozen evenings before making a timid, halfhearted pass.

"Would you like a beer?" was all he could think of to say.

"No, but I'd like a sip of yours, please."

She barely touched the can to her lips, fulgent eyes appraising him warmly over the rim. She lowered the can, lips parted, glistening, and took a step forward and stretched to kiss him. Her hand fastened behind his neck, pulling to alter the distance between them.

Caught by surprise, he automatically put his arms around her, hesitated only a moment, then closed them. Disjointed thoughts crackled and flashed through his brain like fire. Her lips seemed to pulse under his, open, and melt into warmth. He wondered at the fullness of a body that appeared so small. He was afraid to move, afraid the raging need in his loins would betray him. But he failed to take into account the persistence of a determined woman, be she ever so small. She dropped the can of beer into the potted palm by the door, and sent the free hand wandering in search of physical evidence.

"Mmmmmm," she said throatily against his mouth. She broke away long enough to whisper, "The bedroom would be nice."

"The first door on the left." He found himself whispering also.

They raced feverishly to divest themselves of clothing. She won hands down, and stood for a moment revolving slowly, shivering delicately under the almost palpable touch of his eyes.

There were few preliminaries; she seemed to need them even less than he. He tried to prolong it, to stretch the moment into infinity. But soft moans, heavy-lidded eyes, a quicksilver body, and liquid pulsing flesh overwhelmed his good intentions. Soft lips covered his and firm arms clung to his shoulders, holding him down against the thrusting cushion of her body.

He groaned mightily with his release, and she made muted encouraging sounds, urging him on with mouth and hands and the heat of her desire.

She came prancing out of the bathroom, leaped and bounced and landed astraddle him, her body cool and damp from the shower. She stretched out like a cat on the wide shelf of his body and placed her head on his shoulder.

"Neat, huh? Nothing like a good roll in the hay to clear out the old tubes."

He chuckled, no longer appalled by her language. He stroked the curve of her waist to her buttocks, enjoying the sericeous texture of her skin, a purely sensual experience unmarred by urgency.

"You were really wild," she said. "You groaned a lot. I like that. It makes me feel good."

"That's what it's all about—feeling good."

"I know, but there's something special, something *really* special, about knowing you're giving someone you like pleasure."

"Why me? You don't even know me."

"Sure I do. I met you this afternoon, remember."

"You can get in a lot of trouble, making snap judgments like that."

She propped her chin on his chest, her breath warming the underside of his chin. "You mean like with the Trashman?"

"The what?"

"The Trashman, the Merriweather Trashman. That's what they called him on the Cable News Network in Atlanta."

He grunted. "Leave it to the reporters. Catchwords are their stock in trade. But they don't have it right—they're not trash bags."

She blew softly on his neck. "Ricky. You don't think it could be him, do you?"

"No. It isn't Ricky."

"Well, what I forgot to tell you, and I honestly did forget—I was fibbing before—anyhow, it's about Emily's boyfriend. I remembered something after you left. Do you remember the city councilman who shot his wife about two months ago? His name was Hammer, right? Well, Emily was at my apartment when they announced it on the news. And she said her boyfriend had the same name, only it was spelled different—with an *n*. Hamner. Later on that same evening, she called him Duke."

"Duke? Sounds like a nickname."

"I thought so, too, but she only mentioned him that one time."

"Did she happen to mention where he was from?"

"No. Somewhere in Texas, though. She called him a good old boy, a Texas redneck with class."

"That sounds like a small town, maybe."

"Could be. I'm not sure I know what redneck means."

"I'm not, either. Probably something like a hillbilly."

She nodded gravely, her small chin digging into his chest. "That could be. She said his idea of a good time was to ride out into the country in his van and make it under the—" She broke off, staring up at him. "What did I say?"

"Van? What kind of van? Did she say?"

She shook her head, chin skewering his sternum. "She didn't say." She scanned his face intently. "Why?"

"There's a van, a light-colored van, involved in this, we think."

"That's why you were interested in Ricky's van."

"Right." He squirmed and twisted his torso so he could reach his cigarettes on the nightstand by the bed. He fished one out of the package and reached for his lighter.

She took the cigarette out of his mouth and slipped it back into the pack, then wormed her way upward until she could reach his mouth.

"You don't need that," she said, eyelids at half-mast again, lips pursed.

"Why not?"

She gave him a wicked grin. "We don't have time."

Chapter Eleven

Milly Singer was already in the conference room when Pope arrived Monday morning. Hair swept back into a chignon, a cigarette dangling from her mouth, she sat hunched over stacks of F.I.R.s spaced neatly on the table before her. She looked up and nodded curtly when he came in.

"You're early," Pope said, uneasy as always in the presence of a woman who could conceivably be in a volatile state of mind. He cautiously studied what he could see of her lowered face. That told him exactly nothing.

"I have a lot of catching up to do," Milly said, her tone noncommittal. And that told him nothing also.

"Anything I can help you with?"

She slowly stubbed out the cigarette, one hand idly poking at stray hairs that had escaped the sleek chignon. "Yes, there is." She leaned back and looked at him, her eyes thoughtful.

"In your little dissertation last night to Chief Durkin—when you were talking about the Keller case. Maybe I'm wrong, but I got the feeling that you were implying something. About the differences in the Keller killing. I thought about it a lot last night. . . . Were you saying that maybe she was killed for a specific reason? That maybe the other killings were . . . well, a smoke screen to make it look like the work of a maniac? The girl being pregnant, the mysterious boyfriend, her history of promiscuity . . ." She let it trail away, eyes locked on his face.

He grinned and nodded. "Go to the head of the class. I had been thinking along those lines. I didn't realize it showed, though." He pulled out a chair and sat down across from her. "Several things bother me about Keller. The way she was dumped, the fact that we now know she was pregnant—just barely, but pregnant all the same—and the will-o'-the-wisp boyfriend. Well, he's beginning to take on substance, Milly. I know now he drives a van, and I have a name. Duke Hamner. Duke is obviously a nickname, so it won't be as easy to trace him as it could be." He tilted back in the chair, his eyes narrowing. "Another thing bothered me. The plunger. That seemed to be an afterthought, the kind of thing you'd do if you wanted people to think you were a psycho. Why a plunger, of all things?" He brought the chair forward with a thump. "The bag? Well, that was just a convenient way of killing her without having to do something himself—stab, strangle, shoot." He smiled grimly. "Maybe the guy is fastidious. He ties her hands, puts the bag on her head, ties the drawstring, and walks off and lets her die. He doesn't have to *do* anything. No blood, no fuss. All he has to do then is get rid of the body, and that's relatively simple."

"If that's the case, then it could be someone who would normally be a suspect. One of the big three: relative, friend, or lover."

"Yes. In this case, probably lover."

"The father of her baby."

"It seems logical," Pope admitted. He rocked back in his chair and lit a cigarette. He tossed the pack to Milly. She selected one of the low-tar, filtered cigarettes and accepted a light.

"Only one thing bothers me," she said, picking at an imaginary fleck of tobacco on her lip. "The succeeding crimes were more violent, the last one in particular."

"Yeah," Pope said soberly. "That could mean several things —one I don't like to think about much."

"What's that?"

"He's found out that he likes it."

An hour later, Pope and Milly Singer were alone again in the conference room. One by one the members of the small task force had checked in and been assigned to a specific detail. Bert Sheldon had been assigned to Duke Hamner. The names from Dr. Webster's therapy class had been divided and passed out to Forbes and Stevens. Pope had retained two for himself and was shrugging into his brown corduroy jacket when Milly held up a narrow slip of paper.

"What's this, Ham, do you know?"

He took the paper from her. "Where'd you get it?"

"It was among the things in Peter Jackson's billfold. A receipt of some kind?"

"Free Animal Clinic. Ever hear of it?"

She shook her head.

"Looks like a receipt for five dollars, but it doesn't say for what. Far as we know, they didn't have a pet of any kind. Animal clinic. Maybe that's where the cat turd came from. Might be you ought to check and see what it is anyhow. Might be—" He broke off and dropped the paper on the table. "No point guessing. Check it out, huh?"

"Will do. After that, what?"

He turned to the blackboard that covered the entire width of the back wall. "Grab a half dozen names that haven't been checked off. Jackson's relatives are the ones to the left of his name, friends on the right. His business associates are in the brackets below. Let's do the relatives first. There's not many of them."

"All right." Milly tucked the receipt into the outside compartment of her purse that also contained her notebook. "I'm almost finished here." She placed the purse back on the floor beside her, then looked up as Roscoe Tanner's frame filled the doorway. His face was a dull shade of pink and his eyes were stormy. A short, plump woman carrying a large straw handbag and wearing a hat with a wide, floppy brim came in behind him.

"Ham, Milly," he said brusquely. "Somebody I want you to meet." He half-turned toward the woman and waved his hand. "Maybelle Norman, this is Ham Pope and Milly Singer. Ham here is in charge of this investigation." He looked at Ham and grinned evilly. "I think he's the one you need to talk to."

Maybelle Norman bustled around the table and held out a pudgy hand. "Pleased to meet you, I'm sure." She had a broad, round face splotched with freckles as large as dimes, a ridiculously small turned-up nose, and a wattled neck as wrinkled as an empty stomach.

Pope nodded and relinquished her hand to Milly.

"Hi," said Milly.

"Pleased to meet you, I'm sure." She put down her handbag and patted Milly's hand. "My, aren't you pretty."

"Why, thank you." Milly almost, but not quite, blushed.

Tanner hissed in Pope's ear, "She's a private eye! Can you believe it?"

Pope cocked an eye at him, then looked back at the grandmotherly woman still bent over Milly's hand.

"What kind of cream do you use, honey? Your hands are so soft." Her skirt had hiked up in the back, revealing milk-white, puckered flesh with blue ropes of varicose veins. She wore men's white ankle-high socks and blue and white Adidas. Her blouse had struggled free of the skirt and hung below the edge of her blue imitation-leather jacket, and strands of mousy brown hair had pulled loose from the big bun at the back of her neck and dangled listlessly across her plump cheeks.

Pope cleared his throat. "Mrs. Norman? What can I do for you?"

"What was that, honey?" She turned, pushing ineffectually at the dangling hair. "My, I must look a fright."

"I asked what we could do for you."

"Oh, yes." She picked up the handbag and rummaged inside. She came up with a man's billfold, cracked and bulging. She fumbled a moment, then produced a thin plastic card. She held it out to him. "I'm Maybelle Norman, honey. I'm a private investigator."

Pope scanned the card, compared the picture with her face, then handed the card back to her. She looks more like a Dallas bag lady, he thought. "So?" he said.

"I've been retained to investigate the murder of Rochelle and Peter Jackson," she said solemnly.

"By whom?" Pope asked.

She wagged a finger at him, beaming. "You know I can't tell you that."

"You could," Pope said. "I don't see that it matters."

"My client wishes to remain anonymous."

"Well, Mrs. Norman—"

"Maybelle, honey. I'm a bachelor lady."

"All right, Maybelle. I'm sorry, but this is an ongoing police investigation, and—"

"Uh, Ham, I—we've been . . . uh, Chief Durkin said to cooperate with the lady." Tanner, red-faced and grinning, edged toward the door.

"What?"

Tanner shrugged and grimaced ingratiatingly from the doorway. "That's what he said, Ham." He ducked away down the corridor.

Maybelle patted Pope on the shoulder. "Don't be upset, honey. I won't get in your way a bit, and you'll get used to me." She beamed again, then made an exasperated sound and pushed upward on her dentures. She turned back to Milly. "Take care of your teeth, honey. You'll never miss them until—"

"How old are you, Maybelle?" Pope asked abruptly.

"Ham!" Milly glared at him.

"Oh, I don't mind, honey. I know what Ham means. You think

I'm too old to be fooling around playing detective and like that. Well, honey, I'll tell you. It's exciting—most times. I make a little money off of it sometimes. And the best thing of all is I found out that I'm real good at it. Lordy, who'd expect an old lady like me to be a detective? Now, you wouldn't, would you? If you didn't know better, I mean?"

Pope laughed in spite of himself. "I'm not sure I believe it even now."

"Ham," Milly said evenly, "I think you're being pretty crappy."

"That so? Well, I'll tell you what. Maybelle, Milly here can fill you in on what we know about the Jacksons. I don't suppose I have to tell you that if you leak anything to the media, I can, and will, charge you with obstruction of justice. And that goes for your client as well."

"Oh, pooh," Maybelle said, "I know that. I been a detective three years now. Ever since I retired from the Texas Department of Public Safety. I worked near about every unit in the Texas prison system. I was a cop, too, honey. I was a deputy sheriff for ten years, until I got too old and fat." She gave him a benign smile.

"Well, that's different," Pope said genially, making no effort to suppress the sarcasm. "I thought maybe you were new to the business."

"Maybelle," Milly said sweetly, "I was just leaving to check out something on the Jackson case. Why don't you come along? I can fill you in on the way." She snatched up her purse and gave Pope an indignant glare.

Maybelle's dark eyes gleamed. "Why, thank you, honey. That'd be fine. And Sergeant Pope, you don't have to worry about me. I got lips tighter'n a virgin's twat."

Pope couldn't stop a chuckle. He shook his head and walked out with Milly's laughter ringing in his ears.

"See, honey," Maybelle said complacently. "I know how to handle these cops. Just talk a little dirty once in a while. They all love it." She cocked her head reflectively. "Makes you feel pretty good, too."

"Thanks for working me in, Dr. Burdock. I'll try to be brief." Pope settled in the hard wooden chair in front of the massive walnut desk and looked around in vain for an ashtray.

Dr. Phillip Burdock nodded without speaking. He got up and came around to Pope's side of the desk. He dragged another of the hard, uncomfortable chairs to within a few feet of Pope and sat down. "How can I help you, Sergeant?" Only fractionally taller than medium height, he had a slender, compact body and a bushy head of brown hair that combined to make him appear taller. His round face somehow didn't go with the rest of him. Deep-set, penetrating eyes projected an aura of quiet confidence.

"Emily Keller, Doctor. I understand you presided over some of the therapy sessions she attended."

"Yes." Dr. Burdock crossed his legs and, to Pope's relief, produced a pipe and began packing it with tobacco. "She was technically Jim Webster's patient, but we often have interchangeability in the group sessions."

Pope fished out a cigarette and lit it. "Then you were in a position to observe Emily with the other patients. Was there anyone who seemed interested in her? To a greater extent perhaps than the sessions warranted?"

Burdock frowned thoughtfully. "Emily was a very lovely young woman. I'm sure you're aware, Sergeant, that it is very difficult for any reasonably virile man to be around an attractive woman for very long without posturing to some extent, without projecting at least some of the mating signals we all subconsciously exhibit."

"Does that mean someone was on the make for Emily?"

Burdock smiled and held a match to his pipe. "Not necessarily, and offhand I can't think of anyone in particular who was. You must understand that the people in the sessions are normally absorbed in their own problems almost to the total exclusion of outside influence."

Pope shrugged. "Human nature doesn't change, Doctor." He looked at the inch-long ash on his cigarette and wondered where the hell he was going to put it.

"Just a moment." Burdock got up and went around his desk. He came back with an ashtray and put it on the desk in front of Pope.

He settled back in his chair and tamped his pipe with a stained forefinger. His dark eyes searched out Pope's bright, twinkling ones. "Tell me, Sergeant Pope, do you think about sex to any great extent when you have . . . oh, the flu, say, or a severe cramp in your calf muscle, or maybe a splitting headache? I think not. Please believe me when I say the pain our patients feel is just as real as in those somewhat specious analogies."

"To your knowledge, the Keller girl didn't show up at all at the Friday session after Thanksgiving?"

"No. I don't recall seeing her, and she certainly didn't sign the roster."

"And there was no one else missing from the normal lineup of patients?"

He frowned. "Not that I recall. A check with the roster for that day—"

"I have a copy of the roster. Would a patient be missed if he happened to leave the building for a while? Thirty minutes, maybe even less?"

He nodded. "I'm sure he would. Either Dr. Webster or I would have noticed. The group is rather large and we divided it into two. If memory serves, I had six patients and Jim Webster had five on that particular night."

"If you had two separate groups, how would you know what happened in Dr. Webster's group, and vice versa?"

Burdock bobbed his head. "I see what you mean. No, the groups are separate, but the sessions are held in the same room. The basement, or rather what used to be an underground garage. We had it converted into a large room. It's below ground and virtually soundproof." He smiled wryly. "Some of our patients get rather . . . vociferous during regression."

"Then the two groups were in sight of each other?"

"Oh, yes. It's all rather informal. Sometimes a patient will drift from one group to another—"

"Then how do you know some patient didn't just drift out for a while?"

Burdock's laugh held a hint of impatience. "Primarily because there is only one entrance, and the door has an automatic locking device. You can go out, but you can't return unless someone lets you in. That didn't happen."

"Dr. Webster said something about leaving for toilet breaks. I assume, then, that the toilet is somewhere in the room?"

"Yes, it is."

"Do you recall Emily ever mentioning a boyfriend, or maybe even a lover?"

He shook his head slowly, lips pursed. "No, I can't remember her mentioning her social life at all." He clicked the pipe stem against his teeth and smiled faintly. "She was quite young, you know."

Pope stubbed out his cigarette. "I'd like to ask you the same question I asked Dr. Webster. What do you think of our recent spate of killings, Dr. Burdock?"

He puffed silently for a moment, ejecting small, blue-white balls of smoke. "I've been following it with interest. I gather that the police believe the same person—or persons—is responsible?"

"We think so."

He nodded. "Jim and I haven't discussed it, but I imagine our analysis would be much the same. It would appear to be someone in deep and tragic turmoil. Someone with a pool of internal tension so great that it has created a permanent split between the real self, who would not ordinarily be capable of doing something of this nature, and the unreal self, who *must* do it or something equally traumatic in order to relieve inner pressures—either that or die. Anxiety. Tension. Pain. He has undoubtedly been a hotbed of neurosis for years and has finally slipped across a very thin line into psychosis." He hesitated. "Unless he's stopped, I'm very much afraid we haven't heard the last of him. During these periods of acting out, he is without restraint, compassion, a human organism running wild, internal checks gone."

Pope cocked his head, a quizzical smile on his face. "You guys really have a lot of faith in this pain thing."

"I've seen its power, Sergeant Pope," Burdock said quietly. "I've seen what it can do to people. There is no single greater influence in our lives, short of death."

Pope shrugged. "A little pain gives you character." He lit another cigarette.

Burdock's face tightened. "May I suggest that you smoke too much, Sergeant? That you are probably an overeater, since you are somewhat overweight, that your thumbnails are bitten to the quick. These things are the results of pain, symbolic substitution for undifferentiated needs of some sort."

The twinkle in Pope's eyes changed to a glint. "A very glib analysis, Doctor. Maybe I smoke because I happen to like it. Maybe I have a glandular condition. And maybe I have a kinky girlfriend who gets off chewing on thumbnails."

Burdock laughed heartily. "Your point is well taken, Sergeant. One should never make a diagnosis not supported by sufficient data. It's an irritating habit of mine. I tend to make snap judgments of people based on superficial physical traits. Quite often I have to change them."

"We do a lot of that in my business, too, Doctor. I rarely change mine." He rose to leave. "I'm afraid I'm taking up too much of your time."

Burdock shrugged. "I consider it my civic duty to help in any way I can."

Pope nodded. "I wish more people felt like that. Sure make our job a lot easier."

Burdock shook hands with him at the door. "Policemen and doctors, Sergeant. I'm afraid we have one thing in common."

"What's that?"

"Nobody wants us around until the shit has already hit the fan."

Pope chuckled all the way to his car.

Chapter Twelve

The Free Animal Clinic was located on South Ruskin Street, a long, low building of once-white brick sandwiched between an automobile wrecking yard and an antiquated, tin-roofed feed store. The sound of barking dogs could barely be heard above the noise of air hammers and metal saws coming from the salvage yard.

Milly slipped the small Dodge Dart between a rust-colored Chevy and a pale gray van. She leaped out and hurried around the car to help Maybelle.

"Lordy, honey, don't bother about me. I can make it just fine. They just don't make these cars as big as they used to." Maybelle heaved herself through the door and tugged fretfully at her clothing. She looped the handle of her handbag over her arm and looked toward the glass door entrance. "What're we looking for here, honey?"

"I'm not sure, Maybelle. We found a receipt in the Jacksons' records from this place. There was nothing to indicate what it was for. Probably means nothing at all, but we have to check." She held the door for the older woman.

The door opened into a cubbyhole office. One chair, a counter with a small bell, and a hanging potted flower that was dead. There was an open door behind the counter, and an antique swivel chair backed against the wall. No one in sight.

Milly palmed the plunger on the bell. Nothing. No sound except the faint barking of dogs. She waited thirty seconds, grimaced, then did it again.

"Nobody home, looks like," Maybelle said.

"The door was unlocked," Milly said, "surely there's someone here. Anyone could just come in and walk off with the place."

"Not much to walk off with that I can see," Maybelle observed.

Exasperated, Milly reached toward the bell again, then jerked back her hand as a man appeared in the doorway.

"Can I help you, ma'am?" The voice was soft and resonant, and Milly felt a faint fluttering in her chest as her eyes relayed to her brain clear, sharp images of transcendent male beauty. Tall, bronzed, heavily muscled, he stepped lightly into the room and came up to the counter, smiling easily, a young Nordic god in faded denims and red tank top.

God, he's beautiful, Milly thought inanely, forcing herself to look into liquid brown eyes a foot above her own. Bright, sensuous eyes that watched her with a trace of amusement as she fumbled in her purse for the receipt.

She almost giggled as her fingers closed frantically on the piece of paper, the fact that he was easily twelve years her junior doing little to ease her agitation.

"I—I'm Detective Milly Singer. I have this—oh, and this is Maybelle Norman."

The young man nodded pleasantly. "Nice to meet you ladies. My name is Rocky."

"Yes, I . . . well, I have this receipt from here. I wonder, could you tell me why—what it might be for?"

She watched him take the receipt and turn it over in his strong, blunt fingers. He looked up and grinned cheerfully. "Sure. It's from us, all right. A receipt for five dollars. Mr. Jackson must have left a dog or cat with us."

"Oh, I see, you board animals."

"No, ma'am, not like you mean. We accept animals that people are trying to get rid of. Rather than have them dumped on the street somewhere, we'll take them in. We don't charge, but we do ask for a contribution to buy food for a few days."

"Why, I think that's real nice," Maybelle said.

"It certainly is," Milly agreed. "What—how long do you keep them before . . . ?" She let it die away in embarrassment as his finely chiseled features tightened.

"We don't, ma'am. So far, we've always managed to find a home for them somewhere, sooner or later." He gave them a sunny smile. "Sometimes it takes a while."

"Do you sell them?" Milly asked, the cop in her refusing to take things at face value, the woman in her slowly regaining equilibrium.

His lips tightened again. "No, ma'am, we do not," he said firmly.

"That is wonderful," Maybelle said.

"Well, how do you make any money?" Annoyed at her giddy reaction to this yellow-haired hunk of male pulchritude, Milly was determined to find at least a trace of baseness beneath the gold.

He grinned at her as if he understood perfectly. "We don't, ma'am. My father and some other doctors and businessmen pick up the tab. My brother and I do the work."

"Well, that is nice," she finally conceded, returning his smile. Such a pretty boy—but, after all, only a boy, she told herself firmly, feeling a faint fluttering again at the magnetism of his smile, the warm glow in his eyes that seemed to touch her everywhere at once.

"Could you . . . is there any way you could tell me if the Jacksons left a dog or cat or picked one up?"

"Sure," he said. "That's a plain white receipt. That means they dropped one off. If we get a contribution from a new owner, we give them a pink receipt. See?"

"Do you know if it was a dog or cat?"

"I can tell you. Just a moment." He stepped back to the doorway. "Duke. Would you look—do you know their first names?"

"Rochelle and Peter," Maybelle said promptly.

"Rochelle and Peter Jackson," Rocky repeated into the doorway. He leaned against the doorjamb while he waited, lips pursed in a soundless whistle, fingers idly plucking at the seam of his trousers; the movement caused muscles to writhe and jump in his arms. Heavy thigh muscles stretched the material of the tight denims, and Milly felt a seeping weakness when her eyes dropped involuntarily to the thick bulge at his groin. She wrenched her eyes away.

"Here you go," a voice said, and an arm appeared in the doorway, a thick, muscular arm covered with fine golden hair. And then a leg, and Milly watched Rocky separate and become two, her heart pounding crazily in her chest.

"By golly if there ain't two of them," Maybelle said.

"You're twins!" gasped Milly, unable to believe that two such perfect creatures could exist in one world. In *her* world!

"Yes, ma'am, we are," Rocky said, grinning at her reaction, glancing at his brother and winking, obviously enjoying a game often played. Duke smiled faintly from the doorway, then turned and disappeared.

Rocky watched her confusion for a moment longer. He glanced down at the card in his hand. "It was a cat, ma'am. They dropped off a cat. They didn't want to take it to their new house." He looked up. "I remember now. She said they were buying a new house and new furniture, and she didn't want the cat messing up her new stuff." There was a faintly contemptuous edge to his voice. "They could have housebroken it," he finished mildly. He put the card down on the counter. "They didn't even bother asking what we did with them." His handsome face wrinkled in a disapproving scowl.

Milly put the receipt back into her purse. "Yes, people can be unthinking at times."

"Unthinking?" His eyes blazed at her, his voice revealing the boundless passion of a true animal lover. "It's barbaric, is what it amounts to. Plain and simple murder!"

"Reckon I tend to agree with the boy," Maybelle said. "It's a downright shame the way some folks treat their animals. You're right, son. It's murder, all right."

To give her hands something to do, Milly picked up the card, glanced at it, then put it back down. "Well, you may be right. Maybelle, I guess we have what we came for." She turned toward the door. "Thanks, Rocky. We appreciate your help." She let her eyes flow over him once more, then moved resolutely through the door, wondering whether, if she asked her landlord really nice, maybe he would let her have a little dog, or maybe even a cat. . . .

She was halfway back to the station before she realized that Rocky hadn't asked why she wanted the information about the Jacksons. She resolved that in her mind by deciding that he had read about the Jackson murders and was too polite a boy to ask.

Hamilton Pope spent fifteen minutes leafing through a four-month-old copy of *TV Digest* before the buzzer sounded on the attractive brunette's desk. She flicked him a smile and went inside Spencer Good's office.

She was back a second later, the smile still there, but apologetic.

"I'm sorry, sir, but Mr. Good won't be able to see you before the noon broadcast after all."

Pope looked at his watch. "It's only ten."

"I know, sir, but Mr. Good needs to relax before—"

Pope put his arm around the attractive brunette's shoulders and walked her to her desk.

"I'll tell you what, honey. You just sit down here and pretend you see me going out the front door, okay?" He patted her on the head and went through the door into Good's office.

He couldn't find him at first. His eyes groped in the gloom of the large ornate room: a huge desk, dark, probably mahogany, he thought, a deep leather chair, a trophy case, small statuettes gleaming dully—

"What the hell is this? I told Liz I couldn't see you till after the show."

Even with the voice, he had trouble finding him. The couch was wide and long, a dark chocolate color, almost the color of Spencer Good's suit. It wasn't until he sat up that Pope saw the blur of his face.

"There you are," he said genially. He crossed the room.

Good was shaking his head. "I'm sorry. I have to go on in a little while."

"We've got two hours," Pope said. "This won't take long." He found the chair that matched the couch and sat down across from Good.

"I won't have it," Good said. He slammed his feet to the floor, but the thick carpet ruined the effect. "You can't come barging in here like this."

Pope took out his cigarettes. "If this was a bad TV show, right about now I'd be telling you that I'm by-God a cop and this is my town and I'll by-God go where I damn well please."

"Cop or not, you can't come barging in here. I need this time to get my shit together!"

Pope lit the cigarette and smiled at him, his eyes beginning to adjust to the dimness. "I'm a cop and this is my town and I'll by-God go where I damn well please."

"You're abridging my constitutional rights!"

Pope sighed. "As concerns this interview, you've got two. You can talk to me now, or I can get a warrant and take you downtown. That ought to take about two hours. I figger I can be back about twelve-fifteen. What time was that show of yours?"

"This is outrageous blackmail!"

"If I have to do all that," Pope went on calmly, "I'm gonna figger there's some dark, devious reason you don't want to talk to me about Emily Keller. That's gonna make me curious. When I get curious, I dig." He looked around for an ashtray, found none, and raked his ashes into a pewter coffee mug on a table by the chair.

"It's not that," Good said petulantly. "I just don't want to get involved in this silly murder investigation. I hardly knew the girl. I have some standing in this community, and I can't take a chance on having my career jeopardized because I happen to be attending the same physician." He had a long, angular face with an overripe mouth and bushy white hair. He was anchorman for the twelve o'clock news on a local TV station, and immediately afterward hosted a one-hour talk show with guests ranging from the latest punk rock star to the ubiquitous, self-serving politicians. Pope had watched it once or twice, decided he didn't like the vapid, vicious little man, and had never tuned in again.

"Mmm. I thought Webster was a shrink."

"Well, he's that, too, of course."

"You just attend the therapy sessions for a lark?"

"I think that's my business."

"Yes, it is, Mr. Good. For the present, at least. I came here to ask you if you left the therapy session on Friday, November twenty-seventh, at any time?"

"No, of course not. I arrived shortly before seven and left a few minutes after ten o'clock. Why?"

"Did you see anyone else leave?"

"No."

"Do you know of anyone in the therapy group who showed an interest in the Keller girl—beyond the normal relationship that existed in the group, whatever that was?"

"No, I don't believe so."

"Did you ever see Ms. Keller outside the group? For a friendly drink afterward?"

"Absolutely not."

"Did you ever see her with another member of the group?"

"No."

"Do you have a twin brother, Mr. Good?"

His eyes glowed darkly from beneath ledges of bushy hair. "Why—why do you ask that?"

113

"Do you?"

"No—that is, I did. He died at a very early—we were just small children."

"What of, Mr. Good, do you mind telling me?"

He shook his head vaguely. "I—I don't know for sure."

Pope sighed. "It doesn't matter. If you should be lying to me, I'll find out."

"I'm not lying. He is dead."

Pope dropped the cigarette into the pewter cup and rose to his feet. "Very well, Mr. Good. You can go back to sleep now." He crossed the room and went out in silence. The attractive brunette smiled at him, and he patted her on the head again. "Don't disturb Mr. Good for a while, honey. He has to get his . . . thing together."

She shook her head, smiling. "That's shit," she said.

Larry Mumford turned out to be Father Larry Mumford, associate pastor of St. James Catholic Church on Teterboro Boulevard. Pope gleaned that bit of information from a stout, middle-aged lady with an Irish accent who answered the door at the address listed on Dr. Webster's roster of patients in attendance at Emily Keller's therapy sessions.

He was a slender, compact man with thinning black hair and quiet hazel eyes. Pope found him raking leaves in the rear courtyard of the large church, dressed in a blue and white jogging suit and old sneakers. He was whistling tunelessly, and a dozen or so black bags stuffed with debris gave mute testimony to his industriousness. A bright yellow, baseball-style hat with Bell Helicopter's name and logo was perched on the back of his head. He stopped working as Pope approached and gave him a welcoming smile.

"Greetings," he said cheerily. "Whatever your business, it gives me great pleasure to cease my labors." His smile broadened and he raked a slender hand across his brow, extended the other one to Pope as he approached.

Pope shook hands with him and returned the smile. "You're fighting a losing battle, Father. Some of these oaks will lose leaves all winter."

"That's the Lord's truth," the priest said sadly. "That white oak over there will hang on until the new buds come in the spring." He flashed his quick smile again. "Just goes to show that all of God's creations are not meant solely for the convenience of man." Up close, he was not as young as Pope had first thought. In his early forties, Pope estimated, his practiced eyes noting the deeply etched laugh lines at the corners of the slender man's mouth and eyes, the permanent grooves in the high, tanned forehead.

"I'm Detective Sergeant Pope, Father Mumford. I, uh, understand that you're one of . . . that you were, at least, one of Dr. Webster's patients, and that you attended therapy sessions with a Miss Emily Keller."

Father Mumford's smile died and he nodded soberly. "Yes. I've been expecting—or at least thinking that someone from the police might be stopping by." He lifted the hat and ran a hand over his sparse, close-cropped hair. "A terrible thing . . . such a lovely girl . . ." His voice faded, lips still moving as if he were giving a silent benediction.

"Did you know her well, Father?"

"No, not well. I had seen her at perhaps a half dozen sessions up until . . . that time. I had spoken to her perhaps three or four times directly. Nothing very substantial, I'm afraid. Casual conversation. She did tell me once that she had been raised a Catholic, but had since left the Church. I'm not certain why. No one there knew I was a priest."

"Not even Dr. Webster?"

"Dr. Burdock was technically my doctor. No, not even he, that I knew about. We were working on . . . problems that had nothing to do with my calling." He smiled wryly. "Of course, it's possible that someone there was a Catholic and attended my church. We have a rather large congregation and I haven't been there long. I'm sure there are many parishioners I wouldn't recognize by sight yet."

"Can you think of anyone who showed an unusual interest in Emily, someone who may have been attracted to her physically, I mean?"

"No," he said, shaking his head slowly, "not offhand. No, I don't think so."

"You've never seen her with any of the other patients outside the clinic?"

"No."

"How long have you been with St. James, Father?"

The priest gave him a quizzical glance. "Oh, I suppose it's five—no, six months now."

Pope nodded and fished a cigarette from the box of Carltons in his pocket. He lit up and smiled disarmingly through the smoke, his head cocked to one side. "I've been trying to place your accent, Father. Bible Belt? Or maybe farther up? Indiana, Illinois, up in there somewhere?"

He shook his head, smiling. "No. Believe it or not, I was born in Texas. I did spend quite some time in Illinois, however. I hadn't realized it showed. I went to college in Chicago. I suppose one picks up certain nuances."

"Just some words," Pope said. "Somewhere along the line you lost your Texas drawl."

Father Mumford shook his head. "I never really had one. I speak rather rapidly by habit. Perhaps that's the reason."

"I know very little about training for the priesthood, Father, but don't you undergo a certain amount of psychological—"

Father Mumford lifted a hand and smiled faintly. "And you're wondering why a middle-aged priest would be going to a shrink?"

"Yes, I was," Pope said, unabashed. "But you don't have to tell me."

"I don't mind," Father Mumford said quietly. "I have no deep, dark secrets, Sergeant Pope. I could sum it up, I suppose, in one word: guilt."

"Guilt?"

He nodded, his eyes tracing the downward path of an orange and brown leaf dislodged by the wind. "When I was seven, I lost my family. There were six of us. I lost my parents, two brothers, and a sister in a fire. I was the only survivor. I have never understood why."

"Why you lost them?"

"No, why I survived and they didn't. I was the smallest, the weakest. Logically, I should have been the first to succumb. But I was spared. All my life I felt there must have been a reason. When I entered the priesthood, I thought I had found it. I am no longer able to accept the theological concept that everything happens according to a divine plan." He shrugged. "Perhaps it is nothing more than a loss of faith."

"I'm sorry."

"No need to be. We're making progress. Not as much as I'd like, nor as fast, but I seem to be blocking."

Pope fieldstripped the cigarette butt and tossed the filter into the pile of leaves. "The session on the Friday after Thanksgiving, did you happen to notice if anyone left the room for any length of time? Or left and didn't come back?"

The priest lifted his hat again and scratched his head with his little finger while he thought about it. He slowly shook his head. "No. If anyone did, I didn't see them. I think I would have, though. The locking bar on the outside door makes a loud noise when it's activated. I think I would have noticed."

A gust of wind stirred the pile of leaves, lifting a few into the swirling air and into the parking lot next door.

"Well, I'd better let you get on with your work. I appreciate your time, Father."

"Not at all, Sergeant Pope. I wish I could be of more help."

Pope shook hands with him. "Who knows? Maybe you have, Father."

The two men exchanged smiles.

"I hope you catch him, Sergeant Pope."

"We will, Father. It's just a question of time."

Father Mumford nodded and looked around the courtyard. He grimaced. "I believe they're gaining on me." He heaved an exaggerated sigh. "Well, no rest for the wicked, eh?"

"One thing you could do, Father."

"What's that?" His neat eyebrows arched quizzically.

"Pray for a high wind."

Chapter Thirteen

✕✕✕✕✕✕✕✕✕✕

"Sex offenders," Pope said. "Known deviates and recent releases from mental institutions, local and regional. We have to do it, Roscoe. We should have been doing it before now. We can't put it off any longer."

"Jesus," moaned Bert Sheldon. "Sheer numbers alone. Christ, that's a monumental task, Ham."

"And that includes Dallas, Fort Worth, Wichita Falls, Waco —anywhere within a half-day's drive, and that's cutting it too fine."

"Which branch of the service are you commandeering, Ham —Army, Navy, or marines? It would take that many men to talk one-on-one to every known deviate and wacko just in north central Texas." Roscoe Tanner washed his face with his massive hands and clamped down on the butt of his cigar.

"All right," Pope said. "We'll start with known offenders who have violence in their backgrounds, or have committed sexual offenses involving sodomy on men and/or women. Prison releases of the same types, as well as the mental institutions. That should weed it some." Pope stubbed out his cigarette and looked squarely at Tanner. "Now, my question is, where in hell do we get the help?"

Tanner propped his chin wearily on one fist and stared back. "I don't know, Ham."

"You think we can count on Dallas and Fort Worth or

Arlington? They don't have guards on their borders, you know. He could decide to visit their fair cities at any time."

"Some. I don't know for how many." A shudder rippled through him. "Look, getting the names of these yo-yos won't be much of a problem. The computer'll do that for us. It's the interrogation that'll eat us alive." He looked around the table with a tired grin. "A tab run ten inches thick ought to do it."

"Jesus Christ," Stevens said. "You know how many names and addresses that'd be?"

"And half the addresses wouldn't be worth a shit," Forbes put in.

Hackmore Wind cleared his throat. "We could probably count on Sheriff Bigalow for some help."

"Good," said Pope. "That's a start, anyhow."

Roscoe clambered to his feet. "I'm going home. I'm dying on my feet."

"All right, everybody," Pope said. "I know you're all tired, but I want you in here early in the morning. Roscoe, how soon can you get us the list?"

"Some, the local stuff, by ten o'clock. The rest by midafternoon."

"Make that nine o'clock and the rest by noon. How's that?"

"Who the shit is boss around here, anyhow?" Roscoe glowered down at him.

"You are, sir, but make it nine, okay?"

Roscoe's answer was lost in the scraping of chairs and milling of feet as everyone headed for the door. Milly and Hackmore Wind lingered.

Hack looked at Milly dawdling by her chair, then back at Pope. "I think maybe I may be a few hours late tomorrow. Something I want to check on. Okay?"

Pope nodded, his face expressionless. "Anything I should know about?"

Hack fidgeted. "Well, if you don't mind, Ham, I'd just as soon do this on my own. Probably won't amount to much. Just something kinda intrigues me."

"Sure. Something about the case?"

"Yeah, sure. The Keller case—mostly, I think. I'm not real sure if it's anything."

"Okay, buddy. See you when you get back."

"Take it easy." Hack waved at Milly and was gone before Pope could remind him to check with Bigalow regarding the extra help. He started to get up, then thought better of it.

"I'll do it myself," he said aloud.

"What was that, Ham?" Milly came up behind his chair.

"This thing's got me talking to myself."

She ran her fingers lightly across his forehead, then smoothed down his hair. "Tired?"

She was sending him a message. The lilt in her voice told him most of all. Her hands descended to his shoulders, and he captured them with his.

"I'd have to climb up ten rungs just to get to pooped."

"*Too* tired?" She crossed her arms under his chin and rested her chin on his head.

We're beginning to act too much like a married couple, he thought, and felt a sudden fluttering of panic.

"Sorry, dear," he said lightly, "I've got a headache."

She chuckled throatily. She tightened her arms and tilted back his head. She kissed him above each eye. "That'll make it better."

She searched his guileless, twinkling eyes and wondered how much of the seething sensation inside her stemmed from her close encounter with the two Nordic gods earlier in the day. Throughout the long afternoon she had felt giddy and reckless, fretting away the hours plagued by impossible fantasies and long-forgotten yearnings. She placed her hands flat against Ham Pope's hard, wide chest and felt her body flood with weakness.

"My God, Ham," she murmured. "Do I have to rape you?"

"I—Milly, look, I—I have . . . someone staying over."

She found the chuckle somewhere. And prayed fervently that it sounded more natural to him than it did to her. She touched his chin lightly, patted his cheek, and forced herself to kiss his forehead when she wanted to gouge and claw and scream.

"Just teasing, my love," she said huskily. She stepped backward heavily, awkwardly, suddenly conscious of stringy hair and smudged hands, rumpled clothing and the extra ten pounds that strained the seams of her no-nonsense clothing. She felt like she was going to throw up.

"Milly, I—" Pope began, his eyes clouded, his face as miserable-looking as she felt.

"Hey, no sweat, cowboy," she said airily, "I need to wash my hair, anyway." She snatched up her purse and cigarettes. She headed for the door on the other side of the table. She winked at him and smiled sweetly. "Remember your bad back, old man. And when you go beaver dipping, watch out for your partial."

Maybelle's right, she thought glumly, slapping down the tiled corridor in her no-nonsense, flat-heeled shoes, it feels damn good to talk dirty once in a while.

"Can you believe this crap?" Duke wrenched savagely at the newspaper, fought it into a tight crumpled wad, and threw it at the wastebasket in the corner. He paced angrily up and down before the desk. "Maniac! Psycho! Mad killers!" He stopped suddenly and swept his arm in a vicious circle. "It don't matter what they do to you! They can beat, torture, kill—and it don't matter a damn. Nobody cares! But, oh boy, just let us retaliate—then they trot out their little pet phrases about repressed mentalities, diseased minds. Trashman! The bastards can't even get that right." He hunched his shoulders, eyes glazing, lips curling with contempt.

"Just like her," he said softly. "She could never get it right, either. *Little man, little man, little man . . .* There were two of us, goddammit!" He shuddered, straightened slowly to his full height. He wet his lips. "They want maniacs, they want psychos, they want mad killers—damn their souls, we'll give it to them!" He whirled and went back to the desk, picked up the card, ran his thumb lovingly over the words. "I have just the ones," he whispered. "The perfect trio."

He pressed the card between his hands, eyes blank, turned inward toward the visions that danced and cavorted inside his head.

After a while, Rocky made a muted sound, then said hesitantly, "You okay now, Duke?"

"Yeah, little brother, I'm fine, just fine."

"We'll show them, won't we, Duke?"

"We'll blow their bloody minds," Duke said hollowly.

"Do we still have to wait until Wednesday?"

"No," Duke said quietly. "We don't have to wait, we don't have to wait at all."

"Well, how did it go today?" Hack stared longingly at Wendy's pack of cigarettes on the coffee table, watching glumly while she selected one and lit it, exhaling the smoke with obvious relish.

Wendy shook her head slowly, pink lips pursing to blow a perfect smoke ring. "I'm not sure yet, honey. He's very nice, like you said, he seems very compassionate . . ." She let it trail off with another doughnut of smoke. "He put me under the CAT scanner at the hospital and made some tests, blood, X-rays, the usual hocus-pocus they go through when they don't have any idea what's wrong with you."

"Well, didn't he talk to you, tell you anything about his therapy?"

"Oh, yes. We talked for an hour—maybe more."

"What do you think after talking to him?"

She shrugged listlessly. "I don't know, Hack. It sounds a little . . . frightening."

"Frightening? Why?"

"Not so much the therapy . . . the talking and all that. But you have to be isolated a day and a night before the first session. Defense conditioning, he called it. No cigarettes, very little food, no TV or radio, nothing to read. Just me alone with my thoughts, insulated from outside influences. To make me more vulnerable, he said, to put a strain on my defensive mechanisms—whatever they are. It sounds more like brainwashing to me." She reached for another cigarette.

"Throw me one of those," Hack said, surrendering without a whimper.

She lit a cigarette and brought it to him. She lit one for herself and sat back down. "I can't even smoke," she said morosely.

"Anything else?" Hack asked, dragging the sweet smoke deep into his lungs.

"I have to learn to feel," she said, her voice didactic, mechanical. "He said to know is not enough, that we could learn about the things that I've been repressing all my life, and it wouldn't be enough . . . it wouldn't be anything. I have to retrieve them, he said, go through them again. All of them. To be free, to be my real self." She looked at him across the empty space, her lips trying to quirk into a smile, failing. She shivered. "It's scary, Hack. What if I don't like the real me?"

He smiled. "Not likely, babe."

"Or what's more important, Hack, what if you don't like her?"

He got up and came to the couch and took her into his arms. He kissed the tip of her nose. "That's even less likely." He ran his hand over the smooth contours of her body. "Whatever changes inside, this ain't going to change."

"You bastard," she said warmly, clenching her fingers in his hair and tugging downward. "You only love me for my beautiful bod. As long as you've got someplace warm to put that big old thing of yours, you're happy."

"That's right, of course," he said solemnly. "As far as it goes."

Chapter Fourteen

Oldfield, Texas. Population 6,945, according to the rain-streaked sign Hackmore Wind passed out on the state highway. Down from twelve thousand-plus in its oil-boom heyday, according to the gnarled old man who sold him gas, a Pepsi, and a Twinkie at a decrepit service station just inside the city limits.

Once the county seat, a bustling multi-industried little city, Oldfield had watched its future fade with the passage of the interstate highway twelve miles to the east, watched its population dwindle along with local oil exploration in the inflation-riddled, OPEC-dominated seventies. Losing its position as the seat of county government had been the lowest, cruelest blow of all, shifting its status, relegating the proud populace to instant mediocrity, shutting off cash flow, reducing commerce; the glassy-eyed, empty buildings infesting the once-thriving business district were mute evidence of wasted dreams, failed chances, Oldfield's fall from grace.

All this and more Hack learned from the garrulous little man while he munched his Twinkie and drank Pepsi, occasionally prodding the fiery, profane cynic with a judiciously chosen word.

"Town really gone in the dumper, huh?" he said once, raking a long forefinger across his lower teeth to remove the sweet, gummy coating left by the Twinkie.

"Like a plumb bob to hell," the little man rasped, stroking a blade-thin, pockmarked nose and casting a suspicious glance at

Hack, berry-brown eyes glowing with a fundamentalist fervor. "Sold out by them goddamn county commissioners and that bunch of sumbitches down at city hall." He made a deep hawking sound of disgust.

Hack set his empty Pepsi bottle on the counter and spread his hands. "Government. What can you do?" He picked up his credit card receipt and tucked it into his shirt pocket. "You ever hear of a family named Hamner used to live in these parts? Might still do, for all I know."

He stared at Hack intently, one thin hand rasping across beard-stubbled cheeks as withered and wrinkled as a raisin. "What for? You some kind of cop or something?"

Hack laughed. "Do I look like a cop? Nope. Surveyor. Supposed to be a guy named Hamner's got some land around here he wants surveyed."

"Nope," the old man said promptly. "Never heard of them. Lived here all my natural life—" He broke off, the suspicion back in his eyes. "Hey, I didn't see no surveying equipment out there in that pickup of yours."

Hack shrugged and turned toward the door. "Can't do it in the rain, can I? Thought I'd look the job over, see what I got. Well, thanks anyway."

Outside, he trotted to his pickup, shoulders hunched against the biting wind. The rain had slowed to a drizzle, still heavy enough to ensure the use of wipers and keep people off the streets. A little depressed by the old man's bitter soliloquy and his failure to recall the Hamner name, Hack drove through the wet, sizzling streets into downtown Oldfield.

His nerves a little frazzled from the two-hour drive on wet, windy highways, he cruised the empty courthouse square slowly. He stopped abruptly when he passed the sign that read: For Sheriff's Use Only.

He backed up and eased the pickup to a halt a few spaces away.

He paused long enough to light a cigarette from the new pack he had purchased on the way down, then cupped the smoking cylinder in the palm of his hand and dashed for the courthouse door.

He beat the rain off his hat against his leg and pinned his badge to his jacket pocket. He passed a half dozen almost-deserted offices and walked three-fourths of the way down the long, domed corridor before he found the sheriff's substation.

The man behind the scarred oak desk was dozing. Hands coupled across his not inconsiderable paunch, his head sagging forward onto his chest, long legs propped precariously on the edge of the desk. A sports magazine lay open on the floor beside him, and a cigarette with a two-inch ash lay dead in the groove of an ashtray hollowed from a solid chunk of granite.

Hack coughed and shuffled his feet. When the man didn't stir, he walked back to the open door and rapped on the glass panel.

The deputy came awake slowly, one eye opening as if to determine whether what was waiting was worth the effort of two. His feet hit the floor and he yawned prodigiously, a wide, sheepish smile breaking across his face as he spotted the badge on Hack's coat.

"Rough life, huh?" He rose and stretched across the desk to shake hands.

"If you don't weaken," Hack agreed. "I'm Hackmore Wind from Merriweather."

"Gil Stiles. You're a right smart way from home. Business or pleasure?"

Hack returned his smile. "It'd be a pleasure if I can conclude my business satisfactorily."

"Know what you mean. This got anything to do with all that meanness going on up in Merriweather?"

"I'm not sure. Maybe. Just a frayed end that either needs clipping or unraveling."

"Something here in Oldfield, or are you just passing through?"

"I'm not sure about that either," Hack admitted ruefully. "A couple of things I've put together. Maybe a backtrail on somebody who may be involved in the Merriweather thing, then again, maybe not."

"Pull you up one of them chairs over there. Let's hear what you got." Stiles sat back down at his desk, all signs of drowsiness gone. "Got plenty of time to listen, that's for sure." He lit a cigarette and grinned. "Hope it's not one of our leading citizens you're looking for."

Hack sat at the end of the battle-scarred desk. "I've got two things. A man named Duke Hamner who came from Oldfield or hereabouts. I should say they. He's supposed to have a twin brother, name unknown."

"Twins, huh? Any idea how old they might be?"

"We're not sure, but we believe early forties. I can't get much closer."

Stiles's brow clouded and he shook his head slowly, regretfully. "I've lived here all my life, been deputying for about fifteen years now. I think I know every man, woman, child, and cow in the county. I don't know any Hamners. Closest thing I know is a man named Hayner . . ."

"No, it's Hamner. We're pretty positive about that." Hack swallowed his disappointment. It went down hard. "This would probably have been some time ago. Anywhere from fifteen years to maybe as long ago as thirty."

Stiles chuckled. "That's going back some, all right. Thirty years ago I'da been fifteen—" He broke off and sat up straight. "Could it have been as much as thirty-five?"

"Yeah, it could," Hack said quickly. "We're not sure how old the guy is."

"There were two little boys. Yeah, my dad did some carpenter work for their mama one time. I went with him. I was . . . let's see . . . about ten. They were about three, four years younger 'n me. Yeah, sure, I remember. I don't remember their names, though."

"Where was this?"

"Out on Backwater Road. Used ta be out in the county. They annexed it a few years back. Just a little ways out of town here." He shook his head. "You thinking about going out there, it won't do no good. That old house burned down a long time ago. Nobody lived in it for years."

"There must be some kind of records. School, maybe."

"Don't think so," he said. "They never went to our school. I'da remembered that for sure right off. Seems to me the time I saw them, they was too young for school, anyhow. Ain't like it is today. You didn't go until you was seven back then."

"Seven? Or six?"

"Don't get me to lying, but I think it was seven. Anyways, I'm sure they didn't go here. I went through all twelve grades in Oldfield."

Hack nodded reluctantly, his mind scrambling, his hopes dwindling. "How about birth records?"

"Be over to Pierson, the new county seat, if they was born here in the county."

"I'll try over there," Hack said, reaching for a cigarette. He almost fell out of his chair when Stiles suddenly exploded.

"Hamner!" He slammed his hand on the desk. "Goddamn! Sure, Clyde and Mavis Hamner. Goddamn, how dumb can one man be! I hadn't thought of it in years. Biggest killing we ever had in this county, I reckon."

"What?" Hack could feel his pulse begin to hammer gently. "What happened?"

Stiles lit another cigarette, his eyes reaching beyond Hack into the past. "Clyde and Mavis Hamner. They had four kids, an older boy and girl besides them twin boys. The boy was . . . let's see . . . he musta been fourteen, the girl maybe twelve. Both of them were ahead of me in school. The boy was a mean son of a bitch, I remember. The girl was kinda skinny, not bad-looking . . . purty red hair."

"What happened?" Hack prompted gently.

"Just a minute. Let me get it straight in my head. The man, Clyde, well, he was killed in an accident a few months before . . . the massacre." He looked at Hack, his face florid, his eyes sparkling. "I remember most of it, but I read about it in an old magazine story once, too." He wet his lips. "Let's see now. . . . Yeah, it was just a few months after the old man was killed—he wasn't really old, about thirty, I think. Well, anyhow, somebody broke in the house one night . . ." He paused for dramatic effect, eyes locked on Hack's face. "And the son of a bitch killed every one of them."

"All of them?" Hack felt his insides plummet.

"Damn right they—oh, no, wait a minute! I'm getting ahead of myself. They killed the woman and them two oldest kids—the twins was sleeping up in an attic room and they musta slept through the whole thing. That's right. Just the old lady and the two older kids."

"How killed?" Hack expelled his pent-up breath, his heart settling down to a trot again.

Stiles frowned. "I ain't exactly too sure on that. Seems like they might have been strangled or gassed or something like that."

"Gassed?"

"I'm just not sure. I seem to remember reading that, though."

"What happened to the twins?"

He shook his head. "I don't have any idea. I was too young to really pay much attention to that part of it. I know it scared the hell out of everybody for a while. We were locking our doors for the first time in my life. Wouldn't have done no good, though. Whoever it was broke a window, went in that way."

"Any official records that we—"

"Whoo-ee! I wouldn't know where to begin to look down in

that basement. There's a hundred years of records down there, and nobody knows shit about them. Not in any kind of order or anything. We put all our records on film now."

"How about somebody who worked on the case? An ex-sheriff, or a deputy?"

"I was just about to suggest something. Parnell Slocum. He ain't no lawman, but he's lived across the road from that old house all his life. Still does. He's about four, five years older'n me. Crippled feller. Been crippled since he was about fifteen, sixteen. Nice feller. If anybody'd know about the killings, it'd probably be Slocum. He's a writer. Sends a lot of stuff in to them New York magazines, and like that."

"You think the kids could have been sent to an orphanage?"

"I just can't tell you that. I wish I could."

"That would make them forty, forty-one years old now."

"That's about right."

"And you don't know if one of them was named Duke?"

"I don't recall that I ever heard them called by name. It was always just them twin boys, you know what I mean?"

"I understand." Hack rose to his feet and held out his hand. "I appreciate your help, Deputy Stiles. If you're ever in my county and need help, just whistle."

Stiles beamed. "I'll do it. I hope you fellers catch that mother before he decides to try his luck in some of our small towns. I don't envy you the job."

Hack edged toward the door, anxious to leave. "Come see us."

"You come back, hear?"

Chapter Fifteen

Parnell Slocum was a big man trapped in a wasted body. A leonine head with thick silver hair topped wide heavy shoulders that tapered away to shriveled hips and stick legs. He had a thin, sensitive face and dark, brooding eyes that had seen too many high curbs and narrow doorways to ever be trusting again. And yet his smile was wide and warm and free of subterfuge.

"It's true, Deputy Wind. I probably know as much about the Hamners and their tragedy as any living human. But there's a lot that I don't know, that no one will ever know, I suspect."

"We'd very much appreciate anything you can tell me, sir."

Slocum nodded, the lines in his face growing deeper as if in preparation for a reluctant journey to a painful land he had visited too many times before. He sipped iced tea from a brandy goblet and replaced it on the tray attached to the arm of his wheelchair. He cleared his throat and faced Hack squarely.

"They were an odd lot, the Hamners. I say odd, because none of the members of the family appeared to belong to each other. They seemed to me to be six strangers living under the same roof. Except, of course, the twin boys. They were inseparable. They belonged to each other, there was no doubt about that. But there again, their very unity seemed to set them apart from the others. To ostracize them. And that may have accounted for a great deal of the physical and mental abuse they were subjected to."

"Abuse?"

"Yes, abuse. To some extent before, but increasingly so after the father died. I believe Mr. Hamner loved them in his own bumbling, offhand fashion. They adored him. That was obvious. And after he was killed, I believe the mother and the other two children made the boys pay dearly for the love their father gave them. Are you sure you won't have some iced tea, Deputy Wind?"

"No, thank you, sir. I had a Pepsi a little while ago. That'll hold me."

"I have some beer in the refrigerator."

"No, sir. I'm fine."

Slocum sighed and swirled the ice in his glass. "Mrs. Hamner was a shrewish woman. A harridan. A high shrill voice that carried like a screaming blue jay, even from inside the house. I grew to hate that voice. Particularly in the summer when the windows were open. I could hear her screaming at the kids—the twins, ninety percent of the time."

Hack settled back in his chair, then realized belatedly that he should be making notes. He took a small recorder out of his coat pocket. "Will this bother you?"

Slocum shook his head slowly, distractedly. "If those two little boys grew to manhood without some sort of identity crisis, then Texas is not the second-largest state in the union."

"Why do you say that?"

"Their names were Kerry and Perry, but not once in the five or so years they lived there did I hear her call them that."

"What did she call them? Twins?"

"That would be the logical assumption. No. She called them 'little man.'"

"Little man? You mean little men?"

"No," he said heavily. "Little man. Singular. Even though she would sometimes be addressing them both. Little man. It was so idiotic. The two older children did the same thing. They thought it was smart. I was fourteen, and it sometimes confused me. Imagine what it did to formative minds, to be considered half of a whole instead of a unique being. Not to exist except as you relate in terms of another human being, no matter how close, would, I think, be intolerable."

"It'd be pretty confusing," Hack acknowledged. "But as soon as they got old enough to realize, wouldn't—"

"Young minds, Deputy Wind, accept and store information. If at the age of four your parents called you 'dog'—even though you had dogs and understood what dogs were—if they called you 'dog' long enough and convincingly enough, before long you would become convinced that you were a dog. A strange species of dog, perhaps, but a dog, nevertheless."

Hack laughed. "My folks sometimes called me worse than that, I'm afraid."

Slocum forced a tight, austere smile.

Too caught up in the Hamner tragedy to appreciate humor, Hack decided.

"That was a small thing," Slocum said. "Not perhaps particularly damaging in and of itself. But coupled with the abuse . . . If those two little boys escaped without serious psychic trauma, I'll miss my guess." His face tightened. He clenched and unclenched his fingers, watching the movement as if he had never moved them before. "As a matter of fact, I'm relatively certain they did not escape."

Hack's ears pricked up, and he felt a faint acceleration of his heartbeat. "What makes you say that?"

Using his heavily muscled arms, Slocum shifted his position in the wheelchair. He gazed through the window toward the crumbling foundation that was all that remained of the Hamner house.

"Before I answer that, Deputy Wind, I would appreciate an answer to a question of my own. Agreed?"

"Sure," said Hack. "Why not?"

"You haven't said so precisely, but you are investigating the Merriweather murders, are you not?"

"Yes."

He made a half-turn in the wheelchair and faced Hack directly. "From the fact that you are here, I assume you have reason to suspect that the Hamner twins may be in some way implicated in those murders?"

"Yes." Hack nodded. "We have the name Duke Hamner. We're not certain yet just what connection that has with the killings. Maybe nothing. But maybe everything. Duke Hamner and Oldfield and a connection to one of the murdered girls. It's no secret, Mr. Slocum."

"Duke. Yes. Duke and Rocky. Those are nicknames their father gave them. I never heard them called that but a few times, never after he died."

Hack studied him for a moment. "You don't seem shocked or even surprised that we believe the Hamner boys may be implicated. Why is that, Mr. Slocum?"

"Because I wouldn't be at all surprised," he said bluntly.

"When was the last time you saw the boys, sir?"

"When they were six, possibly near seven years of age."

"Then what makes you say you're not surprised . . ."

"Because I'm firmly convinced they killed their mother, sister, and brother." He folded his arms and leaned back in the wheelchair and waited for a reaction, dark gleaming eyes ambushing Hack from beneath thick bushy brows.

"Jesus Christ!" Hack said, stunned, his voice as hollow as an echo, a cool breeze tickling his ears. "Jesus H. Christ," he repeated slowly.

Slocum smiled faintly, apparently satisfied with the response to his proclamation. "It's the only possible explanation to a set of improbable circumstances, Deputy Wind. And I'm firmly convinced, also, that the only reason the investigators didn't reach the same conclusion was their gross ineptitude and their somewhat naive belief in the inherent nobility of man as personified in the

very, very young. I'll have to admit I had a slight advantage
—perhaps more than slight. I happened to know about the abuse,
the callous disregard by the mother, the continual subjection of
the twins to sexual harassment, to sodomy by the older brother and
sister—different in physical expression only. I also happened to
know about the chloroform Mr. Hamner kept in the garage for
occasional use when he brought home a very sick animal from the
animal shelter. And last, but not least, I saw the twins' grandfather
break the window." He sat back and folded his arms again, the
small, almost secretive smile back in place.

"I—I see," Hack stammered. Sexual abuse? sodomy? . . .
chloroform? . . . a broken window? . . . grandfather? Good God,
was he talking to a nut?

Slocum read his mind. "I understand how you must feel, Deputy
Wind. I've given you a lot to assimilate on very short notice. And I
was rather brief. If you'd like, I can elucidate."

"Yes, please," Hack said grimly. "I'd like that a lot."

Slocum steepled his hands in front of his face and rubbed his
forefingers along the bridge of his nose, his eyes directed toward the
window again. "After the father was killed in an automobile
accident, the mother was forced to go to work. She worked at one
of the roadhouses, or honky-tonks they were called, that used to
abound out on the highway. She worked evenings. That, of
course, left the children alone at night. The boy, Carl, told me
that she gave the twins to him and his sister to supervise, to raise.
If I remember correctly, he had Kerry, or Rocky, and his sister
assumed responsibility for Perry, or Duke. Although they never
called them that. They simply adopted their mother's ridiculous
habit of calling them 'little man.'" His voice had become a dry,
didactic monotone, all traces of humor gone from his face.

"How old were they then?"

"I'm not absolutely certain, but I would think between six and
seven." The wrinkles in his face seemed to deepen, as did his

voice. "I still feel guilt," he went on somberly. "Although in my own behalf, I must say I had no idea of the true nature of their . . . bestiality. The girl, Eloise, was as bad as the boy. Perhaps worse, since she was the one with imagination. Carl was something of a dullard. But Eloise . . . she liked to do things." He glanced at Hack, his face expressionless. "As much as I regret it, I had firsthand knowledge of Eloise. She did things to me as well. Things I found incredibly exciting as a boy in the throes of adolescence and just beginning to find the opposite sex intriguing and irresistible." He drained the watery remnants of his iced tea. When he put the glass back on the tray, Hack noticed his hand was shaking.

He lifted his eyes and smiled wryly. "This part is difficult for me to remember, almost impossible for me to relate. I've never told anyone before."

Hack nodded encouragingly, gave him a sympathetic smile. "We all have a past," he said quietly.

Slocum nodded vaguely and leaned back. He took a deep breath. "As I said, Eloise had a vivid imagination and a sadistic streak as well. I rebelled at some of the things she came up with. Abnormal things, I thought, dirty things, painful. She seemed to have an anal fixation of some sort. And she would taunt me. Tell me that even stupid Carl had more nerve than I, that even the twins—" He broke off, a thin white line around his compressed lips. "I should have known right then that the things I was refusing to do . . . that she must have been doing them to the boys. She and her brother together. The two of them were having sexual relations, of course. That's more or less the way I became involved. Carl and I used to hang out together a bit. There was no one else around in the summer. He was continually telling me what a great lay she was . . . with graphic details of their couplings. He would urge me to try her out. Needless to say, I finally did. I was thirteen at the time." He stopped again, avoiding Hack's eyes. "I don't know that it's absolutely necessary to tell you all of this. I'm not proud of my part in it."

"Don't sound too bad so far," Hack said. "We all started sometime. You were just a little younger than some, is all." He grinned engagingly. "I got my first piece on the reservation at eleven. Couldn't even come yet, but it sure tickled."

Slocum smiled grudgingly, acknowledging Hack's efforts to relieve the tension. He pressed down on the arms of the wheelchair and shifted his body. "Carl was simple, a bully with anyone smaller than he was, but Eloise was the clever hand manipulating the strings. Carl sodomized the twins while Eloise watched. Carl told me that—or tried to. I wouldn't listen, pretending to myself that he was bragging, trying to impress me." He stopped and looked out the window, then turned back to Hack and sighed. "I'd like to think that if I had allowed myself to believe it, I would have been forced to stop seeing her, to stop seeing either of them. It was too appalling, even to a thirteen-year-old. She, in turn, had her own ways of using 'her' twin for sexual purposes, but she would not let Carl watch, so I'm not at all certain what she did. I can imagine some of the things, as I'm sure you can."

"What about the mother? Surely she must have known what was going on?"

Slocum made a gesture of disgust, a hawking sound deep in his throat. "She was a lush. And I'm not at all sure she would have done anything if she knew. I think she was more than a little afraid of her older children. Carl was a pretty big boy for his age." He husked something up out of his throat and went on slowly. "Perhaps I shouldn't say this, but I sometimes had the feeling that she was as . . . depraved as her children. Maybe it was the way she looked at me. I was, I think, a fairly perceptive youngster and I had the most peculiar certainty that I could have . . . She was, incidentally, a very attractive woman." He sighed. "I had fantasies." He glanced up at Hack, his eyes clouding, a tinge of red creeping into his face. "She was most certainly involved in the physical abuse, if not the other thing."

"About the murders?" Hack prompted gently.

"Oh, yes. The murders." Slocum steepled his fingers in front of his face again. "It was on a Sunday morning. My parents were in church. I was feeling poorly—it was the beginning of the illness that put me in this damn chair. Of course, we didn't know that at the time. At any rate, I was alone, still in bed. I was reading; the window open—the one facing the Hamner house across the road. I heard a car, an old, noisy car that I recognized the sound of immediately: Mrs. Hamner's parents on one of their infrequent visits. It was perhaps eleven o'clock. I had no interest in the grandparents, but for some reason I got out of bed and went to sit by the window. Something to do, something to watch, I suppose. I was bored to death and feeling a little feverish.

"They were entering the house. I sat in the window seat and waited for my parents to come home. A few minutes later, possibly ten, I saw the grandfather come out of the house and go into the garage. When he came out, he was carrying a hammer. There was something different about him, something I didn't realize until years later when I was reading the police report of the murders. He had changed his shoes. He was wearing a pair of Mr. Hamner's old work shoes. I noticed it, but it made no impression. He went around to the side of the house. At about the center, he leaned forward and struck the wall—one blow. Then he stepped into the flower bed and seemed to stamp, move around, sort of shuffle his feet." He stopped, the wry smile returning to his lined face. "What he was actually doing was breaking a window and making tracks beneath it. I'm positive of that now. At the time, I had no idea what he was doing and cared less. I was feeling worse and I wanted my parents to come home. I sat there a few minutes longer, long enough to see him go back into the garage, dispose of the hammer, and change his shoes again. None of this made an impression on me. The last thing I saw before I returned to bed was the grandmother come out of the house with one of the twins and put him into their car."

"Only one?"

"That's all I saw. I was on my way back to bed. They must have brought the other one out later, because by the time the police got there she had taken them and gone."

"Where did she take them?"

"To her home, I suppose. Yes, I'm sure of it. I heard later that she had taken them to raise. I never saw them again."

"And when the police got there?"

He nodded. "I learned about most of it later. I watched them carry out the bodies later in the day, but I was too sick to get out and by then my parents were too worried about my fever to care what was happening. They took me to the hospital about dark that day."

"What happened?" Hack asked, fighting to keep the impatience out of his voice. "At the Hamners', I mean."

"They were dead, the three of them. Suffocation in all three cases. A strong odor of chloroform. The police assumed someone had broken in, used chloroform to render them unconscious, then tied the bags around their heads—"

"Bags?" Hack's ears were suddenly burning; he felt an involuntary twitching in the muscles of his cheek.

"Cellophane bags." Slocum's eyes bored into Hack's. "Much the same as your Merriweather Trashman. Only plastic bags weren't around back then. The killer—or killers—used cellophane. The kind that used to come with your dry cleaning. He tied the tops closed, then slipped the bags over their heads and tied it around their necks—rather tightly, I understand."

"And you think the twins did that?"

His smile was mirthless, a simple separation of lips over yellowing teeth. "The knots used. What type of knot would you expect a six-year-old to be familiar with?"

Hack thought for a moment. "Bow? Like in a shoelace?"

141

Slocum's eyes gleamed. "Exactly. Precisely that. All the knots used were simple bow knots—and the bonds themselves were . . . ?"

"Shoelaces," Hack said wonderingly.

"Exactly. Shoelaces from shoes found in the house."

"But even so, the mechanics of the thing . . . These were two small boys. How could they subdue anyone as large as you say Carl was, not to mention their adult mother?"

"The simplicity of it is the beauty of it. The boys simply waited until the others were asleep, saturated a cloth with chloroform, and induced a deep state of unconsciousness. They knew about chloroform, what it did. They had watched their father enough times for that. Once their victims were unconscious, it became a simple matter to tie them up, tie the bags over their heads, and let nature take its course. They exhausted the oxygen in the bags and they died, probably quietly and peacefully."

"Jesus Christ," said Hack. He fumbled for his half-empty pack of cigarettes, an uncomfortable chill creeping along his spine, excitement charging his blood, drying his mouth like powdered alum.

"And then," Slocum went on softly, "they inserted various objects in the rectum of the boy and in the vaginas of the females."

Hack gaped at him. "Don't tell me. A plunger, what they call a Plumber's Helper?"

Slocum's eyebrows shot upward. "Yes, that's a very good guess."

"Not a guess," muttered Hack. "A spike?"

"Correct again. An eight-inch spike from a nail box in the garage." He nodded slowly. "I see. Your Trashman is a copycat."

"You said various objects. What else?"

Slocum shrugged. "A screwdriver—there were several on a bench in the garage—and also, in the woman, a long, thin butcher knife from the kitchen."

"And what did the police make of all this?"

"Not much. The verdict was person or persons unknown. They labeled it a random psycho killing. That's the way it stands today."

"You never came forward with what you knew?"

"No," Slocum said heavily. "You must understand. That was the beginning of my illness. I was a very sick boy for months. And what I saw that day meant absolutely nothing to me—then. It wasn't until later, much later, that I became interested in the story. Years later, as a matter of fact. I was having some success in writing, and I thought perhaps there might be a story in our own little murders. My uncle was town marshal at the time, and he brought me all the records on the case. It was only then that I began remembering, putting it all together. I took it to my uncle and he listened politely and made some vague statement about looking into it. But I'm sure he put it down to the wild imaginings of a man who lived alone too much and made his living writing about lurid murders and the like. Nothing ever came of it, of course. But it happened. And it happened the way I think it did. I'd stake my life on that. Something happened. Something snapped in one of those boys, or maybe both of them. One indignity too many, one bit of abuse too much, one episode of sexual harassment too many—something."

"Whatever became of the records?"

"I have them. They laid around here for a while and nobody ever asked for them back. I have them filed in one of my cabinets."

"Could I possibly see them, make copies maybe?"

Slocum rolled his wide shoulders. "You can take them, if you like. I have no use for them. And the town certainly won't miss them."

"Good, thanks. Is there any reference to the disposition of the twins, where the grandmother took them?"

"To be honest with you, I don't recall. All I remember is that they—the woman's parents—lived in Fort Worth somewhere."

Hack lit another cigarette, his long fingers trembling slightly, his nerves gently thrumming. "The twins. They were identical?"

"Yes. Exceedingly so. So much so that I never even tried to tell them apart."

"How about their dispositions?"

"Quiet, reserved, almost shy. One of them, I'm not sure which, was a trifle more aggressive than the other, but not much."

"Was anything ever written about the murders? I mean, a story that someone could possibly read and copy?"

"Yes, as a matter of fact I wrote an article myself about fifteen years ago. It was published by a magazine as part of a series on unsolved family murders. Then again about . . . oh, seven, eight years ago, a man named Raymond Bentley included it in a book he wrote on the subject. It sold rather well, I believe."

"Then all of this is a matter of public record—the plunger, the spike, the screwdriver, the knife, the method of killing used?"

"Oh, yes. I included it in my article as well."

"Do you believe . . ." Hack hesitated, his throat suddenly dry, his heartbeat accelerating again. "Do you believe it's possible that the Merriweather killers could be the Hamner twins? Or at least one of them?"

"Yes," Slocum said instantly. "I think it's possible. There were similar killings in Houston a few years back. I wrote the chief of police there a letter about the Hamner twins, but I never received an answer." He shrugged and smiled. "Another nut letter among many, I suppose."

"We do get them," Hack said. "And confessions. We've had five so far. One man called from New York, wanted to confess over long distance."

"An amazing compulsion." He propelled the wheelchair backward, made a left, then went forward again toward a row of filing cabinets along one wall. "I'll get you the files."

"Would you mind if I made a call? I'll reverse the charges. There's a detective sergeant in Merriweather who might like to hear about this."

Slocum stopped the wheelchair and turned. "Go right ahead. Just promise me one thing. If the Hamner boys are involved, promise you'll call me as soon as you find out. Maybe I can get the drop on the competition."

"You got it," Hack said. He picked up the phone.

Fifteen minutes later, Hack Wind drove straight out of the Slocum driveway, across the road, and into the overgrown driveway of the old Hamner property. He got out of the pickup and picked his way slowly across the weed-infested lot that had once been the Hamners' front lawn. Mimosa and oleander and mesquite grew wild and untended.

All that remained of the house was the concrete foundation and the stump of a rock chimney. He identified the kitchen by the rusted hulk of an ancient refrigerator, the bedrooms by rectangles of rusted coils that had once been bedsprings. Fire-blackened lengths of wood and chunks of concrete littered the spaces between eighteen-inch-high walls of crumbling foundation. Melted blobs of glass skittered and crunched beneath his boots.

He crossed to the approximate center of the structure and stepped up on the foundation. He turned slowly, balancing easily on the six-inch-wide concrete wall, trying to visualize the house the way it would have looked thirty-five years before.

Much like Parnell Slocum's home, he decided, a two-storied frame with a sharply pitched roofline and very little in the way of architectural amenities. Probably painted white. Tall windows with real shutters that closed. An attached garage, one-car, also frame. A front porch with a swing, a lawn chair or two. Maybe a rubber-tire swing in the big oak out front for the kids. All innocuous enough. Nothing to hint at the misery that had existed behind the oversized door that still lay where it had fallen during the fire, charred and shriveled and cracking now with weather and time.

A chill crept across between his ears and made him shiver, the hair seeming to rise on his neck. He took a deep breath and held it until there was stillness inside.

He recognized the house, the replica he had constructed inside his head. He had lived in half a dozen just like it all across the country while his father chased from one bridge construction site to another, he and his mother tagging along, always one step behind the big, brawling man who loved to work the high steel, the higher the better. Up with the eagles he would say, unable to comprehend Hack's deathly fear of heights. Once, determined to cure his only son of cowardice, he had bodily carried the ten-year-old up on the roof of a house much the same as the Hamners', and while the youth lay gasping, spread-eagled across the ridgeline, drooling with terror and soiling himself, he had beaten the fear out of him with a wide leather belt. . . .

Rigid, trembling, Hack leaped down off the foundation, the action wrenching him into the present, out of a past that sometimes seemed trancelike, a vague jumble of images that streamed through his tattered memory like mismatched segments from a dozen hokey grade B movies.

He hesitated at what had once been the front door of the building, feeling an inexplicably poignant bonding with the two small boys who had suffered so much within the once-confining walls, feeling a surge of empathy, a slowly kindling coal of rage.

He had always had a lot of problems with rage. A well-hidden pocket of rage that few people had ever seen because he had learned to master it. Rejection brought it out, as did ridicule, or more than one person ganging up on him in an altercation. On an intellectual level, he understood the cause-effect relationship between his own childhood abuse and the smoldering anger, but felt helpless to do anything about it. And so he kept it hidden, this shameful secret that his own father had not loved him enough to see and understand.

Feeling riven, febrile, impotent, he climbed into his pickup and drove off into the weeping day, the pulse of the dead house fading, the smell of wet mimosa as sharp as yesterday's memories.

Chapter Sixteen

Roscoe Tanner's big feet slapped the floor with confident authority as he came into the conference room, followed by two young men, button-down types with neatly cropped hair and dressed in three-piece polyester suits, one dark brown and one dark blue.

"Hambone!" Roscoe bellowed cheerfully. "Look what I got. Stand up here and shake hands with Agent Rickers and Agent Smith of the United States Federal Bureau of Investigation!" Roscoe came to a sliding halt in front of Pope. Behind his back the two young men exchanged quick glances, as if wondering whether the big man could possibly be putting them on, their bland, clean-shaven features expressionless and quietly watchful.

The blond one stepped forward and held out his hand. "I'm Rickers, Sergeant Hambone."

Pope shook his hand. "Actually, it's Ham Pope."

Rickers held on to Pope's hand and leaned forward. "Hampoke?"

"Hamilton Pope," Pope explained patiently, relaxing his grip and waiting for the younger man to let go.

"Oh, I see," said Rickers. "This is Agent Robert Smith."

Pope shook hands with the second one, who only nodded and grinned.

"Got two more coming," Roscoe enthused. "These gentlemen are willing to help in any way they can. Right, gentlemen?"

Rickers nodded. "We're at your disposal, sir. I was instructed to tell you that our facilities are also at your disposal at any time."

Roscoe held up his hand and began ticking off on his fingers. "I got you four men coming from Dallas, four from Fort Worth, two from Arlington, two from Irving, and four more from other mid-cities towns. We got four Department of Public Safety patrolmen downstairs right now." He beamed at Pope. "According to my tally, that makes twenty, not counting these two gentlemen and the other two agents coming. We might pick up some more help from outlying towns like Weatherford and Mineral Wells and Greenville. How'm I doing, boy?"

"That's a pretty fair start, Roscoe."

"Start? Start! Jesus H. Christ, Ham!"

Pope shrugged. "They're backing up on us over at the gym now, Roscoe. What do you think it's going to be like in a few hours when they really start pouring in?" He turned to the two agents. "Right now we need skilled interrogators more than anything, gentlemen. All right if I put you to work at that?"

"That's what we're here for." Rickers's answer was prompt, but he looked a bit disappointed. The quiet one nodded and smiled.

"Ask the girl at the front desk for an interrogation guideline, then head for the building across the quad from the library. We have booths set up in the gymnasium."

"Very good," said Rickers. The two men whirled and marched out in step.

"Jesus," Roscoe said, "they're getting them younger all the time."

Pope dropped wearily into his chair. After a moment's hesitation, Roscoe sat down on his right. He picked up a pencil and began torturing it with his big fingers.

"I just got off a two-hour stint over in the gym, Ham. Man, I don't know, I'm beginning to think this is all a waste of time. These guys are as slick as snot on linoleum, plus which they lie like a rug."

"What have you got that's better?" Pope leaned back and lit a cigarette, gazed irritably at his superior officer.

"Hell, I don't know. I'm an administrator. What do I know

149

about psycho killers?" The pencil snapped and he tossed the pieces across the table.

"Probably as much as I do," Pope said. "I don't recall ever being introduced to one socially."

"Wiseass." He picked up another pencil. "Don't much look like anyone knows anything about them. I got three different opinions from three different shrinks. Profiles!" He snorted. "We may as well make up our own."

"Why don't you try Webster? He impresses me as being pretty sharp. His approach is different, anyhow. He gave me and Wind a thumbnail profile the other day that I thought was pretty good. Maybe with more information, he could do better. It would sure help to know something about what kind of joker we're up against. And then there's the FBI Academy in Quantico. I've heard that some of their workups are uncanny, right on the mark. Agent Rickers can help us with that."

"I think it's all a crock of shit," Tanner grumbled. "Webster, huh? That the Keller girl's doctor?"

"That's him."

Tanner shrugged. "Can't hurt, I guess. I'll see he gets what he needs. You think he can keep his mouth shut?" He splayed thick sausage fingers on the table, pressed himself to his feet.

Pope smiled thinly. "He didn't want to talk about the Keller girl, and she's dead. Yeah, Roscoe, I think he can."

"We just don't want the media to get hold of that shit about the plungers and spikes. We'd lose what little edge we got."

Pope shook his head. "It's only a matter of time, Roscoe. Too many people involved now. I'm surprised it hasn't leaked already."

Roscoe grinned suddenly. "Would you believe somebody leaked to the media that in both cases the killers gained entry through unlocked windows?"

Pope attempted to work up an answering grin, failed, and settled for cocked eyebrows and a cynical expression. "Good thinking, Roscoe. Maybe it'll make him overconfident if he thinks we're even more inept than we really are." He shuffled through a small stack of telephone messages on the table in front of him. He studied one, frowning, then handed it to Tanner.

"Have any idea who took this message while I was in the gym?"

"Looks like Forbes's chicken-scratching. Who's Huck? And Duke H? And what the hell's this? 'Screwdriver next'?"

"That's Hackmore Wind. Best I could make it out, he called from Oldfield. Must have found out something about Duke Hamner. He was the Keller girl's shy boyfriend. I don't know what screwdriver means."

"Yeah." Tanner dropped the note on the table and grunted uninterestedly. "What's he doing down there? We need him here."

"It's his case, Roscoe." He cocked a shrewd eye at the bigger man. "What have you got against him?"

"He's too damn good-looking."

"Couldn't be because you think he's black, could it?"

"You know better than that, Ham. Hell, some of the best car-wash boys I know are black." Tanner gazed down at him blandly. "You know damn well I used to have a black girlfriend over in Saigon."

"I thought she was Vietnamese."

"Same thing."

"Shit!" Even though he knew he was being baited, Pope felt a tingle of anger. He turned back to the table and picked up a stack of papers. He felt a rough hand grasp his neck and shake.

"No, I don't think he's black," Tanner mimicked. "I think he's a scalp-hunting Indian."

"You're partly right," Pope said, wincing as the playful hand crushed a few more corpuscles. "He's a black Mexican Indian honky, he said."

Tanner's laugh bounced off the walls in a full-throated roar. He squeezed one more time and let go. "Man, I'd trade colors with him any day to be as pretty as he is. Can you imagine? My personality and his looks? Man, I'd screw myself to death."

"What you mean is, you'd have a hair ball the size of a melon."

Tanner laughed again and headed for the door. "Well, I'm going over and slap the shit out of a few perverts. Coming?"

"In a minute. I want to see how the girls are coming along on the tab run."

A bank of phones had been installed in the squad room. Manned by volunteers, primarily wives of policemen, the phones were being used to call the numbers listed by parolees and registered sex offenders in a three-county area. If there was no answer after three callbacks over an interval of time, or if the offender refused to come in, the names and addresses were referred to Lieutenant Lew Quinn, who was coordinating the project. Quinn and his male assistant would make one more effort to persuade the recalcitrant offender to comply. If he still refused, the name was given to a team of officers. It was tiring, often frustrating work, but an air of camaraderie and esprit de corps had sprung up among the women, and several of them had been hard at it for ten straight hours.

Pope circled the room, checking numbers, handing out lavish compliments, listening to inevitable complaints. He soothed, praised, and stroked, and ended up at Lieutenant Quinn's desk listening to the man's elegant Bostonian accent explain in explicit detail to some hapless sex offender what would happen if he didn't get his ass into the Merriweather Police Station immediately. It had to do with a painful and probably impossible method of castration.

Pope gave Quinn a grim smile, formed a circle with his thumb and forefinger, then headed for the gym to help Tanner slap the shit out of some perverts. Why should Roscoe have all the fun, he thought indignantly.

Hackmore Wind worked the first half of the tuna fish sandwich out of its wrapping while he drove the pickup with one hand. He watched the blacktop road and chewed the gummy, tasteless concoction happily.

Wouldn't it be great, he thought, if I could catch this crazy bastard? Or, at least, get the investigation headed in the right direction? He crammed the remainder of the half a sandwich into his mouth and washed it down with a swig of Pepsi.

It could lead to a better job, maybe. A real cop's job. Even a detective job. Anything but this low-pay, dead-end county mountie routine that inevitably led to a Gil Stiles, a sagging paunch, and a boot-scarred desk in some jerkwater town.

He gulped down the rest of the sandwich, washing the bland, oily taste out of his mouth with Pepsi and going over the day's events in his mind. He chortled a bit at the thought of his own cleverness in ferreting out the grandparents' name and address after the skimpy crime report failed to mention it. A chance remark by Parnell Slocum had set him on the right track:

"For all her failings," Slocum had said dryly as Hack was preparing to leave, "Mrs. Hamner never missed a Sunday's church. Sometimes she weaved and staggered a bit, but she always seemed to make it somehow. She got that from her mother, I suppose. That old lady just *looked* religious, and she always went with her when they visited over the weekend. Good Baptists."

Thirty minutes later Hack was poring over ancient, yellowed visitors' ledgers in the basement of Oldfield's only Baptist church. One for each year, with hard backs and lined pages covered with scribbled names and addresses, the tomes were stacked neatly in chronological order. It took less than fifteen minutes to find it.

Mrs. Jason Caudell, 1510 North Bottomly Avenue, Fort Worth, Texas. Guest of Mavis Hamner.

Hack felt like yelling, felt like hugging the short, prim minister's wife who hovered nearby, bright eyes watching his every move through rimless spectacles. Instead, he shook her hand warmly and unleashed his dazzling smile. She fluttered and blushed and followed him to his truck like a puppy scratched on the belly for the first time.

Unable to wait, he had stopped at a telephone booth and called Forth Worth information. There was still, incredibly, a Jason Caudell listed at 1510 North Bottomly. He stood for a moment inside the booth, his hands shaking. Then he lit a cigarette and went into a nearby fast-food grocery and bought a sandwich and a soda. He climbed back into the truck and headed for the interstate and Fort Worth, his blood singing, his imagination running wild.

Now he finished the last of the Pepsi and glanced down to find the mouth of the trash bag dangling from the dash. His dark eyes were off the road for only a second—but a second is enough when a buck deer, wounded and wild with fear, is running for its life.

It came out of nowhere, clearing the ditch in a single bound, and Hack Wind caught only a glimpse, a stop-motion frame, of distended eyes and flaring nostrils before the truck slammed into the animal broadside.

A thudding, jarring crash, and the deer disappeared, rolling and grinding beneath the wheels.

The truck became airborne, smashed back into the highway with a bone-breaking crash that ripped his hands free of the wheel and tossed him sideways into the passenger seat. Rudderless, the wheels bounced, twisted, careened into the line of least resistance: a sloping grassy shoulder and a yawning drop-off to oak trees and muddy water.

Hack lunged for the wheel, then dropped back and covered his head when he felt the truck's center of gravity shifting at an impossible angle.

He had a sensation of blinding light, a flashing, whirling world, a kaleidoscope of visual effects that metamorphosed into a single star. A single black star that rushed at him with incredible speed . . . bringing oblivion.

Chapter Seventeen

~~~~~~~~~~~~~~

"Please," the woman said. "Please don't do that. You'll hurt my baby."

Duke straightened slowly, allowed himself to slip free. He leaned and placed his hands flat on the tight, swollen stomach. He moved his fingers gently, caressingly. "How far along, darling?"

"Six . . . no, almost seven months. Please, the doctor said I shouldn't after six months." She had a soft, round face, dark eyes that welled and bled moisture as she watched him, terror-stricken. Her lips quivered and writhed as she tried to smile.

"Yeah, man. She's telling you the truth. Why don't you just take the money and leave us alone?" Her husband, beside her, flat on his stomach, raised his head as far as it would go and looked at Duke pleadingly. "Come on, man, we won't say anything. I give you my word."

Duke looked at him and laughed. He walked around the bed and leaned his knees on each side of the woman's head. "I've got a problem," he said softly. "What am I supposed to do with this? It won't go away all by itself, it's funny that way." He smiled into her wet, upside-down eyes.

"What?" He smiled tenderly, reassuringly. "What can we do?"

"What, little lady?" he repeated after a moment. "It wouldn't do for me to go around like this, now, would it?"

She wet her lips. "I—I don't know. . . . Maybe . . . maybe I could—"

"No!" The man was shouting, stretching his neck to look over his shoulder. "You lousy son of a bitch!" He struggled against the tape, lifting the woman's leg completely off the bed.

Duke regarded him with glittering eyes. "What was that, little man?"

"I said no, dammit! You can't—you can't make her do that." But there was no conviction in his voice, and the blood drained from his face as Duke walked around the bed again.

"Go get him, boy," Rocky said softly. Duke ignored him.

He stopped at the man's head, slowly, deliberately twisted his hand into the thick yellow hair. He wrenched upward, bending the long slender neck, Adam's apple bobbing, the man's mouth gaping with the strain.

"I don't think we need you anymore," he said gently, his eyes narrowed to slits, opening slowly in sardonic humor as he brought the blue bag across in front of the man's face. He heard a gasp, and the slender figure tried to buck upward to a hands-and-knees position.

Duke laughed. He took a firm, wide-legged stance, gripped the oily hair with one hand, and swung his right leg over the man's head. He backed up and sat down on the heaving shoulders, settled the bag into place with a deft flip of his wrist. He yanked the drawstring tight.

"Whoooo-eee," Rocky said gleefully. "Ride 'em, cowboy!"

Duke let his eyes wander across the woman's smooth abdomen, the tumescent breasts, stopped at her tightly clenched eyes.

"Look," he commanded. "Watch!"

The woman's terror-filled eyes were the trigger that sent the searing waves of joy exploding in his brain. Gasping, gagging sounds whetted the frenzy as the man's body whipped and tossed in blind, mindless convulsions. He held the thrashing body until it was still, then stepped away from the dead man with shaking knees, his head about to burst. He slid slowly to a sitting position against the wall, eyes blank and lusterless.

"Dammit, he was supposed to be mine," Rocky said petulantly. "Why didn't you let me do that?"

"Don't worry, brother, there's enough to go around." Duke glanced up and saw the woman watching, wide eyes filled with horror, her mouth slack, glistening.

Duke wrinkled his lips in a savage grin. "Don't be impatient, bitch, you're next."

"The Red Witch is crying," Rocky observed. "I think she's sad. I think she wants a little action, too." He giggled helplessly.

Duke thought he recognized a trace of hysteria in his brother's voice. "Okay, babe, just a few more minutes, then we'll give her all she can handle."

"But aren't you afraid you'll hurt baby?" Rocky giggled so hard he began hiccuping.

Duke waited patiently until he was finished, settled down. "Fuck baby," he said.

Rocky broke into another spasm of giggling.

Duke leaned his head back against the wall and wearily closed his eyes, ignoring the sounds of Rocky's mirth.

Rocky subsided, and the room grew quiet. Almost quiet. A faint snuffling noise came from the woman's side of the bed. She clenched her eyes and choked back the sobs, trying desperately to shut out the sound of Rocky humming.

Despite the early-morning sunlight flooding the room when the telephone yanked him out of a troubled sleep, he somehow instantly knew; he picked up the receiver and said simply, "Where?"

Roscoe's voice, somber, deflated, weary, gave him the address. "Rossacher's been contacted. There's a plane out of there in thirty minutes. He said he could make it. We'll have a car at the airport."

"How many? Two?"

"Yes . . . I think so. But it must be bad. The rookie who went in is in some kind of shock."

"You have it sealed off?"

"Of course." He sounded offended. "Dammit, Ham, you think you're the only one's got any damn brains?"

"Sorry, Roscoe. I'm ringing off. I'll be there in about ten minutes." He paused, breathing heavily. "Goddammit, Roscoe, this is only Tuesday! That son of a bitch ain't—" He broke off and hung up the receiver. What was he going to say? Wasn't playing fair? He barked a short, mirthless laugh. He dropped his head into his hands and fought down a sudden wave of panic, dark images flooding his mind, his heart quaking at the thought of what was ahead.

He had to go inside a death room again. Jesus. He *had* to do it. He wasn't sure he could.

Pope stopped just outside the doorway, breathing deeply, filling his lungs with air that wasn't yet tainted with the smell of death. His nose tested: the faint coppery odor of blood and something else he couldn't identify.

He could see feet past the edge of the door, but he averted his eyes quickly. Too soon for that. First he must assimilate the ambience, see it as *he* had seen it, feel it as *he* had felt it in the midst of his frenzy, in the throes of his savage blood-lust.

Mechanically, his mind catalogued the items to the right: dresser, chair, hassock, an ashtray on a stand; a cubbyhole dressing room in one corner with mirrors and a metal stool with a cushion, and centered on the end wall a Rotogrande landscape, a pastoral scene of peace and solitude: two spotted fawns curled at the feet of an alert-eyed doe.

The room was dim, almost dark. The way *he* had left it: a small light somewhere to Pope's left and a faint glow of sunlight through the heavy draperies the only illumination.

He moved forward cautiously.

He could see the feet plainly now almost to midcalf: four of them. All pointing upward. Upward? That was different; the others had been two up and two down. Why? A chest of drawers came into view. Smooth dark wood—pecan or walnut? He found himself trying to decide which, and abruptly realized he was deliberately stalling, creating a diversion.

He moved forward again.

He stopped, puzzling over a wastebasket that had materialized out of the gloom, filled to overflowing with a gray material of some sort with red flowers. A thick ropy strand of something that could have been a belt extended over the side, hung limply. The woman's clothing? Her bathrobe, perhaps? Or maybe the man's—

Dammit, Pope, get on with it!

He moved forward a step, another.

Shallow breaths. The blood smell was cloying, the unidentifiable odor burning in his sinuses, clutching at his throat. He could see the bodies dimly. Side by side, belly-up, like giant, defenseless infants presenting their vulnerability to the world. He suddenly realized he was talking to himself and closed his mouth with a snap. Then he opened it again. It was sound; it beat hell out of the deathly stillness.

"Why different?" he asked himself almost musingly, his voice a low, droning monotone. "Why is the man on his back? Why not like the others? Why did he change the pattern? Why are they both facing the same way? Why? Why?"

He moved again, leaning forward slightly in his effort to see.

"The bags are there, just the same. And her right arm and leg are taped to the bedpost; the same. There's tape on her left wrist and leg, his left wrist and leg— Aha! He had been tied, after all. Cut loose after he was dead and turned around and over. Why? Why bother?"

He leaned forward and peered closely at the woman, his brow wrinkling.

At first glance, she appeared grotesquely obese, full, heavy breasts and a pendulous stomach sagging to one side. But her legs were long and slender, her upper torso thin, her arms and wrists fine-boned and delicate. A numbing chill swept over him, clotting his throat.

Pregnant. My God, she was pregnant! Three victims instead of two. What kind of monster could do this? What kind of rotten son of a—

His heart lurched suddenly. How long could a baby live? Maybe the child was still alive! He took an involuntary step forward, reached to touch her, then drew his hand back with a curse as he saw the smooth wooden handle of the skewer protruding from the lower side of her stomach. The hope died. He felt like he was going to vomit, felt his heart grow cold and hard as stone at this unbelievable madness, this darkness of the soul.

He wrenched his eyes away from the woman, stood upright, sucking in air in huge, ragged gulps, forcing the scalding rage out of his mind, groping for detachment. He reached for a cigarette, then let his hand fall, empty, and turned resolutely to the man.

He had been tall and slender, the long sinewy legs of a runner, well-muscled arms and chest, an almost hairless body. Pope leaned forward, his eyes straining in the gloom.

There was something wrong below the chest, an unnatural concavity and red markings: a straight red line crisscrossed with diagonal lines intersecting at the center to form a series of X's that extended from the sternum to the groin, a hairless groin with a long pale penis that draped limply over the edge of the bed almost to the floor—*almost to the floor!*

He leaned closer still, eyes focused on the incredible phallus.

"Oh, sweet Jesus!" He lunged backward violently, one hand clamped to his mouth, the other pressing against his rolling stomach. He crashed into the wall, stumbled along it to the corner. He thought for a second that he might conquer it, but his mind's eye created an instant replay and his stomach responded with a vengeance.

He turned his face to the pink, rough-textured wall. He slid to his knees and began vomiting.

He was pale and shaken when he came out. Roscoe stepped forward and took his arm. "Hey, man, you okay?"

"Sure," said Pope, lying, knowing he would never be all right again. He turned and looked back toward the house, then at the sun.

"Tell them the vomit in the southwest corner of the room belongs to me." He held out his hand with the two balled-up fit-alls he had worn. Roscoe took them silently, his eyes quizzical, his broad face warped with concern.

Pope looked toward the street, at the curiously silent group of reporters grouped around the Channel 5 news truck. Normally they would be yelling questions, trying to press past the cordon of policemen; instead, they stood silent, watching. A few cameras were rolling; he could feel their blind eyes.

"Musta been bad," Roscoe ventured.

Pope nodded and sucked cigarette smoke deep into his lungs. He made his voice light, unfeeling. "She was pregnant—six, maybe seven months. He used a barbecue skewer on the baby. He opened the man, emptied his insides . . . cut out his genitals. He left a string of intestines hanging out where his penis used to be." He breathed deeply. "He sewed up the man with red yarn. He put the rest of the man's intestines in a wastebasket. Then I think he washed the man down. There wasn't a lot of blood on him."

"Jesus," breathed Tanner, his face slowly losing color.

"One more thing," Pope said.

"My God, what else?"

"He left a message."

Tanner's eyes snapped wide.

" 'Pain,' " said Pope. "That's all, just, 'pain.' On the dresser mirror in blood. 'Pain.' " He looked past the newsmen and reporters to the field of mesquite across the road. Leafless, desiccated limbs pointing toward the sky like horny, fleshless fingers. He glanced back at Tanner's mottled face. "We need to find Hack Wind."

Tanner looked startled. "Wind? Why?"

"Screwdriver," Pope said. "The woman had a screwdriver inserted in her vagina. Wind's note said 'screwdriver next,' remember?"

"Jesus, that's right! How in hell would he know a thing like that?"

"That's why we have to find him," Pope explained patiently.

A siren wailed in the distance, coming closer. The two men turned toward the corner and watched the rotating lights of the speeding squad car.

"That'll be your man Rossacher, I expect," said Tanner.

The car squealed to a dramatic halt at the curb. A tall man in a pearl-gray topcoat with matching flat-brimmed hat stepped out almost before it stopped rolling. He reached back inside and snatched up a thick black briefcase. He came briskly up the walk and stopped in front of Pope.

He held out a thin, long-fingered hand. "Good to see you again, Mr. Pope. It has been too long." His face was long and lean, weather-stained and austere.

"Too long," Pope agreed. "Dr. Rossacher, this is Captain Roscoe Tanner."

"Captain Tanner."

"I've heard a lot about you, Dr. Rossacher."

Rossacher nodded, his cold gray eyes sweeping over Tanner fleetingly, then back to Pope. "You've been in." It was a statement.

"I have. And I think maybe I'd better prepare you for this one."

Rossacher smiled thinly and placed a hand on Pope's shoulder. "No need, Mr. Pope. At one time or another, I've seen all the horrors man can perpetrate against man."

Pope's smile was fully as sparse. "I don't know, Doctor. This one is special."

Rossacher's eyebrows lifted in ironic amusement. The hand on Pope's shoulder squeezed, gave a pat. "Trust me, Ham."

"Okay," Pope said doubtfully. He turned and walked the thin man to the stoop. "Just be prepared for the worst." He handed the doctor a plastic package containing a pair of fit-alls.

Rossacher kicked off his loafers and leaned his shoulder against the doorjamb to slip on the fit-alls. He stepped through the door and smiled back at Pope. "Just like the Boy Scouts, I'm always prepared." He disappeared inside.

"The puke in the southwest corner is mine," Pope said after him, not sure, not really much caring if he heard. He was the best, but that didn't keep him from being an egotistical prick.

He appeared in the doorway a few minutes later, his ruddy face a curious shade of gray. He had shed his coat, and he brushed ineffectually at a stain on the leg of his jumpsuit.

His eyes searched out Pope. "Perhaps you should have prepared me, after all." He smiled his thin smile. "I want your three best men. I do hope you have the Pierson with the Jacobi accelerator pump and the Klaus microfilter."

Tanner looked at Pope. "What's he talking about?"

"Vacuum cleaner."

Tanner shrugged. "I dunno, I think we got a Hoover." He turned and pointed a finger at the small knot of men around the lab truck. He held up three fingers. One of the men leaped into the truck and began passing out equipment.

Rossacher reached out one long arm and touched Pope on the shoulder. "He left a calling card," he said softly. He carefully unzipped a breast pocket on the jumpsuit. He took out a small glassine envelope slightly larger than a postage stamp.

Tanner leaned forward and peered closely. "What the hell is it? I don't see anything."

"Feel," Rossacher said succinctly.

Pope got there first. He took the envelope and pressed thumb and forefinger along the sides gently. His blue eyes widened, shot upward to meet Rossacher's. "Contact lens."

"Exactly." Rossacher's voice carried a trace of pride. "I found it tucked neatly at the edge of her buttock."

"He's a planter," Pope said doubtfully. "You'll probably find a couple of hairs. A red and a blond."

"What'll this tell us if it is legit?" Tanner's huge fingers swallowed the envelope.

"His prescription, for one thing, and if we're lucky it will have the manufacturer's mark on it somewhere." Rossacher carefully stowed the lens in his briefcase and snapped it shut. He stepped out the doorway to allow his small team to come inside.

"How long, do you think?" Pope asked.

Rossacher shook his head impatiently. "I have no idea. It depends." He looked at Tanner. "You'll have a car standing by to take me to the airport?"

"Yes."

Rossacher nodded briefly. "And I'd like to be at the autopsy. Please schedule it for tomorrow afternoon. I'll be back by then. Say, three o'clock."

"Whatever you say, Doc. It's your show."

"Good." He whirled and went back inside.

"Bossy little prick," Tanner said sourly.

Pope laughed. "If that lens is legit, he's already earned his pay."

Tanner wasn't convinced. "Yeah, maybe. We'd have found it anyhow."

Pope moved down the sidewalk toward his Dodge at the curb. "But would we have known what to do with it?" He stopped beside his car and lit a cigarette, watching the group of reporters across the street. "Gird your loins, Roscoe. You're about to be attacked by ravening wolves."

"Where you going?"

Pope climbed in and put the key in the ignition. "Home to have some breakfast, first thing." He switched on the motor, his face suddenly thoughtful. He sighed. "No, on second thought, I guess I'll just have a beer."

Chapter Eighteen

⨯⨯⨯⨯⨯⨯⨯⨯⨯⨯⨯

"Hackmore Wind's wife called," Milly greeted him. "She's frantic. He didn't come home at all last night."

"Hmm." Pope dropped his briefcase on the conference table and pulled out a chair. "And we didn't hear, either?"

"Not exactly," Milly said coolly, her voice very close to icy. "I located Oldfield and called the counties in between here and there. He had an accident. He's in Fairfield Hospital with a couple of broken ribs and a slight concussion."

"Well, I'll be damned. Did you tell his wife?"

Milly nodded, her eyes back on her work. "She's probably on her way down there right now."

"Good work, Milly."

"Just doing my job, sir." Her tone had definitely crossed into the frigid zone.

Pope studied her bowed head for a moment, decided he had better leave well enough alone. Women. He wondered uneasily if she had somehow learned about Nancy Lessor. He felt a sudden flash of indignation. Well, dammit, they didn't have any commitments did they? He had not objected when she dated other men, had he? And she had always made damn sure he found out about it. He watched her flying hands as she sorted through the interrogation reports and wondered if she was trying to tell him something. He shook his head irritably. That didn't make any sense. He had offered to let her move in with him. Several times,

166

in fact. And she had given him that shitty little grin he never understood and shaken her head.

He glared at the part in her hair and tried to think of something to say that wouldn't be too obvious. Something businesslike.

"By the way," he said, "did you find out anything about that receipt?"

Milly looked up and frowned. "Receipt? Oh, you mean from the Free Animal Clinic." She shrugged. "They ask for contributions from people who want to get rid of pets. The Jacksons dropped off a cat they didn't want."

"That's a hell of a thing," Pope said, his tone ingratiating in spite of an effort to keep it neutral. "People want pets, they should keep them."

Milly shrugged again and went back to work. "It's a tough world." She looked up a moment later. "You should get to know Rocky. That's his sentiment exactly."

"Who's Rocky?"

"A beautiful hunk who runs the Free Animal Clinic." She leered and waggled her wrist, forgetting for a moment her antagonism. "God, he's gorgeous. And so's his twin brother." She paused reflectively. "A little musclebound, maybe."

Pope's ears pricked up. "How old?"

Milly's face reddened. "Old enough."

"How old?" pressed Pope, happy to have her talking again.

"Twenty maybe, twenty-one, somewhere in there."

"Little young for you, huh?"

"Oh?" Back to icy again. "Since when do men have a monopoly on hot young bodies?"

Damn! So she did know about Nancy Lessor. He pushed away from the table. "Well, guess I better go give them a hand in the gym."

"Yes," Milly said evenly. "I think that would be nice."

* * *

167

He went instead to his small office and the telephone on the desk. He dialed information and then placed a call to Fairfield Hospital in Freestone County. He asked for Hackmore Wind's room and was routed to the nurses' station instead.

"This is Detective Sergeant Pope of the Merriweather police. I need to talk to Deputy Wind, please."

"I'm sorry, sir," the nurse said, unimpressed. "Mr. Wind isn't allowed to take calls as yet."

"But I only need to talk to him for just a second."

"I'm sorry, sir. Perhaps after doctor makes his rounds."

"Well, perhaps," Pope said testily, "you could connect me with doctor."

"I'm sorry, sir, doctor is unavailable now. He's making rounds."

"Is Mrs. Wind there yet?"

"I haven't seen her, sir."

"Would you mind asking her to call me when she arrives?"

"Of course, sir."

"Does that mean you mind? Or will you have her call?"

"I'll give her your message, sir."

"Could you tell me anything about his condition?"

"He's doing as well as can be expected, sir."

"Thanks, I really appreciate it. You've been most helpful." He slammed down the receiver, almost immediately ashamed of his petty behavior. He lit a cigarette and started to get up. He sat back down as Maybelle Norman bustled through the door.

"Oh, there you are!" She was wearing a pale yellow dress and a man's cardigan sweater, carrying the same floppy hat and straw handbag, lined face florid as usual from exertion and good humor.

"Hello, Maybelle. I heard about you helping out on the phones. Thanks."

She waved a plump hand. "Everybody's got to help, something like this comes along." She sat down in his visitor's chair with a sigh. "I heard about the . . . new ones." She fanned her face with the brim of her hat, bright eyes gleaming like a ferret's.

"I don't think you want to know about these, Maybelle."

"Trashman getting carried away, is he?" She rocked back and forth in the chair, perspiration gleaming on her broad forehead, a friendly smile that invited confidence.

Pope nodded moodily. "I think you could say that."

"What I wanted to ask you," Maybelle said, "is that I seem to remember reading or hearing something about a van, a light-colored van at the Jacksons'."

"That's right. A van was sighted in the vicinity at about the time of the murders. Not corroborated."

"Could it be something like a . . . say, a light gray, maybe?"

"Could be." He eyed her intently. "What's on your mind, Maybelle?"

Her hand fluttered at her throat, an amazingly girlish gesture considering its size and shape. "Nothing . . . not anything, really. I was just wondering."

He gazed at her for another long moment, scanned the bland face, innocent eyes. He cleared his throat harshly. "Don't hold out on me, Maybelle. This is too important."

"I wouldn't do that, Ham," she replied quietly. "It's nothing —really. If I thought it was, I'd tell you. Okay?"

"You do that, Maybelle. This is real life, you know. It's not 'Rockford' or 'Magnum, P.I.'"

She bobbed her head. "I know. I sure appreciate you letting me in on it even a little bit. Makes me feel like I'm earning my money."

"You still don't want to tell me who your client is?"

"I'll tell you this much, Ham. It's someone very close to Rochelle Jackson—a relative."

"Okay. That's good enough. I can't say I blame whoever it is. The police aren't doing such a hot job with it." He stubbed his cigarette in the ashtray.

"You're doing all you can, I'm sure. What else can you do?"

"A lot, according to the newspapers." He stood up and pushed his chair in to the desk.

"You can't pay no attention to them. Bunch of Monday morning quarterbacks." Maybelle gave him an encouraging smile and hoisted herself to her feet. She tugged at her dress and walked ahead of him out of the office. She looked over her shoulder. "Is my slip showing, honey?"

Policewoman Merry Childs poked her head around the conference room door. "Ham. There's a phone call for you in your office. Want me to have the desk transfer it in here?"

"Yes, Merry, thank you."

He got up and lit a cigarette and moved to the end of the table by the phone. When it rang, he jerked it up impatiently. "Pope."

"Sergeant Pope?"

"Yes, this is Pope."

"Uh . . . this is Spencer Good, Sergeant. I've, uh, been thinking. I wasn't exactly . . . well, I didn't tell you the whole truth the other day."

Pope sucked on the cigarette and said nothing.

"I—well, about my brother. He's not really . . . Had you found out about that yet?"

"Just go on, Mr. Good," Pope said coldly.

"Okay, okay. It's just that he's been in there so long I think of him as dead."

"Exactly how long? And where has he been?"

"Ever since—I'll bet you know about this already?"

"Let's just play like I don't know anything, Mr. Good."

"Well, they put him in there when he was eighteen. For life, it was supposed to be."

"After he did what?"

"What?"

"What did he do, Mr. Good?"

"Oh. . . . Well, he did that . . . thing to that girl. He spent ten years in the nut . . . institution before they even tried him. Then he got life."

"You said that, Mr. Good," Pope said patiently. "What did he do to get sent to the institution?"

"He cut her up." He spat it out in a soft liquid rush as if he couldn't bear to hear the words. Either that, or the thought turned him to mush inside. Pope couldn't tell which.

"Is he still inside?"

"Oh, yes, I'm . . . sure he is."

"Don't lie to me again, Mr. Good."

"I don't really know."

"Don't you visit him?"

"No—not for years and years. He was just too . . . mean."

"What's his name?"

"It's Good, like mine."

"His first name, Mr. Good?"

"Oh. Hector Roy, Hector Roy Good."

"What prison?"

"Huntsville."

"Is there anything else I should know, Mr. Good? Anything else you lied about?"

"No, absolutely not."

"What type of vehicle do you drive, Mr. Good?"

"Why—a Bonneville. That's Pontiac. It's a year old. Why?"

"Do you own a van?"

"No."

"All right. Thanks for calling. We'll be in touch." Pope dropped the receiver in the cradle and tried to put Spencer Good in the scene he had witnessed that morning. It wouldn't jell somehow. He added the gist of the conversation to his notes and attempted to wash the resurrected images out of his mind again. They wouldn't go, and he could suddenly smell the copper of blood and the unidentified odor that he now knew came from inside human bodies.

171

He wasn't sure if he could ever go into a death room again. It was something he would have to think about, make up his mind about. It was his job, and it was either do it or quit. Maybe he would quit.

He went into the squad room and found the G tab run. It had been worked, but there were a number of names with a large asterisk in the left margin. This indicated that the name had been given to a team of detectives, that all attempts by phone had failed to produce results.

Pope found himself holding his breath as he leafed rapidly through the flimsy sheets. Gondell, Goneph, Gonte—Good! Hector Roy Good. Paroled August 2, after serving sixteen years of a life sentence for murder. A large asterisk by the name.

His heart pounded. He walked along the line of busy women to Lew Quinn's desk.

"Hector Roy Good, Lew. Who's working him?"

Quinn gave him a sharp look, then ran a pencil down a list on his desk. "Nobody yet, Ham. There's three ahead of him. Why? Anything special?"

"I don't know. . . . Put me down for him. Me and . . . Singer, I guess." He went back to the tab run and copied down the address. He was on his way to pick up Milly when he remembered the gun.

He detoured to his office. Feeling a slight tingling along his nerve ends, he unlocked the bottom drawer. He picked up the holstered revolver gingerly, the smooth, worn leather cool to his fingers, the bone handle rough and hard against his palm. He clipped it to his belt and removed the gun. He flipped open the cylinder and stared at the empty chambers, slick and slightly oily from its last cleaning.

Seven years, he thought, seven years and it could be yesterday. He suddenly felt fragmented, unwanted images of a dark, dim hallway flashing off the cutting-room floor in his mind: a dark, dim hallway and a hulking Lieutenant Roscoe Tanner stalking fifteen feet ahead of his backup team with about as much caution as a bull elk in heat; a dark, slim shape materializing from a doorway, the deliberate practiced crouch, the long-barreled gun held in both hands, pointed at the back of Roscoe Tanner's head. . . .

No time for anything except panic reaction: a warning cry from Pope's constricted throat, and the feel of the bone gun-butt slamming into his palm—once, twice, three times. The slim shape leaped, did a delicate tippy-toe routine, and dissolved onto the threadbare carpet, a limp, lank pretzel of lifeless arms and legs.

Someone ripped the ski cap from the small head. And someone else used a flashlight to halo the fifteen-year-old face with the delicate bones, long fringed lashes, and the fan of shoulder-length yellow hair.

And then, seconds later, the other half of the father-daughter robbery team appeared at the end of the corridor, a paper sack of money in one hand, a sawed-off double barrel in the other. The gun lifted, lined up down the narrow hallway. The others were still kneeling beside the dead girl; Pope emptied his gun into the man, screaming with fear and despair. He heard, dimly, the roar of the shotgun, stood limply in a rain of falling plaster from the ruined ceiling.

He remembered the thud of his gun on the carpet, the hot smothering July night as he picked his way through the curious faces that came out of the woodwork. And he remembered precious little else. . . .

He closed the cylinder and pushed the drawer shut with his toe. He made it all the way to the door before he came back and opened it again and took out the bullets.

Chapter Nineteen

✕✕✕✕✕✕✕✕✕✕✕

Wendy finished tucking Hack into the passenger seat of her Dodge. She trotted around the front of the car and slid under the wheel. Tall, lissome, she had fair skin and strawberry-blond hair. Her face was angular, a short straight nose and full lips. Attractive, bordering on lovely, she had a sensuous grace that was entirely unaffected, which lifted her a notch or two above the crowd, kept her from being just another pretty girl.

She lit two cigarettes and passed him one. "Are you sure you can handle two hours of sitting like that?"

Hack worked the lever on the side of the seat, allowed it to tilt backward two notches. He leaned back with a sigh. "Yeah, I'll be okay. Just don't scare me into jumping, is all." He burlesqued a frightened face and winced when he moved more than he intended.

She chuckled throatily and started the engine. "Well," she said tartly, "I haven't hit a deer lately."

He lifted his head. "That damn thing came out of absolutely nowhere. Damnedest thing you ever saw. Just like he came up through the pavement." He lay back and closed his eyes. "I never see one that big when I'm hunting."

She waited until they were on the interstate, settled into the right lane at a cruise-controlled sixty. She flipped her cigarette into the airstream outside the car. "They had another one last night, Hack. I heard it on the radio coming down."

174

His eyes opened slowly, bewildered. "Another . . . You mean the Trashman?"

She nodded. "A man and his wife. Carlson was their name." She hesitated. "She was seven months pregnant. Glenna and John," she added sadly. "In their early twenties."

"Jesus Christ! He wasn't due until Wednesday!"

"Maybe nobody told him that."

"Oh, Christ! That goddamn deer!"

She threw him a startled glance. "What're you talking about?"

"I *know*, Wendy! I know who the Trashman is. The Hamner twins—Duke and Rocky Hamner, real names Kerry and Perry. I lost a whole day and night because of that damn deer. We could have maybe—"

"You don't know that for sure, honey. How can you know for sure?"

"I do know, dammit! It's too much of a coincidence—the plungers, the spike—" He broke off and took a deep breath and began to tell her about it.

After he finished, she drove quietly for a moment. She lit them each another cigarette, then drifted into the passing lane to go around a laboring eighteen-wheeler jetting black smoke and bellowing in helpless anger.

"I'll admit it sounds right, but like Mr. Slocum says, it could be someone who read about the Hamner killings and is copying them." She shook blond tresses. "I'm not convinced that two six-year-olds could do something like that."

Hack smoked in grim silence. He opened the glove compartment and took out a Texas map. He studied it for a moment, then folded it and put it back. "When we get to Ennis, take a left on Highway 287."

"Why 287? That'll take us to Fort Worth."

"There's a reason for that," Hack said belligerently. "That's where I want to go. Bottomly Avenue. I'll direct you when we get to the interchange."

"Hack!" There was alarm in her voice. "Honey, you're in no condition to go looking—"

He twisted in the seat and gripped her arm, ignoring the stabbing in his ribs. "Just do it, Wen, please. This is my lead. I dug it out. I have to follow it." He leaned back in the seat and closed his eyes again, a film of sweat on his dark brow. "Kick it up to sixty-five," he said.

Obediently, Wendy reset the cruise control. "We'll get a ticket," she prophesied.

He smiled without opening his eyes. "I'll fix it. Too bad you don't have a light and siren on this jalopy."

They drove for a while in silence, through wide, flat fields beginning to swell and roll gently the farther north they progressed, distant farmhouses surrounded by cottonwoods and elms, the faraway horizon limited by the deep, dark shadow of scrub oak forests.

"How did it go yesterday?" he asked suddenly.

"Oh, all right, I guess. We talked, talked, talked. I was there all afternoon. He took me to see the isolation room." She stopped and laughed dryly. "I see what he means by isolation."

"Is it in the same building?"

"Yes. Of course, you don't have to stay there. You can go to a motel room if you prefer. But why spend thirty dollars for a drab motel room when I can get all the drab I want right there?"

"Sounds pretty grim."

She shrugged. "Not so bad, I guess. It's clean. A bed, table, and chair. A small bathroom. Plenty of hot water. I'll probably spend the night soaking in the tub. Nothing else to do."

"No TV?"

"No TV or radio either. No newspaper, no magazines. No nothing. Just me and my pain."

Hack laughed. "He's pretty high on pain. He gave me and Ham a little lecture on the terrible consequences of repressed pain."

She brushed her hair away from her face so she could see him in her peripheral vision. "Didn't you have any childhood fears? Rejection, feeling unloved, neglect, any of the stuff he talks about?"

He shook his head slowly. "Naw. I had pretty good parents. The only rejection I felt was being a black Mexican Indian honky in a honky world."

Her hand reached impulsively for his, the almost translucent white skin a sharp contrast against the dark warmth of his.

"I wish you'd stop saying that. You're beautiful, even if you don't know it."

"And smart, too," he said.

"That's right. You have a fine brain. You inherited the best of all four races."

"You bet. Only twenty-six and already a deputy sheriff."

"You don't have to be a lawman, you know. There are other things."

"I dunno. Now that the demand for astronauts and brain surgeons has slowed down, there ain't a hell of a lot left that I'm qualified for."

"You could go back to college. You only lack a year—"

"A year and a half, and anyhow, this is about as close as I can come to my lifelong ambition to be a gunslinger."

She retrieved her hand. "I can't talk to you."

"I thought we were having a nice conversation. We were talking real good, I thought."

"*I* was talking. You were being a wiseass."

"That's jive-ass. When you gonna learn my language? Jive-ass turkey. I think that has a nice ring to it. Very expressive. You get the idea right off. Say it: you're a jive-ass turkey, Hack." He knew he should shut up, wondered even as he was babbling what perversity drove him to instant brutal retaliation at the slightest hint of rejection by her, by almost anyone with a pure white skin. He sometimes wondered if marrying Wendy hadn't been a form of self-flagellation.

177

"I'm sorry. I know you were only trying to be funny." She found his hand again and squeezed it.

"Yeah, that's me, I'm a very funny man." Embarrassed, ashamed, yet not quite able to admit it, he leaned his head back and pretended he wanted to sleep. Trying to analyze his own attitude objectively had too often proved to be a fruitless task.

The house at 1510 North Bottomly Avenue was small and badly in need of repair. It was also dark and silent. Hack and Wendy stood on the concrete porch while he punched the bell, then ended up pounding lustily.

"They gotta be old," Hack muttered. "Maybe they're hard of hearing."

"I don't think they're home, honey." Wendy glanced nervously toward the street, toward the two young black men walking slowly past, watching them with open curiosity, undisguised hostility.

Hack turned awkwardly, his forearm pressed against his side. "I guess not."

A sliding window protested loudly in the house next door. A voice as thick and liquid as cold maple syrup yelled at them, "You-all lookin' for pore old Mr. Caudell?"

Hack walked to the edge of the porch. "Yes, ma'am, we are. He does live here, doesn't he?" He smiled at the round black face. Gold teeth flashed back at him.

"He shore did. But they done took him away last week. Pore old man living by hisself thattaway. Somebody ought to be ashamed of theirselves."

"Do you know where they took him?"

"Probably John Peter. He didn't have no money—not unless that fancy grandson of his'n sent him some. He sure ain't been by to see him none."

"Do you know who his grandson is?"

"Nossir. Don't know nothin' about him. I only lived here three years. He ain't been by here in that time that I knows about. Pore old Mr. Caudell talked about him all the time, is all I knows."

"Did he mention what he did—what kind of work he does? His grandson, I mean?"

"Nossir. Don't remember him sayin' that about him. Just said he was rich." She made an indignant noise. "You'd think he'd take better care of his grandpa. Old man couldn't hardly get around at all the last year or so."

"You think he went to John Peter Smith Hospital, then?"

"Yessir. Don't know where else they'd take him wifout some money."

"He went away in an ambulance?"

"Yessir. It was an ambulance."

Hack thanked her and turned away. He was suddenly light-headed, the bright afternoon air around him filled with black dots and twinkling stars.

"Hey," he said thickly. "I guess I don't feel as good as I thought."

"I told you," Wendy hissed in his ear as she slipped a hand around his waist and draped his arm across her shoulder. "You're pale as a ghost."

"Just get me to the car, hon, I'll be all right."

She half-carried him down the walk, suddenly aware that the two black youths had turned and come back. They were standing a few feet in front of the car.

"Hey, momma, you need some help?" He was tall and lean, with a basketball afro. His buddy laughed and bopped around in a circle and clapped his hands.

"No, thank you, I can manage." She opened the door, balancing Hack on her hip. She backed him into the seat and watched him fold limply against the backrest, his head lolling.

"What the hell happened?" he muttered. She picked up his feet and stuffed them in the car.

"Hey, momma!" The voice was right behind her and she leaped backward and slammed the door. "Looks like your man done petered out on you. Maybe we ought to get it on? Whatcha say, momma?" A long ropy arm snaked out to lean against the car and block her way. The other hand reached out to her hair. "Mmm, look at that purty yeller hair."

"Naw, that ain't yeller, that's gold hair." His companion had come up on the other side of her, his arm also against the car. Not as tall as his friend, he was even thinner, with a tight cap of kinky hair.

"Get out of my way. Please." She tried to slip under the first man's arm, but he bent a skinny leg and blocked her with his knee. She felt a hand cup her buttock and squeeze.

"Stop it!" She backed against the car as they edged closer, her eyes casting frantically about for aid. No one on the street. But her sweeping eyes saw the round black face of the woman they had talked to, watched in disbelief as she slowly closed the window, her face impassive.

A hand touched her breast, another slid between her clenched thighs and began to move upward. She saw the tall one's grinning mouth move toward her own, and she wrenched her body in a violent attempt to escape. She kicked out her foot and felt her leg captured between the tall one's thighs. She felt his erection pressing against her leg, and panic surged in her throat like vomit. They forced her back against the car window. The tall one gripped her jaw in his fist and grinned and licked his lips.

"You . . . can't . . . do this," she whispered through clamped teeth.

The tall one pressed against her, pinning her against the car. The other one began pulling up her skirt. "Why not, momma? I does it standing up all the time."

"My—my husband—"

"That motherfucker! He's out like a light. Come on, man, get them panties off her!" He brought both her hands together and held them in one of his. He fumbled with his clothing, and she shuddered at his bare hardness against her thighs. She felt the blood draining from her face, her body going limp, felt something moving down her back and wondered vaguely if they were taking off her bra.

"Hey, man!" The sound in her roaring ears was so faint she almost missed it. But there was a familiar ring to it, and she almost fell as the hands suddenly went away. She braced herself against the car and opened her eyes.

"Hey, man," Hack said again. "Where you mothers want it? Make it easy on yourselves. In the gut or in the head? It's all the same to me."

"Hey, bro, we was just . . ." The tall one's voice faded as the gun at the end of the long arm dropped toward his dangling penis. "Hey, man—don't!"

Hack swung the gun toward the other one. "How about you, snotface? Your partner gets it in the balls. Where do you want it?"

"Come on, man, we wasn't out to hurt your woman. We just—"

"You hurt her, you son of a bitch! Just putting your filthy hands on her, you hurt her, scumbag! Goddammit! Where do you want it?" He snaked the hammer back to full cock. "Get in the car, Wendy. I wanna be ready to roll when I waste these shitbags." He cranked the glass down the rest of the way and leaned out the window. He waited until she was behind the wheel, then stopped the weaving gun and pointed it at the tall man's groin.

"Say good-bye to love, motherfucker!" He took deliberate aim.

The tall man screamed, turned, and ran. Hack raised the gun barrel and squeezed the trigger. There was a dry click.

He looked at the second man. "Dammit, a dud. Let's see if it can happen again." He pointed it at the second man's genitals and pulled back the hammer. The second man turned and ran. Hack pointed it at the sky and pulled the trigger. The roar was deafening.

"You okay?" He leaned across and touched her cheek, stroking

181

gently, his taut features shifting from cold, hard rage to compassion, dark eyes still charged with flaring emotion.

Wendy nodded dumbly, leaning into his comforting touch.

"Can you drive okay?"

She bobbed her head.

"Then get us to hell out of here. I think I'm going out again."

Chapter Twenty

Pope filled Milly in on what he knew about Hector Roy Good while they drove.

"He's spent the last twenty-three years behind bars of one kind or another. Released last August. I don't have the details, but it had something to do with the dismemberment of a young girl. His twin brother is Spencer Good, the TV anchorman."

"Sounds like a jolly type," Milly said. "Do you think he could be our man?"

Pope shrugged. "He could be. But if he is, he's changed his M.O. Maybe he learned a little finesse in the joint."

Milly looked out at the dreary, dripping day and shivered. "Creeps like him give me the horrors."

"I'm sorry, Milly. If there had been anyone else available . . ." He let it fade under her withering glance.

"You'd what? Chosen a man? You listen to me, Hamilton Pope! I'm just as good a cop as you or any of those other hairy-legged brutes. Just not as strong—maybe. And don't you forget it!"

"That's not what I meant," Pope said reasonably. "It's just not right for a woman to be exposed to scum like—"

"Don't try to protect me, Ham," she said crisply. "I don't need it." She lit a cigarette and wiped her side of the foggy windshield. "Durant Street, it's the next one past that Gulf station. One-fifteen north will be to the right," she added unnecessarily.

183

She checked the house numbers as soon as they turned the corner. "It should be in the middle of the block . . . there, that yellow frame." She pointed to a two-story wooden house badly in need of paint. A late-model Pontiac sedan and a battered Toyota station wagon sat side by side in the driveway.

Pope nodded and eased the car to the curb two houses away. "Let them know we're here," he said.

Milly picked up the mike. She pressed the switch, then pecked it against her palm. "It's not working, Ham."

"Oh, hell, I forgot the damn thing's broken."

"Again? Or still?"

"Still," he muttered. "We better go back to that Gulf station and call in for a backup—"

"Whatsa matter, tough guy?" she jeered softly. "You're not afraid of one little psycho, are you? Don't worry, honey, I'll protect you." She patted his hand consolingly, a mean little smile tugging at the corners of her mouth.

His eyes found hers and locked, his face expressionless. He opened the car door. "Okay, officer, you got it."

He touched her arm at the bottom of the short steps. "Wait right here until you see me go in."

She nodded and opened the clasp of her purse.

He heard sounds inside when he punched the bell: an excited jabbering, quickly hushed. The muffled thud of feet on a wooden floor, and then silence. He was ready to pound when the doorknob rattled and the door swung open slowly. Six inches, pause, and then a foot.

It was Spencer Good's face with a burr haircut and a jagged scar down one cheek, thinner, pallid, meaner. The eyes were different, sly, darting, suspicious. The face stared at him silently.

Pope held up his shield. "Hector Roy Good. I'm Sergeant Pope, we'd like to come in and talk—"

He saw the right shoulder dip, the eyes flicker, the shotgun coming up, and he was on his way to the right and the wall beside the door. Even so, he felt the sharp tug of the balled shot as it passed through the billowing tail of his raincoat. His head rang and his left hand stung with a thousand needles of fire from the expanding powder blast.

The gun had leaped into his hand of its own volition, cocked and spearing toward the door, waiting for movement. There was none.

He yelled something at Milly and saw her head bob through the porch railing as she disappeared around the side of the house.

He slipped out of his raincoat and tossed it through the doorway. Nothing. He followed in a running dive with his heart in his mouth and his stomach screaming in dismay. He came to his knees in time to see a short, fat man disappear through a doorway, a bundle of clothing under his arm.

He climbed stiffly to his feet and went after him. He passed another doorway: a glimpse of a thin, naked figure spread-eagled on a black bed, a raised head with a startled female face and no signs of blood.

In time, thank God! He thudded clumsily onward.

The short, fat man was hopping on one leg trying to get the other leg into his pants. He squawked and dropped the pants and threw his hands in the air when he saw the gun. "Don't shoot! Don't shoot, please!" His pudgy legs were shaking and urine dribbled unnoticed from a short, thick penis almost hidden by groin fat.

Pope stepped close and swept his foot behind the quaking knees. The fat man fell, screaming, rolling in his own urine, trying to crawl. Pope pounced on him, snapped handcuffs on the surprisingly tiny wrists.

"Where is he? Where did he go?" He pressed the ashen face into the wet carpet. "Goddammit, answer me!"

"I don't know . . . don't know," the man blubbered. "Out . . . the back . . ."

Pope's heart lurched. Milly! He was on his feet and running

185

when the first clap of thunder sounded—and again. An answering blam, blam, blam, and then a final one, and he burst through the open rear door and into the backyard into eerie silence.

He slid to a halt, crouching, frantically searching among the trees and bushes for Milly's green windbreaker. His heart was bursting, choking him; the only part of him not shaking was the hand holding the gun.

"Back here, Ham." Her voice was weak and strained, and he whirled, expecting the worst.

She was standing by the corner of the house, shakily punching new loads into her .38. She gestured with her head. "Over there . . . behind that . . . that . . . whatever the hell it is . . . that bush, the red one." Only the fact that she was leaning against the house and her quivering voice betrayed her.

"You okay?"

She nodded impatiently. "Check him, Ham. Make sure the b-b-bastard's dead." She seemed reluctant to leave her support. He knew how she felt.

Pope grinned at her and turned away. Now that he knew where to look, he could see the shotgun and a pair of arms, the hands curled into fists in the long, dead grass. Nevertheless, he approached the man cautiously.

On his back; the open, sightless eyes stared uncaring into the peppering rain. He wore nothing except shorts—briefs, nylon or maybe silk. He couldn't tell which without touching, and he wasn't about to do that. He touched a finger to the stilled neck artery, noted the three bloody holes on the thin chest that he could have covered with the span of one big hand. There was no fourth hole that he could see. Three out of four ain't bad, he thought. He wondered what the man's back would look like, but he didn't look.

He went back to Milly. "The b-b-bastard's dead, all right," he said, grinning, watching her carefully.

She bobbed her head in grim satisfaction and tried to smile. Her chin quivered, and he saw her eyes roll warningly. He stepped in quickly and put his arms around her.

"You did a hell of a job, Detective Milly Singer. But it's not over. There's a fat slug in there who needs interrogating, and a little girl who's been through a lot. So, let's go, Singer." He brushed her forehead with puckered lips.

She bobbed her head again and dropped the .38 into her purse. Her hand came out with a sodden mass of Kleenex. "Oh, shit! Everything's wet."

"Here." He produced a relatively dry handkerchief from his inside coat pocket and gave it to her. "Wash it before you return it, will you?"

She smiled feebly and blew her nose. She breathed deeply and walked ahead of him across the muddy yard.

"Looks like they were all prepared." Roscoe Tanner, his face three shades lighter than normal, stood over the TV tray draped with a white, fluffy towel. "Skinning knife, butcher knife, meat saw, cleaver—Jesus H. Christ!" He backed away from the tray and looked at Pope, his eyes bright and hot. "They were going to cut her up," he said hollowly, wonderingly.

Pope nodded. "That was Hector Roy's thing. A little fun and games, then quarter the evidence. There was a rubber sheet under the girl on the bed. It's padded with an absorbent liner. Helps a lot with the blood. He didn't have the sheet the last time. That's one of the things that tripped him up, the blood soaked into his mattress."

"Jesus. Another few minutes . . ."

Pope shook his head. "They hadn't even touched her yet—a little stroking, maybe. I think they were all set up for a long winter evening's entertainment. They had a big bowl of pretzels and six quarts of beer." He turned and led the way out of the property room, nodding his thanks to the young officer at the door.

"The girl was okay, though?" Tanner slowed his stride to match that of the shorter man.

Pope smiled faintly. "Pissed off at us, is all."

Tanner's head jerked around, his face incredulous. "Pissed off! Godalmighty, why?"

Pope lit a cigarette and stopped at a trio of squat, battered vending machines. "She's a pro. Thirteen years old. The fat one, Paul Hermann, picked her up down on South Street. They promised her fifty each if they could tie her up and pretend they were raping her. Whore or not, she's still a kid, and that made perfect sense to her. She pretends all the time. She was pissed because she didn't get her money." He dropped coins into one of the machines and motioned for Tanner to make a selection.

"Nobody told her?" Tanner punched coffee, black.

"I wanted to, but Milly wouldn't let me. Said she would explain it to her later—after things had quieted down a bit."

"Sounds like a tough little girl."

"That's not the half of it." Pope didn't try to squelch his rumbling laugh. "The little squirt told Milly she wanted to see the fat man again, to be sure she could identify him at the trial. That made some kind of sense, so Milly brought her into the bedroom. The fat asshole was still naked, and the girl walked right up to him. She spit in his face. He leaned backward to get away from her, and she kneed him in the nuts. I couldn't have done a better job myself. He puked all over the floor."

"Victim brutality," Tanner said when he stopped chuckling. "Some bleeding-heart lawyer will probably use that in court."

"I doubt if he'll mention it when he sees the size of the little girl." Pope made his own selection, watched the mud-colored liquid stream into a white Styrofoam cup.

"How did Milly handle icing that asshole?"

"Controlled. Tight. Wound up inside. She's running on raw nerve alone. I'd like to help her, but it's something you have to work out for yourself." He tasted the concoction he had ordered, made a face, then dumped it back into the machine's drip tray. Despite his empathy for Milly, he couldn't suppress a faint trickle of relief, a sneaky feeling of gratitude that it had been her and not him. The thought appalled him, but the feeling wouldn't go away.

"You don't think they're our men?" Tanner's voice contained a faint trace of hope. "Maybe they're just changing their M.O."

"No chance, Roscoe. We found no gloves, surgical or otherwise, no bags. They tied her with clothesline. Even the knots were different. The Trashman uses bow knots on everything. They planned this last night, according to Hermann."

Tanner shoved his hands into his pockets and walked around the room, his massive face disgruntled. He came back to stand in front of Pope. "Heard from your man Rossacher. They ID'd that contact lens. It's made by Orsen Optical in Milwaukee. FBI's got a man on the way over there to pick up a list of the distributors in Texas. Only problem is, Orsen is one of the biggest manufacturers in the country. They sell a new type of soft lens that everybody's using." He grimaced heavily. "Another impossible task ahead of us. Rossacher translated the prescription into its numerical equivalent, so now all we'll have to do is get a copy to everybody concerned with the contact industry. Do you have any idea how many eye doctors there are in Texas? Optical stores?"

"Don't knock it. It's our first piece of hard physical evidence. I doubt if we can use it to catch him, but after he's caught, it'll tie him to the scene." He stopped and grimaced in turn. "If it wasn't planted."

"Even if it wasn't planted, he could've got the damn things in Big Ball, North Dakota, or somewhere," Tanner said dispiritedly. "Anything else?"

"A smudge of grease on the carpet and some talcum powder on the woman that he says probably came out of the gloves." He hesitated. "Two hairs. One red, one blond. Same as before."

Pope nodded calmly, not bothering to look at the big man. "He's consistent. He gets hung up on something, he stays with it."

He stopped and stared thoughtfully at Tanner. "Kinda makes him look like a dummy. Maybe that's the reason for it."

"I reckon you're right about the hairs," Tanner said grudgingly. "Nobody's going to lose just one hair each time. What I don't get is why we haven't found some real hairs. You'd think with all that activity, he'd lose at least a cock hair. Them little boogers come out all the time." He grinned suddenly. "On women, too."

"He's smart enough to know that. Something like a pair of men's elastic briefs or cutoff panty hose with a slit would prevent that."

"Goddamn pervert. I'd like to get that son of a bitch alone for just five—hell, no, just two minutes."

"Bloodthirsty savage." Pope threw up his hands in mock fright. Suddenly, for the first time in days, he felt good. Very nearly lighthearted. His sympathy for Milly notwithstanding, it had been a good afternoon's work. One animal scum dead, and another behind bars. One little girl spared a night of unbelievable horror and a gruesome death. At least one positive thing had come out of the Trashman's madness.

Chapter Twenty-one

※※※※※※※※※

"Could I get you a cup of coffee, Sergeant Pope?" Dr. James Webster, compact and athletic in a tailored burnt-orange jumpsuit, cocked an inquiring eyebrow at him from the electric coffee-maker on top of the filing cabinet. A bottle of Coffee Mate and a bowl half-filled with artificial sweetener sat beside the coffeepot.

"Don't mind if I do. Black, please."

"Bravo. Coffee is like tequila—if you can't stand the taste, you shouldn't drink it."

Pope lit a cigarette. "Caffeine and nicotine. I guess I'm addicted to both."

"Maybe not." Dr. Webster handed him a steaming mug of coffee on a small, round tray. "Smoking can be a form of acting out, the same way as overeating, compulsive sex, drinking too much—well, you get the idea." He sat down behind his desk with an apologetic smile. "Sermonizing again. I talk to so few people other than my patients, I find it difficult to keep the subject away from my work."

"You're lucky you find your work so interesting."

"I do. Immensely. In turn, I would think your line of work would have its moments."

Pope laughed. "Moments are right. Ninety-nine percent dull, slogging routine, and the other one percent enough to kill you and often does." He blew across the top of his coffee. "You look to be in pretty good shape. Handball, tennis, or golf?"

Webster laughed. "Certainly not golf. I believe more old doctors die of coronaries on golf courses than any other place. A little handball, but mostly workouts in a small gym we have here in what used to be an underground garage. Not much, a few lightweight barbells, a few machines." He opened his center drawer and removed a large manila envelope. He placed it on his desk and laced his fingers on top of it. "Consistency is the key, rather than maximum effort on an intermittent basis. Ten minutes a day of the correct exercise can maintain one at a rather high level of physical efficiency." He cocked an eye again, the ripple effect spreading into the tight skin on his bald head. "You appear reasonably fit, Sergeant. Do you follow any particular routine?"

Pope grinned ruefully. "Not much, other than muscling a fork lip-high forty or fifty times a day."

He laughed and picked up the envelope, his face undergoing a rapid transformation from humor to seriousness. "Very well. To get to why you're here, Sergeant. I've gone over all the data your office submitted. I'm very much afraid my determination is much the same as it was on your previous visit. I believe what we're seeing here is the result of a very severe split. The—"

"Split? I don't think I understand."

"A split from the real self into the unreal self. This is, simply, a phenomenon that occurs when the psychic integrity of a human mind is threatened, when it is confronted by trauma—or pernicious information—that it finds itself incapable of assimilating, incapable of understanding within the framework of normal quotidian existence. Thus threatened, the organism makes an effort to sustain its continuity by suppressing the anomaly, removing it from conscious perception. If the deleterious condition persists and the inevitable tension is great enough, the organism can, and sometimes does, project itself into a state of dissociative reaction."

"And that means exactly what?"

"He removes himself mentally from the source of discomfort or pain." He hesitated. "But that does not mean the underlying tension and pain will simply go away, even though he has managed by subterfuge to avoid its immediate consequences. It festers and grows, and sooner or later must find a suitable outlet. Unfortunately, what is and what is not a suitable outlet is subject to the determination of the individual. If the original oppression is severe, as in the case of excessive physical and/or sexual abuse of a continuous nature, the symbolic need for expression can become just as extreme, may well result in sociopathic behavior. Because feelings usually close down along with a shift in the ego state, the individual is often left without the restraints that dictate normal, civilized human behavior, and since symbolic fulfillment can never satisfy real human needs, the illness is self-perpetuating and can be, and often is, exponentially progressive."

"I'm not sure I got quite all of that," Pope said. "Are we back to your ocean of pain again?"

Webster smiled. "Exactly. This individual is undergoing extreme stress. Very possibly unbearable emotional pain. The fact that it is mental pain makes it no less real. He has shut down normal human considerations: compassion, empathy, gentleness —all the things that keep us from being jungle animals. He is an animal in pain, and he is striking out. I would venture that the method he uses in striking out has a lot to say about why."

"He's broken his pattern. He was working a four-day cycle. This time he jumped it to two. Do you think he's losing control, running wild?"

Webster rubbed his chin and shook his head. "It's hard to say, Sergeant. It could be a matter of convenience, or other mitigating factors we aren't aware of. Then again, what little restraint he has may be crumbling—losing his governor, so to speak."

"Do you think it's a good bet that he has had mental problems—been institutionalized, treated—in the past?"

"There again, it's difficult to hazard a guess. Very likely he has. But not necessarily. A lot of us—most of us, I think—go through life with our wants and desires unfulfilled to a degree. It's the degree that matters. The small needs we were forced to suppress during our early years, for one reason or another, we can accept and accommodate without undue stress and tension. We gratify them in small, harmless ways. Perhaps we go all our lives with some inexplicable yearning, some longing for an indefinable something that never materializes, an intangible something that we can find no words to express. We put it down to nostalgia, a desire to relive our lives. But it is a small hurt that we are experiencing. Enough small hurts, Sergeant, and you have a very large pain." He broke off and rocked slowly in his swivel chair. "Your Trashman, Sergeant, I'm afraid has a very large pain indeed."

"My Trashman, as you put it, *is* a very large pain indeed."

A fleeting smile crossed Webster's face. "Yes, I suppose he is." He rocked forward and ran a hand across his bald pate. "I wish I could give you a clearer picture, Sergeant Pope. Some idiosyncrasy, some eccentricity, some behavior trait that could help you. But the sad thing is, there probably aren't any. He can act and appear as normal as you and I . . . until the need for acting out seizes him, until he's caught up in frenzy, his own particular brand of compulsion." He grimaced and rubbed his eyes. "Ours is an inexact science at best, a science of intangibles. However, I'm certain that, if he would allow it, we could help him."

Pope returned his gaze coolly. "Why would you want to?" He finished his coffee and rose to his feet.

"He's still a human being, Sergeant Pope," he said gently.

"Not anymore, Doctor. The moment he put that first bag around someone's neck and tied the knot, he lost his human status, as far as I'm concerned. He became a predator of the worst kind. I buy this pain theory of yours only up to a point. We all have unfulfilled desires and wants and needs. And maybe that makes us act a little irrational at times. And that's okay, as long as it doesn't infringe on another person's rights—particularly his right to live. With all its inequities, its sometimes injustices, the law is all we have to protect those human rights. Only sometimes it doesn't go far enough or fast enough. When a man willfully takes a human life, he puts himself outside the brotherhood of man, and he should be dealt with accordingly. I'm not a Christian, Dr. Webster, but the Good Book says it plain: an eye for an eye."

"You're not exactly a liberal, are you, Sergeant?"

Pope shrugged. "I'm not even sure what that means. I only know that life is a one-time thing. When it's gone, it's gone. There's no coming back and doing it again. When you're dead, the world has ended. It no longer exists. If you have been murdered, your killer has effectively destroyed the world for all time."

"But only as you perceive it."

Pope raised his eyebrows. "You can't perceive anything if you're dead."

Webster laughed. He came around the desk with the manila envelope in his hand. "I've enjoyed talking to you, Sergeant Pope. You're a straightforward, no-nonsense man. While I don't necessarily agree with you, I admire your frankness." He turned abruptly and went back to his desk. "There was one thing in connection with the Carlson killings." He opened the envelope and shuffled through the photos. He selected one, then reached across and picked up a pair of black-rimmed glasses from his desk. "Here. This one. I couldn't quite make out what that is in the wastebasket." He held the picture in the light from his desk lamp, brow wrinkled with perplexity, the glasses giving him an owlish, studious look.

Pope glanced at the photo and waited until the doctor looked up. "Guts," he said succinctly, his twinkling eyes sharply contrasting with the harshness of his tone.

"Oh! Oh, yes, I see. Well . . ." He replaced the photo in the envelope and pressed apart the fastener. He smiled wryly and touched Pope lightly on the shoulder. "I'm not a Christian either, Sergeant Pope, but I wish you Godspeed in your search."

Pope smiled thinly and shook his hand. He crossed to the door.

"I'm beginning to think I'm going to need God's help. I'm not doing so hot on my own."

"You'll find him," Webster declared confidently. "It's only a matter of time. He's bound to make a mistake."

"Yeah," Pope sighed, "but at what cost? How many more dead bodies?"

Maybelle Norman clumped wearily into the conference room. She leaned on the table and waited patiently until Pope completed his phone call. Her lumpy body sagged with exhaustion and her head still rang with the echoes of endless telephone calls.

"Honey, I'm gonna call it a day. If I hear one more telephone ring, something's gonna short-circuit for sure."

Pope chuckled. "Sure thing, Maybelle. We really appreciate your help. I know it's a tiring, frustrating job. Are you staying in Merriweather, or are you driving back and forth to Dallas?"

"Grapevine, honey. I have a niece lives up there. Lord, no, I wouldn't fight that traffic to Dallas every day for anything. Only takes about ten minutes up 157, and I'm at my niece's." She removed the floppy-brimmed hat from her suitcase-sized bag and plopped it on her head. She smiled at him and waggled plump fingers. "See you tomorrow, honey."

"Take it easy, Maybelle."

On the way down the corridor, she fumbled in the handbag for the Baby Ruth she knew to be lurking somewhere among all the junk. Her hunt unsuccessful, she grunted in exasperation, and when she reached her small Ford she banged the bag on the hood and began to search in earnest, mouth watering, her sweet tooth howling for blessed surcease.

Her hand touched slick, crinkly paper, and she smacked her lips in satisfaction. Person needs a little quick energy, she told herself self-righteously, ignoring the almost infinitesimal pangs of her conscience. Especially after a hard day's work.

Chewing happily, she switched on the engine and drove off the parking lot.

She was a mile outside the city limits of Merriweather and down to her last bite of Baby Ruth when the gray van came up behind her. Close. Riding her rear bumper, edging out into the opposite lane only to whip back as approaching cars cut into the necessary passing lead time.

Maybelle glanced at her speedometer—fifty-five. Fast enough on this narrow road, the legal speed limit anyhow, by gum. She increased her speed to sixty. And still the van hung close, impatient, somehow menacing, two blurred faces glaring at her through the large, wide windshield.

"What's the matter with them idiots?" she muttered. She reduced her speed and edged off onto the paved shoulder, waving a plump arm for them to pass.

The van whooshed past, a bronzed face and a muscular arm hanging out of the window on the passenger side. The face was jeering, the arm outstretched with one finger rigidly extended.

"Why, that's them boys!" she said aloud, incredulously. "Them two purty, polite boys from that clinic." Her face composed itself along disapproving lines. "Just goes to show you can't never judge a kid by the way he acts around grown-ups." She regained the highway and worked a bit of peanut from behind her teeth with her tongue. "Wonder where they're going in such an all-fired hurry?" The van was a light-colored van, too, she thought, and a sudden chill traced its way along her spine.

But that can't be, she told herself vehemently, two such nice, clean-cut boys, just kids really. And everybody knows the Trashman is older. Ham does, anyhow. And he's the one should know if anybody does. But what if he's wrong? What if there are two of them? Maybe younger. Maybe . . .

She topped the small hill and saw the van turn off the highway near the center of the small valley ahead. She veered off onto the shoulder again and allowed a group of piled-up cars to go around her. She slowed to fifty when she neared the approximate location of the van's departure from the highway. There was no cross street or intersecting road that she could see, and she was almost past the small dirt road when she caught a glimpse of the van's taillights through the trees. Another quick glance. A tall, lithe figure carrying something black and heavy into the woods. A trash bag? Dumping trash in the woods? Coming all the way out here to dump trash, when there was a dumpster at the wrecking yard next door?

"Not likely," she muttered. She drove over the next hill and turned around in the first available lane.

The van was coming out of the woods when she came slowly back over the hill. She eased off onto the shoulder again and came to a stop. She waited until the van had turned right and was out of sight before she pulled back into the flow of traffic. She drove down the hill and turned into the narrow, rutted road.

The bags weren't difficult to find. Two of them. Ripped apart to allow the elements and predators easy access to the contents. Holding her breath, her heart fluttering in her fat breast, Maybelle found a stick and spread them apart.

Eleven kittens, she counted, five puppies, and two small Pomeranians. Their feet taped together, their heads in impossible juxtaposition to their bodies.

"They wrung their necks," she whispered into the stillness around her, the chill back on her spine, a slow, heavy anger stirring. "After all that Rocky's big talk, they wrung their little necks." She glared into the gathering darkness. "Them little bastards!" she spat.

"Aw, to hell with it," Duke said. He dropped the folded newspaper into the wastebasket. "They're trying to get our goat. Make us angry enough to do something dumb. The newspapers work hand-in-glove with the stupid cops, and them two assholes probably dictated that bunch of tripe to that bastard Bogard."

"Think we ought to slow down for a while?" Rocky asked hesitantly.

Duke whirled, his hand slicing downward in a swift, savage motion. "No! I'm not afraid of them." He paced across the room to the wall, then turned and came back to the center. He dropped suddenly to the floor and began doing push-ups. He counted to twenty-five silently, then relaxed to the carpet with his cheek on the back of his folded hands.

"We can't quit, Rock. It's the only time we're alive. We're dead, man. In between times there's nothing. We have to do what he wants." He sighed and propped his chin on a doubled hand. "Just like in Oldfield, Rock. Remember? I was dead until we did them. Then I came alive. The first time in my life I was really alive. I like that feeling, babe. I like being alive. And it's the only way we can be." He climbed slowly to his feet and sat on a corner of the desk. "Do you think about them a lot, Rock?"

"No!" Rocky's voice was muffled, faraway, disembodied.

"Yes, you do. The same way I do. I think about them, and I feel good for a little while. But it never lasts. It goes away, and it gets harder all the time to bring it back. I wish we could do it all over again. Kill the Red Witch and Carl over and over again. I mean, really kill them again and again. Every time the . . . feelings get too bad. Then maybe we wouldn't have to . . ." His voice faded, ended in another deep sigh. "But that can't be, can it, babe?"

"Do you ever feel sorry for . . . you know . . . *them* . . . the ones we play little man with?"

"No." Duke's voice was cold and flat. "Nobody felt sorry for us. Only Daddy . . . a little, but not enough."

"He was nice," Rocky said.

"He was weak," Duke said harshly. "Too weak to stand up to the bitch. All he wanted to do was put his dick in her." He giggled suddenly, a muffled, childish sound. "We put our dick in her, too, Rock, only ours was bigger than Daddy's."

"And sharper," Rocky added around Duke's giggle.

Duke locked his hands together and pushed, feeling with satisfaction the swell of extended muscles, the rush of blood through his veins. He locked his hands behind his head and pulled forward, arching his neck against the thrust of his hands.

"Have you got the next ones picked out, Duke?"

"Maybe. I'm not sure yet. We'll have to do a little more groundwork first."

"Can I bite them this time, Duke? I didn't get to do that with the Carlsons. I missed that, Duke." Rocky's voice was thready, plaintive.

Duke clasped his hands around his knee and pressed backward against straining thigh muscles. "Sure, babe." He grunted with exertion. "You can bite them all you want."

Chapter Twenty-two

"Hack, I don't want to go," Wendy said plaintively. "I don't want to go off and leave you, and besides, I think this whole thing is silly and much too expensive."

"I'm feeling fine," Hack said, "and it's damn well not silly and I don't care how much it costs. If it cures your headaches, I'll go in hock for ten years. Anyhow, we've got pretty good insurance."

"Honey, I'm grateful, I really am, but I just don't want to go off and leave you alone." Fluffy, honey hair framed her lovely face, the translucent skin of her brow wrinkled with concern.

He crossed the room and pulled her to her feet. "Go. I don't want to hear any more about it." He kissed her. "Anyhow, Ham Pope is coming by in a little while. He'll be around for a couple of hours."

"Well," she said doubtfully, "you have Dr. Webster's number. There's no phone in the isolation room, but he'll see that I get word right away. Promise?" She slipped her arms around his waist and squeezed.

"Oh, shit," Hack gasped.

"Oh! Oh, honey, I'm sorry!" She pressed one slender hand against her mouth, her face pale. "Did I hurt you? I know I'm not going now! You're in worse shape than you say—and now, dammit, I've hurt you!"

He forced a smile. He whirled her around and slapped her rump. "Go! Go, before you kill me." He followed behind her, slapping her rear with his palm. "Giddyap! Gee! Haw! Git along there little dogies." He finished by cupping her buttocks in his hands at the door. She looked up at him with laughing, protesting eyes.

"You're an idiot!"

"Uh-huh," he said, pinning her arms before she could squeeze him again. He kissed her gently, lingeringly, savoring the soft warmth of her lips. He pulled back abruptly. "Enough." He grinned crookedly. "A little more of that, and you won't be going anywhere except to bed."

"Why?" she asked innocently. "I'm not sleepy."

He smiled lazily and touched her cheek, knuckled it gently. His face suddenly sobered. "They wouldn't have tried that if they hadn't thought I was black," he said.

"Oh, Hack!"

"It's true," he said quietly. "It's a kind of reverse discrimination. They have contempt for a white woman who sleeps with a black man."

"Hack, please don't say that." She blinked her eyes rapidly, stifling a sob.

"But it's all right," he said, smiling again. "Who cares what a couple of nigger street kids think?" He wiped a finger across her cheek. "I'm sorry. I'm stupid. This is no time to air my insecurities." He leaned forward and kissed her cheek. "Tomorrow night, okay? I'll pick up the car tomorrow and stop by for you after the session. Okay?" He hesitated. "I really want this to work, Wen. More than anything." He closed the door before she could reply.

She stood there for a while, uncertain, wanting to go back in but afraid to do so, afraid that it might be the worst possible thing for her to do. That he was insecure in her love she had known for a long time. She felt helpless to do anything about it. Loving reassurances did little to compensate for what he considered the incontrovertible evidence of the headaches when they made love. The damn headaches. Blinding pain that came out of nowhere, without warning: intermittent, but almost always when they had sex. As a consequence, she found it very nearly impossible to respond to him. Afraid that the pounding of her blood, the heightened excitement would surely bring on the pain, she would find her responses shutting down, her emotions choking. And he would know; she would feel the change in him, the often half-savage rush to reach completion before his feelings, in turn, shut down.

Her face as clouded and troubled as her heart, she turned and went down the walk to her car.

Maybelle Norman took the last sip of her Pepsi before dropping a quarter into the scarred and battered telephone outside the 7-Eleven grocery store. She dialed a number, listened until she heard the first ring, then began rummaging in her purse for a stick of gum.

Seven rings later, savoring the tart flavor of her spearmint gum, she grunted in satisfaction as she heard the answering click, a harried-sounding female voice.

"SPCA. Can we help you?"

"You folks must be mighty busy down there, missy. This here phone rung eight or nine times."

"Yes, ma'am, we are. Can I help you?"

"It ain't me so much that needs the help. It's them boys down here in Merriweather killing cats—"

"I'm sorry, ma'am, if someone killed your cat, but we have no punitive powers. I'd suggest you go to the police—"

"Nobody killed my cat. I don't even like cats. But I sure don't want to see them killed, their pore little necks wrung—not to mention the little dogs."

"I'm sorry, I don't believe I understand. Are you reporting a case of cruelty to animals?"

"I don't know how cruel they was, but they wrung their little necks."

"Who?"

"Them good-looking boys down at the Free Animal Clinic, that's who."

"You mean Rocky and Duke? Oh, ma'am, you must be mistaken. Rocky and Duke are fine boys, both of them. Why, they accept animals from people all—"

"Yeah, and then they take them out and wring their necks."

"Oh, you must be mistaken! You must have them mixed up with some other—"

"Hah!" Maybelle barked. "It ain't likely I'd mistake them two boys for anybody else. I ain't that old yet."

"Well, I just can't believe—where did all this happen?"

"Right here in Merriweather. Well, actually, out on the highway to Grapevine about four miles. A little patch of woods right off the road."

"Well, I'm sorry. We're way off over here in Fort Worth. I don't even know if that would be in our jurisdiction."

"It's dang sure Tarrant County. Ain't that your jurisdiction?"

"What kind of proof do you have?"

"Proof? I got about fifteen or sixteen little dead dogs and cats, that's what proof I got."

"Are you planning to bring them over?"

"Bring—Lord, honey, I couldn't bring myself to touch the pore little things."

"You left them where they were, then?"

"Of course I did. Right where them boys throwed them."

"And you saw them wring—kill them?"

"Well, no, they didn't stand out there beside the road wringing their necks. I saw them go back into the woods, and I waited and went back there and found them right where they dumped them."

"Let me get this straight. You saw Rocky and Duke drive back into a patch of woods, then you went in there later and found some dead animals . . . and now you're saying they killed them? How do you know? You said yourself you didn't see them."

"I saw them—one of them—carrying two bags from the van to the little dump they got back there—"

"Dump? You mean there were other bags lying around?"

"Well . . . well, yes, I guess there was, but they—"

"Then you don't really know if the bags you saw, the bags with the dead animals inside, were in fact the ones the boy was carrying?"

"They was right where he was walking, and besides, they would have access to a lot of—"

"I'm sorry. I'm just not at all convinced that you saw what you thought you saw. I really don't see what we could do, in any event. You didn't actually see them do it. You have no real evidence. At least, not against Duke and Rocky—"

"What you mean is, you ain't gonna do anything about it?"

"I simply feel that you must have the wrong boys. I've known Rocky and Duke for several years now. They're fine decent kids. And they love animals. Why, they—"

"Yeah," Maybelle said. "I know, they're a couple of swell kids."

"They are," the woman said emphatically, defiantly. Then her tone softened. "Look . . . please understand. If you just had something tangible, something with a little credibility that we could make some noise with—"

"How's this?" Maybelle said, and slammed the receiver down.

"What's this business about the screwdriver? How in hell did you know that?" Pope pulled the tab on the can of Bud and pushed himself back to the first position in the recliner. He crossed his legs at the ankle and gave his full attention to the handsome young man across the room.

Hack eased to a sitting position on one end of the couch. He sat stiffly upright, his hand pressed against his side, his face a curious mixture of pain and eagerness.

"Oldfield, Ham. A man named Parnell Slocum. He lived across the street from the Hamner family. In guessing about the screwdriver, all I did was follow a blueprint of a murder that happened in that house thirty-four or -five years ago. It could have been a knife; a knife was used also. On the woman—the Hamner twins' mother."

"Why don't you start at the beginning? What you're saying is damned interesting, but I'm not making much sense out of it."

"Okay." Hack settled back against the couch and began talking. For twenty minutes he talked, covering the Hamner history from a brutal mass murder in Oldfield, Texas, thirty-five-odd years before to an old man being carted away in an ambulance a week ago. And not once did the twinkling blue eyes of the hard-faced man across from him leave his face. The beer, forgotten, grew warm in Pope's big hand; his cigarette burned to an ash in the ashtray and went out. He didn't bother to light another.

Hack finished and leaned forward, an enigmatic smile on his handsome face. He pulled out a handkerchief and wiped his forehead. His dark skin showed no change, but he felt pale inside, weak, a high, fine edge of excitement bubbling in his veins.

"Well, what do you think, Ham?"

Pope blew soundlessly through heavy lips. Twins. And he had been so sure it was just one man trying to make it look like two. Maybe he was getting old. Twins. At least one of them smart enough to lay a clumsy false trail indicating two, expecting him to see through it and jump to the opposite conclusion. And he had done exactly what they wished him to do. Twins. Hell. That would explain a few things that had been bothering him about the one-man theory. The ease of control, for instance. Two men would ensure docility where one might not. Nowhere had there been a sign of resistance. No forced entry. The victims in each case must have allowed them inside. Possibly under duress, but maybe not, either.

"Ham?" Hack was staring at him, perplexed. "What do you think?"

A slow grin spread across Pope's heavy features. "You did a hell of a job, Hack Wind. There must be a connection somewhere. Too much coincidence. It could easily be the twins themselves, or at least one of them. And as much as I hate to admit it, it would fit within the framework of Dr. Webster's profile on our killer. He said the killer must have been abused or mistreated or rejected as a child—or maybe all three. That fits the Hamner twins exactly. The problem is, now how do we find them? Bert Sheldon has been working almost exclusively on Duke Hamner—"

"We have their first names now," Hack said eagerly. "Perry and Kerry. Duke and Rocky were nicknames."

"Good enough for a start. How about the old man?"

Hack shook his head. "He had a stroke, Ham. He's only come around once or twice since they took him in. And then only for short periods. He's not making any sense, according to what the head nurse told me."

"That's a bad break. He's the one person who could identify the Hamners, at least point us in the right direction. There's a good possibility they've changed their names."

"Even so," Hack said, "forty-one-year-old twins aren't all that common."

"They'd only be noticed if they went around a lot together or, of course, lived together. Somehow, I kind of doubt that last. And, too, people change when they get older. They may not look so much alike now."

Hack nodded, his brow furrowed in concentration. "There must be a way. Aren't there organizations of twins . . ."

"Sure, but there's no guarantee they'd be members. That's easy to check."

"How about Social Security? No damn good if they have different identities, I suppose."

"Service records. They'd have been about right for Vietnam." Pope took out his notebook and made notes. "We need to get someone on the old man twenty-four hours a day. Just in case he comes out of it and can talk."

"I'll take the first shift tomorrow," Hack said. "Wendy will be at Webster's all day, and I'll go nuts sitting around here. May as well be there."

"Fine. Call me when you're ready to leave, and I'll get someone over there."

"Okay."

Pope closed the notebook. "There's one thing you don't know about. They found a contact lens at the Carlson scene. We have the manufacturer and the local distributor, and we're getting set up to go all out to find the doctor who wrote that particular prescription. If and when we find him, we hope he can give us the patient's name from the prescription. I have my doubts that it can be done—there must be a lot of people with the same eye problems. About the most we can hope for is another damn list of names. But who the hell knows? Maybe one of those names will ring somebody's bell." He shrugged and smiled. "But it's a new direction, and it makes Roscoe happy. Visible movement. He's taking a lot of heat."

Hack smiled wryly. "It'd be ironic as hell if he, or they, get caught because of simple vanity. Despite what they'll tell you, it's the only reason people wear contacts in the first place."

Pope nodded and leaned back and reached for a cigarette. His hand stopped halfway to his pocket, hung there while he slowly straightened again. Something tugged at his brain. A tiny click. A tumbler falling into place. He sat frozen, waiting for the other tumbler to fall, the door to swing open. He could feel it. An insistent, nagging thought on the rim of his brain, prodding gently, persistently. He closed his eyes and tried to blank his mind to make entry easier, his memory cells more accessible.

Goddammit, what was it? The contact lens. It had something to do with the lens. He waited.

Nothing; it wouldn't come. He opened his eyes to find Hack watching him curiously. He shook his head. "Something. I almost remembered something. But I lost it."

"About the case?"

"I think so. I'm not sure. Hell, yes, it must have been!"

"It'll come back," Hack said. "Just try to forget about it. It'll jump into your head when you least expect it."

Pope pushed himself to his feet. "I'll touch bases with Sheldon, see what he's come up with on Duke Hamner. And I'll get something working on the twins. You gonna be okay by yourself?"

"Sure, Ham, I'm fine."

Pope crossed to shake his hand. "You did a good job, Hack. I want you to know that if we bust this thing with your leads, you get the credit."

"Hey, man, it doesn't matter," Hack protested, embarrassed but pleased.

"Sure it matters. You're young and ambitious. You might want to run for sheriff someday."

"Not likely," Hack said. "It's a dead-end job." He struggled to his feet and followed Pope to the door. "I'd like to get into something a little more interesting."

Pope eyed him critically, a glint of humor in his eyes. "Like detective work?"

Hack smiled sheepishly. "Maybe."

Pope lit a cigarette and slipped on a pair of thin leather gloves. "It's dull, tedious work most of the time. But it does have its moments, I guess. When this thing is over, we'll have a talk with Tanner. . . . Who knows?" He tapped the younger man lightly on the arm and walked down the steps and out to his car.

Hack stepped out on the porch. "Hey, Ham. I'll see you . . . and thanks."

Pope started his car and continued around the circular driveway that led him between the sparkling white cottage and a large flower garden bordered with sprawling pfitzers and towering junipers. On a square concrete pedestal in the center, a blue and white windmill whirred lazily in the breeze. Neatly spaced pecan trees, leafless limbs bowed with clusters of pecans, bordered the crushed gravel driveway, fallen nuts snapping and crackling beneath the Dodge's tires like ancient fragile bones.

Must be four or five acres here, he thought. A sheepherder's cottage with the grounds of a mansion. Must be nice to live out like this, peace and quiet, birds singing, squirrels racing through the pecans, no road noise, no city taxes.

But look at that golf-course lawn. He sighed. Who needed the aggravation?

Chapter Twenty-three

✕✕✕✕✕✕✕✕✕✕✕

He felt his heart leap when he saw the small blue car parked in his driveway, the soft glow of light behind the draperies on the front window of his house. He parked the Dodge on the street and walked across the grass, acutely aware of the acceleration of his heartbeat, the pleasant fullness in his loins. It had been a long time since he had come home to someone waiting for him, even longer since the waiting someone expected nothing of him except himself. The last five years with Alice had been anything but pleasant. Cold glances and hostile words, frustration and acrimony.

Filled with a nagging discontent with her lot in life, a policeman's wife with little money and less excitement, Alice Pope had gone back into real estate as soon as her children were in junior high school. Lovelier with approaching middle age than she had ever been as a young girl, she had met John Freelander at a real estate convention in Los Angeles. A whirlwind romance with suave, handsome Freelander, who rubbed elbows daily with the stars, and staid, small-town cop Hamilton Pope didn't stand a chance. Sixteen years of marriage did little to tip the scales when balanced against a lavish home in Westwood, a summer cottage at the beach. Alice Pope had never looked back.

The door was unlocked, and Pope saw her tan coat hanging on the closet doorknob. The kitchen was dark, as was the small den, and he followed the glow of light down the hallway to the bedroom, his feet whispering in the carpet, the only sound in the small, still house.

He stopped dead in the doorway.

She was spread-eagled on the bed, nude. Her face tilted toward the doorway, eyes open, the tip of her tongue a splash of pink in one corner of her mouth.

His heart slammed painfully against his ribs and his knees turned to water. He gripped the doorjamb to keep from collapsing.

She sat up. "Oh, hi, honey! Lord, I thought you were never—what's the matter?"

"Oh, Jesus!" He staggered to the bed. "Jesus H. Christ, Nancy! You scared the living hell out of me!"

"What?" Her eyes grew wide with astonishment. "What did I do? I wanted to surprise you and be all ready. You must have seen my car."

He laughed shakily. "You did that, all right. Jesus, when I saw your tongue hanging out of your mouth, I thought—"

"My tongue? Oh, I was licking this damn little zit in the corner of my mouth. Oh, I see." She gave him a fiendish grin. "You thought the Trashman had got me." She bounced to her knees and threw her arms around his neck. "Scared the shit out of you, huh?" She planted a warm, wet kiss on his cheek. "That's for being scared for me." She stripped his coat over his shoulders, grinning wickedly. "Get naked, old man, you're up next."

It was dark by the time Maybelle Norman returned to Merriweather. She drove by the Free Animal Clinic slowly, then pulled into the driveway of the silent wrecking yard and came back. The building was dark, the van in its accustomed place near the door. She wheeled in beside it.

It took less than half a minute to open the van door, even less to wedge the sound-actuated recorder beneath the seat, padding it to prevent vibration with the small hand towel she had brought for that purpose. The mike she pinned to the underside of the seat, the pickup head an eighth of an inch back from the edge. From there, she went to the rear of the van, knelt painfully on one knee, and wiped clean a spot on the inner curve of the bumper. She felt rather than heard the tiny click as the small, magnetized metal box snapped into place.

A minute later, breathing hard from her exertions, she was on her way back to Grapevine. A hundred yards away, she flipped a switch and listened to the beeping sound coming from her dashboard. A mile down the highway, she checked it again. The sound was fainter; another half mile, and it was gone.

"Sanctimonious little shits," she muttered. "You think you got everybody fooled. Well, you might fool them SPCA idiots with your sweet manners and good looks, but you ain't got Maybelle Norman fooled one little iota. Just you talk about it a little bit, next time. That's all I ask." On the way to Grapevine, she stopped at a Dairy Queen and bought a hot fudge sundae. She felt she had earned it.

Chapter Twenty-four

∾∾∾∾∾∾∾∾∾∾∾∾

The sound of thunder woke Hamilton Pope. Pale gray dawn sifting through the thin draperies on the large window at the head of the bed provided enough light for him to see his watch. Seven o'clock. He swung his feet to the carpet and automatically reached for a cigarette. He walked to the sliding glass door. Another gloomy, weeping day. A heavy, dripping mist hanging like an old unbleached sheet just above the trees he could see from the door, oaks and mimosas and elms, a small pecan that he had been babying along for five years without a single nut to show for it.

Behind him, Nancy snored softly and hiccuped. He walked back to the edge of the bed. Fragile and unblemished despite the freckles, her face had the vital glow of youth and good health. She stirred and sighed, her lips pursed as if she had been caught in the act of blowing a kiss, her expression almost startled, as if there were things in her dreams she wasn't supposed to see.

He padded silently down the hall and into the kitchen. After a breakfast of bacon, eggs, toast, and milk, he slipped back into the bathroom, closed the door, and shaved.

He left her sleeping.

Roscoe Tanner was waiting for him in the conference room, his face as dark as the day outside, the crippled remnants of two pencils on the table in front of him. Lighted cigars in two different ashtrays gave mute testimony to his agitation.

"I just got took over the coals by His Honor the dipshit mayor and that candy-assed Chief Durkin!"

"Good morning, Roscoe." Pope sat down at the head of the table and opened his case.

"Did you hear what I said?" Tanner slammed a hand on the table.

"I heard you. You want an expression of goddamned sympathy, or what?" He went on unloading the briefcase.

"You could at least acknowledge the fact that I just got my ass ate out by two all-time experts."

"Okay," Pope said calmly, "you got your ass ate out. Now, where do we stand on the contact lens? And what have we heard from Rossacher?"

"You're a cold sucker, Ham, you know that? You're just like that damn hound dog of mine. What he can't eat he buries, and what he can't bury he pisses on."

Pope gave him a puzzled frown. "I don't get your point. You mean I'm greedy, or selfish, or what?" He smiled faintly. "Or maybe unfeeling?"

"You figger it out," Tanner said sullenly.

"I'm not insensitive to your problems, Roscoe. You want to chew me out? Go ahead. You want to kick some ass? Wait'll everybody gets in, and we'll line up and you can take your best thirty-five-yard swing at our butts. That make you happy?"

"Won't do no good," Tanner grumbled. He smiled suddenly. "Nobody pays any attention when I kick ass. I'm too damn soft around here."

"You're too damn soft around everywhere," Pope agreed. "Where we at on the eye doctor survey?"

"We've covered everybody in Merriweather. No dice. Most of the mid-cities area, and we're working on Fort Worth and Dallas. One problem is, these yo-yos keep such short hours, and I have a bad feeling some of them ain't even bothering to check."

215

"And he may have got the damn things in Snowbird, Wisconsin."

"Yeah, there's that," Tanner agreed soberly.

"Well, it's a piece of hard evidence. We catch him and it'll tie his ass to the scene." Pope debated taking the time to tell Roscoe what Hack had learned. He decided he'd better.

"That's what we . . . okay, *I*, thought about them hairs, too."

Pope nodded. He lit a cigarette and launched into the story about Hack and Oldfield and the Hamner twins. While he talked, the other members of the small task force straggled in one by one. Bert Sheldon in particular pricked up his ears when he heard the name Hamner.

"There ain't a lot of Hamners around," Sheldon said when Pope had finished, "and none of them admit to the nickname Duke. And no Perrys or Kerrys."

"How about service record?" Milly asked. "Wasn't someone checking on that?"

Sheldon shook his head. "No record."

"Musta changed his name," Tanner growled.

"But why would he do that?" Milly glanced around the table. "If he's a psycho who's just gone haywire, he couldn't have anticipated that, could he? How would he have known five years ago, say, that he was going to go ape and start wasting people?"

"Unless," Sheldon said slowly, "he's done it before and knew it was only a matter of time, or had already changed his name because he's wanted somewhere else."

"But he *has* done it before." Pope glanced around the table. "If Hack Wind's source in Oldfield is right, he did it when he was six years old."

"Wasn't there some mass murdering going on in Houston five or six years ago?" Forbes looked up from his newspaper and picked his nose thoughtfully. "Yeah. And they never caught the perp, either, that I remember."

"Right." Cal Stevens slapped the table. "Cousin of mine's on the force down there. He was working on it. We were talking about it at the family reunion a couple years ago."

"Anything similar to ours?" Pope asked.

"I don't remember," Stevens admitted. "My cousin tends to brag a lot. I didn't pay much attention."

"I know some people down there," Sheldon said. "I'll check it out."

Pope turned to Tanner. "Roscoe, think you could get your FBI buddies to check around the country for us? Maybe this guy's been moving around a lot, doing his thing and moving on. I understand they've set up some kind of new computer information bank in Quantico. Mass murders, random killings, things like that. If he's done this before, the same way, they might be able to help us. We can also send in a request to their Behavioral Science Unit for a profile. See how close it comes to Dr. Webster's."

Tanner gave him a quizzical look that quickly became cynical. "We've already done that, remember? Rickers is handling it. What's the matter, Ham, that little blonde draining your brain?" He waited a second, then added, "Too?"

"Just seeing if you were on your toes, Roscoe," Pope said, his tone as casual as a yawn, his eyes avoiding contact with Milly's, his brain conjuring up various methods of hideous revenge on Tanner.

"Uh-huh," Tanner said, all set to continue with his needling until Pope turned his head and stared at him. He grinned and shrugged instead.

"Much noise as the media's been making, we oughta be hearing from somebody." Forbes, out of sync with the conversation as usual, looked up from the sports page.

"Maybe he changes his M.O.," Milly said, her voice as dry and noncommittal as her expression.

Pope pushed away from the table. "Too many maybes," he said crisply. "Let's get cracking. The son of a bitch could hit anytime now." If he hasn't already, he thought. He lit a cigarette and glanced around at the small group. "Any of you running out of assignments?"

A chorus of boos and hisses answered him.

"I'm getting cauliflower lip," Stevens said. "And everybody lies."

"So what's new, partner?" Sheldon drawled. "Nobody promised you it was an easy life being a cop."

"Nobody told me I'd have to wear Sears and Roebuck suits and eat sorry junk food, either."

"You wear nice boots, though," Milly observed cheerily.

"Hell, I always wore boots, even when I was a kid in Jersey." Stevens propped a gleaming Justin on a chair and flicked at the toe with his handkerchief.

"Bert," Pope said, "the twins would be about forty-one now and maybe still have blond or light brown hair. They were normal-sized six-year-olds, so medium height and weight would probably be a good bet. It's all we have, anyhow." He turned to Roscoe. "Wind's baby-sitting their grandfather. We have to get one of our people over to John Peter Smith about four to relieve him. We need to try for some kind of description if the old man comes out of it, their new names if they've changed them."

Roscoe nodded without comment. He splayed sausage fingers on the table and unfolded from his chair until he towered over them. "Let's go brand some steers," he said cheerfully.

It was a long, frustrating day for Hamilton Pope. He spent the morning reviewing the field interrogation reports on the sex offenders. So far, to a man, they had managed to come up with alibis for at least one of the killing times. He separated them into two categories: those that could be verified with a phone call, and those that had to be checked by detectives. He drank too much coffee and smoked innumerable cigarettes. He caught himself

staring into space a lot, shoulders hunched, a feeling of helpless-
ness, of impending catastrophe, slowly pressing him toward numbness.

This is all a goddamned waste of time, he thought morosely.
You don't catch a Trashman with dull, tedious routine. You get
lucky and catch him over his kill with bloody hands and dripping
fangs, or . . . what? Or you don't catch him. He just goes on and
on. Picking his victims at will, slaughtering them at the dictates of
his diseased mind. Maybe as helpless in his compulsion as his
pursuers were in their bumbling ineptitude, as incapable of
stopping as they were incapable of stopping him.

Maybe Webster is right, he thought. Maybe the pain is so great,
so terrible, that he must seek relief at any cost. Pain. The killer
himself had said it in the word painted on the mirror in blood. Was
it a cry for help?

A new thought struck him, and he sat bolt upright, a cigarette
dangling forgotten from the corner of his mouth.

What if he doesn't know he's doing it?

There were precedents: the Boston Strangler, the Hillside
Strangler in California. If the mind-dabblers could be believed, the
annals of crime were filled with monsters who buried their
bestiality below their conscious minds, who lived apparently
normal lives and periodically unleashed their savagery on their
neighbors and friends.

In view of Hack's new evidence of the twins, he wondered why
in his own mind he persisted in thinking in terms of one killer. But
deep down around the edge of his consciousness, he knew. The
Jackson apartment. The presence of evil he had sensed, had seen
in the formless miasma that had hovered for one terrifying
moment over the bed. One presence. One evil. One killer. He
shivered and went back to the interrogation reports.

At two o'clock, Hack Wind came into the conference room.
One look at his grim face told Pope they had lost their gamble. He

lit a cigarette and watched the young man ease gingerly into a chair.

"Dead?"

Hack nodded glumly. "An hour ago." He tugged a small notebook from his shirt pocket. He opened it, glanced inside briefly, then closed it and dropped it on the table. "He rallied for a couple of minutes. Said some things. Nonsense mostly, rambling. I got one thing from him. And it ain't good." He took a deep breath. "The twins weren't named Hamner. Hamner was their stepdaddy. Only the two older kids belonged to him. Evidently he never adopted the twins, so they had their real father's name."

"Their real name?" He asked it without hope.

Hack shook his head. "Never got it out of him. He went out again before he could say, and never came to again."

"Bad break," Pope said matter-of-factly. He stacked the remaining reports in a pile. "Up to taking a drive?"

"Sure, where to?"

"The old man's house. Maybe there's something—a letter, a Christmas card, something with a name."

"Good idea," Hack said. He heaved a sigh and shoved to his feet. "We're back at the starting gate, I reckon. It could be anybody."

Pope clapped him on the shoulder. "Not quite. We know a hell of a lot of people it ain't."

They walked down the corridor to Roscoe Tanner's office. The big man stood slumped at a window, scowling out into the glowering day.

Pope stopped just inside the doorway. "Roscoe. We need three or four good men to meet us at 1510 North Bottomly Avenue in Fort Worth. Call that captain buddy of yours. Tell him we need *good* men."

Tanner turned and stared at him woodenly, then walked back to his desk and wrote down the address. He looked up and came to attention and saluted smartly, his face expressionless. "Yes, sir, anything else, *sir?*"

"Yeah," Pope said sourly. "Up your ass, Captain." He turned and left.

"It's getting to all of us," he told Hack as they climbed into his car.

They found the notebook in the drawer of the nightstand by the bed within the first five minutes. While the others went on with the search, Pope took it to the cramped living room and sat at one end of the sagging Naugahyde couch. He turned on a small reading lamp. The writing was erratic, sometimes small and neat, at others an almost illegible scrawl.

I'm not feeling well at all anymore. Another of those spells again last night with my left side. A light stroke, I would imagine. My vision was blurred and my left side was paralyzed for a time. It's just a matter of time, I believe.

Since this is not intended to be a medical chronicle of my last days on earth, I'll get on with what I have to say, what I feel I must say. Indeed, what I should have told someone before this.

The man they are calling the Merriweather Trashman is my grandson Kerry.

I'm as certain of that as I am that I'm ninety-five years old and dying. He is killing people again, the way he killed them in Chicago, in Houston, the way he killed them that first time in Oldfield, Texas.

That is not to say that what he did in Oldfield was not justified. I fully believe it was. My daughter for her indiffer-ence, her neglect, her selfish indulgences in the ways of the world. My grandson Carl for his brutal, unfeeling treatment of the boys, his sadism. My granddaughter Eloise for her evil. The bite marks on Kerry's body that fateful morning were

Eloise's. She was also the leading player in the tragic scene that led to my grandson Perry's death. For that deed alone, her death was warranted by his hands.

My wife and I found them. The three of them dead. My grandson Kerry sitting quietly at the top of the stairs, the can of chloroform on the step beside him, a trace of blood on his cheek, another on his nightgown. He smiled at us, a sweet smile, a ghastly smile, and said:

"They killed Perry, Grandpa. The Red Witch put a screwdriver in his poop-hole and he screamed and died. Then Mama and Carl and the Red Witch put him in the sinkhole behind the windmill."

My grandson did what he had to do in the only way he knew how. My wife and I decided he had been punished enough. I broke a side window and left footprints outside. We took Kerry home with us to raise. It wasn't difficult. He was a quiet, well-behaved child. Intelligent, responsive, he seemed happy . . . yet I had the terrible feeling that he never really felt anything. . . .

It ended abruptly, the last few words almost impossible to decipher. Pope stared down at the notebook in a blind fury. "You old son of a bitch! Dammit, you haven't told us anything! You haven't told us his last name!"

"What's the matter?" Hack stood in the doorway.

Pope tossed the notebook at him and lit a cigarette with shaking hands. He sucked at the cigarette savagely. "What a goddamned fucked-up family! This old bastard has evidently known for years that his wacked-out grandson has been killing people all over the country. And what does he do? He keeps his damned mouth shut until he's dying, and then he writes a sad little dissertation on why he had a right to!"

Hack flipped through the rest of the empty pages. "That's all there is, all right. We haven't found anything else, either."

"We won't," Pope said grimly. "That old man has probably made sure of that."

"I don't know, Ham. Maybe he thought he *was* telling us who his grandson was. Or maybe he meant to and didn't get to it in time. He was old. Old people don't always think too straight. Maybe he just assumed that everyone knew who his grandson was."

"It still amounts to the same thing. Zilch." Pope clambered to his feet. "Let's get it finished and get the hell out of here."

Chapter Twenty-five

~~~~~~~~~~~~~~~

Hamilton Pope spent a fitful, sleepless night. Alone. By ten o'clock he had made a half dozen trips to the phone to call Nancy, but something inside him, some last vestige of pride, wouldn't let him go through with it. He consoled himself with the thought that maybe she had gone back on the swing shift at the café and was just too busy to call.

He watched the ten o'clock news, the first fifteen minutes of which was given over entirely to a rehash of the Trashman murders. Police ineptitude was the central theme of the program, thinly veiled behind a barrage of "authorities are baffled" or "police are at a loss to explain" or, the most blunt of all, "law enforcement officials have no comment."

He snapped off the set and showered and went to bed. He was up again at one o'clock, and again at three, this time to stay. A can of beer, a cigarette, and a chair by the front-room window. He watched the reflection of Merriweather's lights on low-hanging clouds and wondered what *he* was doing. Was someone somewhere picking up the tab for one little boy's misery thirty-five years ago? Pain for pain, indignity for indignity?

Don't do it anymore, he pleaded silently. Come in to me. Maybe Webster is right. Maybe you can be helped. There are things they can do to help with the pressure, to ease the tension, to stop you from *having* to do it. Stop now, Kerry, before I catch you. Then it will be too late. So help me God, if you make me hunt you down, if you do it again, I'll kill you on sight.

He leaned his head against the back of the chair and closed his eyes and watched the stream of faces parade across the screen of his lids. Wyverns and hobgoblins from long-ago nightmares, leering and gesticulating; quiet faces, bleached and still with death. He heard the dim thunder of jets at DFW Airport, and along about dawn he dozed a little.

The Dodge had a mind of its own. Without consciously willing it, he found himself making the turn that would take him past the Hamburger Box instead of to police headquarters.

"Well, hell, since I'm in the neighborhood, anyhow," he muttered, unable to keep from smiling a little.

She saw him coming through the door and came to meet him, her dazzling smile in place, but somehow strained, her eyes as bright as ever, but evasive.

She took his hand. "Let's sit back here," she said. She made a production out of getting him seated, brushed perfunctorily at the table with a napkin. "I'll get coffee," she murmured, but he caught her wrist.

"No coffee, Nan. I only have a minute. I missed . . . I just wanted to see how you were."

She dropped into the seat across from him and smiled brightly, her eyes on the knot in his tie. "I'm fine, Ham. You look good today."

"Thought you might have had to change shifts or something . . . since you didn't show up last night." He laughed lightly to indicate that it wasn't really all that big a thing.

"Well, I—I was busy, Ham," she said, a small, plaintive voice to match her size. Her eyes dropped to her hands clasped on the table. She began picking at a ragged thumbnail.

"Sure," he said quickly. "Sure, I can understand that. Girls have to do things . . . wash their hair, do up their clothes . . . all kinds of things men don't . . ."

She raised her face, freckles stark against pale skin. "I wasn't doing any of those things, Ham," she said quietly. "I was in—I was with my husband."

He swallowed. "I—I thought you were divorced," he said hollowly.

"All right, my ex-husband."

He nodded and studied his hands, the thick blunt fingers with dirty nails, the tiny brown spots that were the first signs of age. "He stopped by for a one-nighter, huh?"

"No, Ham." She took one of his hands in hers, tried to pry open the clenched fingers. When she couldn't budge them, she settled for his thumb. She wrapped her fingers around it; it looked rough and gross and immense in her dainty fist. And felt warm. She leaned forward across the table, her face earnest and suddenly flushed.

"He wants me back, Ham."

"I thought . . . it was over. I thought you despised him. You said he was a runner, that he was a bum, that you couldn't live your life without some sort of . . . continuity."

"I know," she said miserably. "He hasn't changed all that much, I don't think. But I—I . . . You remember when I told you that the young ones wanted to own you body and soul?"

He nodded woodenly.

"Well . . . he does." She leaned over his hand, her face hidden. "He owns me body and soul, Ham. I—I just didn't know it."

"Well," he said, the sound of his voice unfamiliar, thick and husky out of the spreading void inside him. "Well, I guess there isn't much more to be said, is there?"

"I didn't . . . I don't want to hurt you," she said fiercely, dramatically. Her eyes came up to search his face. "You're not hurt, are you?"

He laughed lightly, another unfamiliar sound. "Nothing that won't heal with a generous dose of one part self-pity and three parts vodka." He tried to look amused. "You're a good piece of ass, girl." There *had* to be some hurt on her side. "Good pieces of ass don't grow on trees." It just wasn't fair otherwise.

She stared at him for a moment, her eyes wide. Then she smiled slowly and squeezed his thumb. "I'd be a lot meaner than that if it was me. You're a softie, Ham Pope." She raised his hand and nipped at the ball of his thumb.

He reached across with his other hand and took her wrist and slipped his thumb free. Her skin felt cool and smooth. He felt a slicing stab of pain somewhere in his chest. He dropped her hand and got to his feet.

"See you around, kid," he said, and winked. "You never had much chance with me, anyhow."

Her voice followed him. "Ham! If it doesn't work out between me and Bob . . ." She let it trail away when he didn't look back.

He marched solidly through the door, aware that she was watching, aware that the others, the fat cook and the skinny brunette, were watching also. He looked off and tried to think of something he could do to show his utter unconcern, how little he cared. Some gesture. A yawn, maybe. Or the one-finger salute.

In the end, he looked up and waved.

"Is there something I can do for you, madam?"

Maybelle Norman backed slowly, awkwardly out of the door of the van. She took small shuffling steps, as if she were battling the last stages of crippling arthritis. By the time she turned to face the owner of the voice, the recorder was safely in her handbag and she was beaming.

"Uh-oh," she said gaily. "I done got myself caught." She tugged at her dress and straightened the scarf at her throat while she took the measure of the man before her.

"It's the van," she gushed. "My Henry's been wanting to buy one of these here Ford vans for a while now. I just happened to see this one, and I just thought I'd sneak a look inside, see what they looked like. I sure hope you don't mind." She paused, finally catching sight of the turned-around collar. "Reverend."

The man smiled genially. "Of course not. Help yourself. Get behind the wheel if you'd care to, drive it around the block." His hand went into his pocket. "I have a key."

"Oh, no, thank you kindly. I just wanted to see how it looked inside. Henry'd like this one fine. It's got that there cruise control thing on it. This is last year's, ain't it, Reverend?"

"No, it's two years old." He cleared his throat. "It's Father, ma'am. Father Mumford of St. James."

Maybelle smiled politely and bobbed her head, thinking it would be a mighty cool day in hell before she, a good Baptist, called any living man "Father."

"Sure looks mighty fine. Them boys must take real good care of it. It does belong to them two good-looking boys that run this place, don't it?"

He smiled and took a thin, aluminum-covered cigar out of his pocket. "No, ma'am. Actually, it belongs to the clinic, but they're about the only ones who drive it."

"Well, I'm here to tell you they're two mighty fine boys. They was telling me and this friend of mine the other day about the way they take them poor little dogs and cats in off the street. That's something unusual in young folks these days."

He nodded soberly. "Yes, ma'am, they're fine boys."

"Well, I sure appreciate your hospitality and for not getting mad at me for prying around your van."

"That's quite all right. Glad to be of service." He smiled again and went toward the clinic.

What a nice, friendly man, Maybelle thought, even if he is one of them priests. Maybe I ought to tell him about them boys killing them cats and dogs. She kept up her limping, shuffling act until she was behind the wheel of her car. She stripped the paper from a Hershey bar and chewed reflectively. Probably wouldn't believe me, though, she told herself. Just like them idiots down at the SPCA. Well, they could just get their own evidence. Too bad about the homer, though. She'd just have to sneak back and get it later. The whole thing was kinda dumb when you set down and thought about it. Even if she'd caught them boys talking about killing animals on the tape, it probably wouldn't have amounted to a hill of beans since them SPCA people didn't want to do anything about it. She sniffed disgustedly, watching the friendly priest come to the door of the clinic and look out, puffing smoke.

She folded the last four squares of the chocolate together and deposited it daintily in her mouth, wondering about a religion that let its ministers smoke cigars and drink whiskey and the Lord knew what else. She shook her head, started the car, and drove out of the parking lot. Once she was safely into the flow of traffic, she felt around in the handbag for the recorder. She put it on the seat beside her and pushed the rewind button. She counted to fifteen, stopped it, then pushed the button marked "Play."

"Might as well see if the danged thing worked," she said aloud. She was sucking noisily at a bit of chocolate between her teeth when the recorder clicked on and Rocky began talking.

"I think it's time we discussed your father now, Wendy."

"My father? I thought we finished with him yesterday. There just isn't much to tell about my father." She tried for an air of amused indifference, ended on a note of irritability.

Dr. Phillip Burdock shook his head impatiently. "Nonsense, Wendy. You lived in the house with the man for nineteen years of your life. You can't just dispose of that kind of relationship with a few well-chosen words about strictness, parsimony, and taciturnity. During your regression session yesterday, you said there was very little physical intimacy between you and your father. And yet later during the hypnotic segment of the session, there was a spontaneous outburst concerning him. Do you recall it?"

"No." Wendy moved uneasily in the hard wooden chair. She

229

uncrossed her legs and crossed them the other way. Her fingers tightened on the smooth, round arms. "No, I do not."

"You said, 'Don't do that, Daddy! Stop it!' Do you recall now?"

"Oh, that. I was probably protesting a spanking or something."

"Nonsense," the doctor repeated firmly. "A child does not protest mere punishment in that manner, certainly not in that tone of voice. What was happening, Wendy? What was your father doing to you?"

"I don't remember," she said sullenly.

"Of course you remember. You started to relive it yesterday, but you backed away. What was it, Wendy? Bring it out. You won't be free of it until you do. You don't have to tell me. Go back. Remember it. Relive it. Put it where it belongs—in the past."

"I don't remember anything," she said, panic in her voice. Her hands had dropped from the arms of the chair, were laced together and cupped at her groin. Eyes closed tightly, she pressed against the back of the chair, straining, her face slowly suffusing with blood. "I don't remember anything!" she yelled suddenly, eyes snapping wide, then closed again. "I don't," she moaned.

"Yes, you do," Burdock pressed. "Go back and live it, Wendy. If he hurt you, then, fine, feel the pain. But he can't hurt you now. Feel it, Wendy. Feel it and be done with it."

"I can't," she whimpered, arms folded tightly across her bosom, slender legs crossed and clamped together, body coiling protectively around her center.

"Do it," the doctor urged softly, soothingly. "Let it through, live it again, here, now, where you're safe."

"No—no, please, don't make me." Her voice was changing, becoming plaintive, precatory, a childish whine.

"Wendy," Burdock said sternly. "Tell me! Tell me what happened with your father!"

She shook her head wildly, blond hair flying, spilling across her shoulders, covering her face. But she was starting slowly to unwind from the fetal curve, stretching her legs in a taut, resistant bow, hands pushing outward as if warding off an assailant, lips curving in a grinning rictus of rage and dismay.

Her back arched suddenly and she clamped her hands over her pubic area. "Don't, Daddy, please! Daddy, don't! Please don't do that!" Tears streamed from under tightly closed lids, and her body became rigid, a bow, sliding slowly out of the chair to the floor. She curled on her side, hands locked between her thighs. "Stop it!" she screamed, again and again, until her voice was hoarse and ragged. "Don't," she yelled once more, her feet lashing out like a battering ram. Her body convulsed; she shuddered. She slowly curled into a fetal position and began sobbing.

Dr. Burdock sat quietly waiting, a curious mixture of compassion and satisfaction on his face. He held a match to his pipe, his plump cheeks billowing in and out like those of an asthmatic chipmunk.

It had been quiet in the room for some time when Wendy spoke from the floor. "The lousy son of a bitch tried to ball me. It started when I was eight, right after Mama died. I fought him off for two years before Uncle Roger caught him at it. He threatened to kill him if it ever happened again. By the time I was fourteen, I'd convinced myself it had never happened, that it was just a bad dream. But even when I was little, when we used to play . . . he would put his hands on me . . . his fingers in me. I knew it was bad, but I didn't know why. I just knew I couldn't tell Mama. I quit playing with him when I was around six. I wouldn't even kiss him unless I had to." Her voice was a dull monotone, weary and dry. "By the time I was eighteen, I couldn't remember why I didn't like him."

"It's a good beginning, Wendy."

"You mean there's more?" It was a sad attempt at humor.

"A lot more, I think. You tell me."

She lay silently for a moment, one arm across her forehead. "Yes, I guess there is."

"It won't be easy. There'll be a lot of pain. But when it's over, when it's behind you, you'll be free to feel. You won't have to run and hide behind things like headaches."

"Do I have to stay in that monk cell again tonight?"

"I think you should."

She sighed and rolled gracefully to her feet. She ran her fingers through her hair and smiled ruefully. "I really threw a worm fit, didn't I?"

Burdock returned her smile. "I've seen worse."

Wendy grimaced and shook her head. "God help you."

Burdock laughed. "It's not as bad as all that, and it has its compensations."

Wendy glanced at her watch. "What do I do the rest of the day?"

Burdock laughed again. "I don't care what you do until one o'clock, but I want you back in here at that time. You're mine for the rest of the day, and we have a lot of ground to cover." He crossed to the door and stopped. He turned and smiled. "Have a nice lunch."

Chapter Twenty-six

"You look tired," Milly said from across the table. She adjusted the paper in the typewriter she had purloined from the squad room. "Not much sleep last night?" She concentrated on the paper alignment, her head bowed.

Pope studied the top of her head for a moment. He washed his face with his hands. "Not much," he agreed. "I kept expecting the damn phone to ring. And every time it's rung in here today, my stomach's squirted another pint of acid."

"You think he hit somewhere last night?"

"I don't know," Pope said wearily. "It's been two days—well, three, counting today. If he doesn't have some kind of pattern the way we thought, he could hit anytime."

"Or never," she said.

"Yeah, or never. Maybe the son of a bitch got hit by a truck. Fat chance."

"We're down to the last dozen eye doctors in north central Texas."

"Yeah," Pope said morosely. "But I never really expected anything to come out of that. Working back from a prescription is like climbing up a slide with your socks on. Damn near impossible."

He got up and paced up and down beside the long table. "I can't believe this crap. Not one damned bit closer than we were in the beginning. And what we've found out, we haven't been able to

233

use. That last twin seems to have disappeared—" He broke off as two figures who could almost have passed for twins themselves appeared in the doorway. FBI Agent Rickers and his shadow, Agent Smith. Breaking stride with his partner, Agent Rickers came around Pope's side of the table, extending a sheaf of papers in his hand.

"We have your workup from BSU, Sergeant Pope." He handed Pope two of the papers. "And, as Captain Tanner requested, we queried the Justice Department in Washington." He gave Pope the remaining two sheets, hesitated, then said diffidently, "It would seem your Trashman is not a beginner."

"We suspected as much," Pope said, scanning the report from Washington, whistling softly. "Milly, listen to this. Fourteen killings in and around Chicago—couples in each case—all in the years nineteen seventy-one and seventy-two. Ten in Houston and environs—couples again—spread out over the years seventy-seven and seventy-eight. Almost identical M.O. In all cases, semitransparent bags and insertion of objects in anus and—well, just like ours here. Jesus Christ." He turned to the two silently waiting men. "We really appreciate this. Great work. Fast, too." He smiled dryly. "We rarely get this kind of service out of Washington."

Rickers nodded soberly. "Mass murder is all the rage right now. Everybody gets excited. There's so much of it going on around the country that it's finally worked its way to the top. Everybody's gearing up to fight it."

"It's about time," Agent Smith said, speaking for the first time since Pope had met him.

Pope nodded and lit a cigarette. They discussed the Trashman's methods and probable state of mind for a few minutes, Pope successfully hiding his impatience to get to the FBI's profile of the Trashman. He expected no startling revelations, but he was aware that the Behavorial Science Unit had come up with some very ingenious bits of profiling in the past, providing various law enforcement agencies with glove-fit descriptions that included almost everything about the perp except the address and telephone number.

After the two men had gone, Pope sat down again across from Milly. She was poring over the report from Washington, her face pale, lips stretched thin in a dismayed grimace.

"My God, Ham, can you believe all of these people killed by one person?"

Pope lit another cigarette and nodded. "I can believe it. Look at Henry Lucas. He's claiming over two hundred. Our man is small potatoes compared to him."

Milly gave him a quick, hard look, opened her mouth to say something, then closed it and dropped her head over the paper again. Pope watched her for a moment, then grinned and picked up the profile sheets.

The top one was a short cover letter explaining that the profile was not intended primarily as a deep psychological portrait of the perpetrator, but was instead, it was hoped, an insightful interpretation of the facts presented in the crime scene photos, the autopsy report, and accompanying police reports. It went on to issue a mild warning that investigating officers should not accept the psychological profile too literally in conducting their investigation. It was meant only as a guide and not as a blueprint.

Pope picked up the last two sheets and read through them quickly. He put them down again, feeling a sensitive nerve-ending tingling somewhere in his back. He looked up to find Milly watching him intently.

"How's it look?" Milly asked.

Pope took a pen out of his pocket and made a check mark a third of the way down the first sheet. He slid the sheets across the table at Milly.

"Read it from where I marked. The stuff above that don't mean much. Read it aloud, if you don't mind. I'm not sure I absorbed it all the first time." His voice was dry and light, and Milly threw him another quick look before she began reading.

On viewing the exhibits submitted for evaluation, it is immediately apparent that we are dealing here with a well-organized male perpetrator who feels that he is in absolute control at all times, a sadistic personality undoubtedly suffering from a serious psychological disorder.

A preponderance of the evidence points in this direction. He is cunning, a planner, a stalker. He obviously knows his victims to a degree or at least something about them. He comes prepared with his own weapon (the bags) and his symbolic implements (the plungers, spikes, screwdrivers, and the like). To maintain mastery of the situation is all-important to him—hence the taping of the victims. The lack of serious physical maltreatment either before or after death would argue against personal animosity, would suggest random selection, but according to certain criteria. The bite marks, actually minimal in number, would indicate a degree of sadism in the killer's personality. The disembowelment of the Carlson man suggests a growing contempt for the victims.

There are some conflicting and confusing elements, in that both the women and the men were forcibly raped and sodomized in all cases, with semen deposited in copious amounts. This would argue against the one-man theory, as would the bite marks since they are clearly irrational impulsive actions and are not compatible with the calm, methodical image the perpetrator presents in other areas. However, it is quite possible that these were well-planned anomalies to serve the same purpose as the planted hair, to distract and confuse. Psychotics generally like to play games, confound the authorities, thus displaying their own superior intellect. A grandiose delusion, perhaps, but he will believe it most implicitly.

In view of the above analysis and other, more intangible factors such as history and experience, we feel that the following general description may well parallel the vital statistics of your killer.

White mature male between thirty-five and fifty. A friendly, well-mannered man, intelligent, possibly an intellectual with better than average education. More than likely not married—it would be difficult for him to sustain a relationship for very long. Possibly of normal height and weight, he would have to be muscular to a degree. Quiet, nonaggressive, but outgoing, a man who would inspire confidence in others, confidence and trust—witness the apparent ease with which he overcomes and immobilizes his victims.

And last but not least, we believe the ritual of the plungers, spikes, knives, etc., is role-playing, a projection of some love-hate relationship he experienced as a young adult or as a child. Sexual abuse as a child would be a good bet. A childhood background check of any and all suspects would be indicated.

Milly ceased reading and Pope clicked his tongue in a sound somewhere between humor and derision. "That would fit my twins, I guess."

"Twins?" Milly raised her head.

"Yeah, the Hamner twins—only now we find out there's probably only one of them left, and his name isn't Hamner. If that old man knew what he was talking about and was telling the truth."

"What kind of twins?"

"Twins, twins! How many kinds are there?" He got up and began pacing again.

"I mean, how old?"

"Forty-one, maybe forty-two."

Milly's head dropped back over her typewriter. "Oh."

Pope stopped and looked down at her. "What's that 'oh' supposed to mean?"

Milly shrugged. "It's just that I know some twins."

Pope waved his hand. "Don't we all. How old?"

"Twenty, probably. Maybe even nineteen. Young."

Pope was no longer listening. "There is a way we can find out if the old man was telling the truth. We can dig up the overflow tank from the windmill on the old Hamner place. That is, if it's still there and if there's only one or two of them."

"Sounds like a pretty big job."

Pope shook his head. "No, they're usually small. A few yards across. A backhoe could do it in a couple of hours or less."

"Sounds expensive. You know what our budget's like since Reaganomics."

"Hack Wind's got a deputy buddy down there. Maybe he can con him into doing it for us. Solve a thirty-five-year-old murder and all that good stuff. It just might work."

Milly threw him a cynical glance. "You're tricky, Pope, really tricky. Remember what happened to Tricky Dick Nixon."

"Uh-huh," he said absently. He turned and headed out of the room, then leaped to one side to avoid colliding with a panting, red-faced Maybelle Norman hurtling through the door, her bulky, ancient body in the last stages of collapse.

"This . . . this . . ." Maybelle stammered, thrusting something into Pope's hands. She dropped into a chair and grabbed her heaving sides. "Play . . ." she gasped.

Pope's gaze dropped from her face to the small rectangular object in his hands. A tape recorder, roughly the size of two packs of cigarettes end to end.

"What is it?" Milly stood up and looked at Maybelle with concern.

"My God, Maybelle, you look sick," Milly said.

Maybelle made pushing motions with her plump hands. "Play," she implored. "It's them . . . it's them little sons of bitches . . . them twins!"

Milly and Pope exchanged glances. Pope placed the recorder on the table and pressed the play button. The recorder clicked, shrilled loudly with the sound of a car motor firing, racing, fading to a hum; the sound of a horn, a raucous laugh, a low wolf whistle; finally a voice:

"How far out do they live?" The voice had a tinny, mechanical sound, the result of poor reproduction by the walnut-sized amplifier. The faint hum of a car motor could be heard in the background, the occasional sound of a faraway horn.

"Not far. Half mile or so outside the city limits." The second voice was almost identical to the first, a shade deeper, more resonant.

"What's their house number?"

"They don't have one, they're on a route number. But don't worry about that, I followed her home. Just look for a small white house back off the road forty or fifty yards. A white rock circular driveway with some kind of rock flower garden in front of the house. Oh, yeah, and a small windmill."

"Sounds cute. What do they look like?"

"Young, mid-twenties, good-looking. She reminds me of the Red Witch a little, only prettier. He's pretty enough to be a girl almost." He cleared his throat and laughed softly. "Don't worry, Rocky, I think you'll like him. He's got nice tight buns."

"Man, I'm ready right now," Rocky said, and hooted with laughter.

"So am I, brother, but one more day won't make much difference. Give us a chance to anticipate a little bit, decide exactly what we want to do this time. Besides, we have to do them together, and they won't be available until tomorrow night."

"Shit, man, I don't need—" The rest was lost in the sudden

239

blare of rock music. Someone cursed and the music shut off just as suddenly.

"Hey, Duke, come on, man, I like that."

"You remember our deal," Duke said firmly. "You won't torment me with your damn rock music, and I won't bitch about you smoking. Anyhow, we're almost there. Watch for a white rock lane bordered with big pecan trees. Look for a big two-story house with green shutters. It's just a little way past that."

"Aren't you afraid this is a little too close to him, Duke? I know you think the police are stupid, but this might focus attention on him. After all, she's—"

"Forget it, Rock. I made the choice for a reason."

"What reason, Duke? Because she looks like the Red Witch? Are you gonna do her the same way?"

"Don't worry about it, dammit! I do the planning, remember? Just like I've always done. And don't even think about him. He wouldn't piss in our mouths if our guts were on fire. He's been trying to dump us ever since Oldfield—well, since that time in Fort Worth, anyhow."

"I know that, Duke, but if he gets in—"

The sound ceased abruptly. Pope leaned over the recorder. The tiny spindles weren't moving. He looked at Maybelle inquiringly.

She spread plump hands. "It's the end of the tape, I guess. I only had part of a reel. I taped my little niece singing—"

"Shit!" Pope said. He pushed the rewind button.

"What do you think, Ham?" Maybelle asked anxiously. "Ain't it them?"

Pope leaned back slowly, the skin on his face taut, prickling. "Where in hell did you get this, Maybelle?" His eyes were narrowed to tiny slits, icy beams of light spearing from under the lids.

"Why—why them twin boys." She looked to Milly for aid. "You know, them boys at that animal clinic."

240

"The Free Animal Clinic," Milly said mechanically, her eyes growing, groping for understanding. "They're the twins I was talking about, Ham. They—"

"Twenty years old? It can't be, goddammit!"

"You heard them," Maybelle said. "You heard them, what they are planning."

"Where'd you have the tape planted?"

"In that gray van of theirs. Under the driver's seat."

"Why?"

"Well, it wasn't about this—I had no idea. . . . I followed them the other day when they went into the woods in that van. They dumped a bunch of kittens and little dogs they had wrung the necks of—"

"But why did you plant the recorder, Maybelle?"

"I thought if I could get something, them talking maybe about killing them animals, I'd take it to the SPCA and make them do something, take them out there and show them . . ."

"How long was it in there?"

"I planted it yesterday. Just overnight, is all. I got it back a little while ago. I almost got caught."

"Then it's tonight, Ham!" Milly's face was ashen. "They're going to hit again tonight."

"Not necessarily," Pope said gruffly. "Maybe they made the trip this morning. That'd make it tomorrow night. Let's run it again, see if we can figure something out."

They were halfway through the tape when Roscoe Tanner came in. Rather than explain, Pope rewound it and ran it through again.

When it was over, there was a moment of dead silence. Tanner stared at Pope, dumbfounded, his mouth gaping in a silly half-grin, half-grimace, big hands curling into freckled fists, eyes shining.

"Jesus H. Christ! Is that what I think it is?"

Pope ignored him, his square face remote, and Maybelle and Milly rushed to fill Tanner in. While they talked, Pope's mind raced frantically, belated shock reaction bringing a surging rush of adrenaline; he felt feverish, incandescent, unable to fit this new information into the vague crazy-quilt mosaic he had been trying to assemble over the past ten days. He put his head in his hands and forced himself to concentrate.

It wouldn't fit. No matter how he twisted and squirmed and rearranged, the Free Animal Clinic twins were square pegs in round holes. If he accepted the premise of the Hamner twins and Oldfield, there was no possible way . . . unless . . . maybe . . .

Maybe what?

Maybe the Oldfield murders had absolutely nothing to do with the current murders.

Maybe Hack had been right. Maybe the killers had read about the Hamner killings and had been so enthralled with their mystical cosmic implications that they had decided to make the Hamner twins' methods their own. Who the hell knew when you were dealing with fruitcakes?

Or, maybe it was possible that a man could hate so much that he could bring up two young boys to carry on his tradition of cold-blooded murder. That could account for the young twins, explain the "he" they referred to. Their father? An uncle? Another brother?

But what about the old man's accusation against his grandson Kerry? Delusion? A dying old man's idea of retribution for a thoughtless grandson's neglect? Not so, Pope thought. The underlying theme of the old man's last words had been sorrow, not vengeance. His head whirling, he broke into the animated conversation going on around him.

"Milly! The twins at the animal clinic, what were their full names?"

Milly jumped at the harshness in his voice. "I—I don't know, Ham. It—it was such a routine . . ." Her voice trailed away, her face scarlet.

242

"They was stunning boys," Maybelle said, as if that excused the dereliction.

"I say we pick the little sons of bitches up," Roscoe thundered. He slammed a beefy fist on the table. "And I mean right now!"

Pope ignored him. He picked up the phone and dialed information. He asked for and received a number, and dialed again.

"Animal Clinic." It was a young voice, vigorous, vibrant.

"Who's speaking, please?"

"This is Rocky."

"Rocky? Rocky McNutt from TCU?"

"No, sir, my name is Burdock. Rocky Burdock."

"I'm sorry," Pope said slowly. "I have the wrong Rocky—oh, wait. Would your father be Dr. Phillip Burdock, by any chance?"

"Yes, sir. He's my dad."

"Thank you." Pope broke the connection and dialed an inside number immediately.

"Sally? Ham Pope. Look, I want everything you can find on Dr. Phillip Burdock. And that means everything. Go to Washington. We've been cleared for priority service by the FBI. I want to know where he was born, raised, service record if any, the whole damn bit. Okay. We needed it yesterday, Sally. Right. Feed it to me at 654 as it comes in. B-u-r-d-o-c-k, just like it sounds. Go!"

"Well," Roscoe said truculently, "are we gonna pick them up or not?"

"I say no," Ham said. "At least, not for a while. Let's get some people over there and keep that van under surveillance. If it moves, we move. Not until. I want to find out about these kids and their father first."

"What for?" Roscoe glared at him. "You heard the damned tape."

"Yeah, I did, Roscoe. But I don't think you did. Who was the *he* they were referring to? If these two kids are involved in this, then there's bound to be someone else." He shook his head slowly. "That kid Rocky didn't sound like either of the voices on the tape."

"It was their van. Voices always sound different on them little recorders."

Pope stared at him, smiling faintly.

"I want—" Tanner began, but Pope quickly cut him off.

"Milly, I saw Sheldon outside. Pick up him and two others —take those kids from the FBI if there's nobody else—and get over there. Two cars. Don't let that van out of your sight." Ham winked at her behind Tanner's back. "Come on, let's move it!"

"I'm going, too." Maybelle Norman grabbed her bag and waddled after Milly.

"Hey," Tanner yelled. "You can't—"

"Let her go, Roscoe," Pope interrupted him again. "She deserves a little of the action. She brought us the tape."

"Dammit, she's a civilian!"

"She's a rent-a-cop. There's a difference. Besides, we have orders to cooperate, remember?"

"It's your ass, buddy, if she gets hers shot off or something," Tanner said grimly. He looked at his watch. "You get one hour. Then I'm picking them little bastards up. We got to get us some movement in this case, a little visible action."

"Right or wrong, eh, Roscoe?"

"Two suspects in hand is two better than we had an hour ago."

"So we blow the whole damn case by moving too fast. If those two kids are doing this, Roscoe, there's a guiding hand somewhere behind them. And it goes back to the Hamner killings. It makes no sense any other way. And the nicknames Rocky and Duke. I suppose it's just a coincidence that the Hamner twins were called Rocky and Duke, too."

"Could be," Tanner said stolidly. "Must be thousands of kids across the country call themselves Rocky and Duke. They're macho gang names, like."

"Bullshit! This is Merriweather, not New York. We don't have gangs."

"Hell, Ham, I'm not arguing with you. I just want to arrest somebody, goddammit!"

Pope laughed and got to his feet. "I'm going down and goose Sally a bit. Coming?"

"Naw. I'm gonna round up some troops and put them on standby. In exactly fifty-six minutes, I'm gonna arrest me some killers. You coming, or not?"

Pope walked out without answering. Tanner watched him leave, then slammed an open hand on the table, muttered something obscene and disrespectful under his breath, and got up and followed him.

Chapter Twenty-seven

~~~~~~~~~~~~

"No local priors." Sally Minelli fingered the fuzz on her upper lip. "I went to the AMA for his medical background. He attended medical school at Indiana University at Bloomington, interned in Houston, graduate school in Houston, and practiced there for three years with a Dr. James Webster."

"When did they come here?"

"About six years ago."

"Any reason for the change?"

She shrugged burly shoulders. "None listed. Change of scenery, I suppose."

"No word from Washington?"

"Not yet. Want me to send a follow-up?"

Pope shook his head. "No time. My hour's up. If I know Tanner, he's on his way. If you don't hear anything in another thirty minutes, you might jog them a little. Remind them they promised us premium service."

"You got it, Sarge." She showed him a set of small, even teeth.

That little moustache don't look half bad, he thought as he climbed the stairs to wait for Tanner. If she'd just lose about thirty pounds and get that little wart taken off her chin.

Pope took no part in the interrogation of the Burdock twins. They were brought in through the back entrance and hustled into separate interrogation rooms. Forbes and Sheldon drew Rocky, and Tanner and Stevens and Milly were in the room with Duke. Pope drifted in behind them and leaned against the wall.

"All right, Duke. First of all, what's your full name?"

"Connie Albert Burdock."

"And your father is Dr. Phillip Burdock? Is that right?"

"Yes, sir. And I'd like to call him." He looked past Tanner at Milly, and turned on a dazzling, appealing smile.

"We're attempting to do that right now, Duke. What do you say you answer a few questions while we're getting your father for you? That be okay?" Tanner sat down across the table from the muscular young man, his broad face damp and flushed, eyes bright with excitement.

"Questions about what? I don't even know what I'm doing here."

"Just some questions. You'll understand as we go along. Okay?"

"Yeah, I guess so." He stood up abruptly, shrugged out of a lightweight yellow nylon windbreaker, hanging it neatly on his chair, then checking casually the fit of T-shirt and denims, muscles rippling.

"November twenty-seventh, Duke. Think you might tell us where you and your brother were that night?"

"November . . . that was the day after Thanksgiving?"

"Right. Where were you and Rocky that night, Duke?"

"Lessee. . . . Yeah, we went to a movie . . . then we stopped at McDonald's for a burger . . . then we went home. Yeah."

"What movie, Duke?"

"Aw, it was one of them movies down at the Airport Mall. I forget what they're called."

"What movie did you see, Duke?"

"Lessee. . . . Clint Eastwood—no, no, it wasn't him. It was that other one, the one who died . . . Steve McQueen, yeah, that's him. He was playing in something about . . . hunting. Yeah, *The Hunter*. That's the one, *The Hunter*." He looked at

Milly again and smiled, bringing his hands together on the table, clenching, sending shock waves of rippling muscles across his chest, pecs contracting and expanding like wild creatures beneath the thin cloth of the T-shirt.

"What time did you get home?"

"Midnight . . . somewhere around there."

"And you stayed home the rest of the night?"

"Sure. Where else would we go?"

"What vehicle did you take to the movie?"

"What vehicle? Why, our car, of course. We only got one vehicle. Me and Rocky's got a Chevy Camaro between us."

"You ever take the gray van? Like maybe when your car's not running, or something?"

"Hasn't happened yet. We—me and Rocky—take good care of our car."

"Okay, Duke, let's go to December first. That's a Tuesday. Where were you and Rocky on the first of December?"

"If it was a Tuesday, that's easy. We go to class at TCJC until ten o'clock and Dad makes us be home by eleven. So that's where we were."

"You went home then after school and didn't go out again?"

"Yeah, if it was a Tuesday. We go three nights a week. Monday, Tuesday, and Thursday."

"All right, Duke. Let's try December fifth. That would be on a Saturday. The Saturday a week or so after Thanksgiving. Tell us about that." Tanner's voice had taken on a faint note of desperation, a fine sheen of sweat glistening on his wide upper lip.

"Let me think. . . . Saturday night? Okay, Saturday night. . . . Yeah, we were at a party."

"Until what time?"

"All night."

"An all-night party? That musta been some party, Duke. Where do you go to a party like that?"

"Mr. Briggs's house—you know Mr. Jeeter Briggs, the city councilman?"

"Mr. Jeeter Briggs, the councilman, huh? I've known Jeeter quite a spell, Duke. I've never known him to throw an all-night party before." Tanner leaned forward, voice deepening, resonant, a revival of hope in gleaming eyes. "Tell me about the party, Duke."

"Oh, the party didn't go on all night. It broke up about midnight. Me and Rocky just stayed all night at that little ranch he has out of town a ways, out toward Weatherford."

"And Jeeter Briggs was there?"

"Sure he was there. It was his party. A birthday party for his daughter, Clarisse."

"Any particular reason why you stayed all night?"

"Sure. Our car battery was down and it was raining, and I don't think he wanted to get out to give us a jump start. So he asked us to stay the night. And we did."

Milly picked up her notebook and quietly left the room.

"And Monday, December seventh? I suppose you went to school and straight home?" Tanner's voice had gone as flat as a racing slick, deep-set eyes harried.

"Yes, sir. Daddy won't let us mess around with dates and stuff during the week. We have to get up to go to work, you know."

Tanner stalked around the table toward Pope. "Why don't you ask him some questions, Ham?" His face was flushed and the sheen of perspiration had worked its way upward to his broad brow.

Pope shrugged and pushed away from the wall. He gave Tanner a thin, dry smile. "Damn, Roscoe, I can't think of a thing you missed." He turned and followed Milly out the door.

An hour later, Milly came into the conference room and sat down across from him. There was a silly, lopsided grin on her face. She waited until she had a cigarette going.

"It all checks, Ham. Every damn bit of it. They go to school Monday, Tuesday, and Thursday. They haven't missed a day this year. They did go to Councilman Briggs's party. I talked to him personally. It happened just the way Duke said it happened. The only thing I haven't checked is whether they were home those other nights. I wasn't sure if you wanted me to bring their mother into it right now." She flipped a page. "I checked the Airport Theatre. *The Hunter* was playing there on the Friday after Thanksgiving."

Pope nodded. "Saturday night was the Jacksons'. If they didn't do that one, then there's no reason to think they did the others. I was having a hard time with it all along, Milly. The only thing that would have made sense with them as the killers was if the surviving Hamner twin had somehow got hold of them and trained them to do his killing for him. Maybe he was even their daddy, I thought." He stopped and shoved a sheet of paper across to her, smiling tiredly. "But Dr. Burdock was born in Chicago, Illinois, forty-two years ago. He went all the way through school there, went on to medical school in Indiana."

"Jesus," Milly sighed. She slumped in her chair and cupped her chin in both hands. "Back to square one."

"Maybe not," Ham said. "We still have three or four ophthalmologists to check out. And we know they're planning on striking tonight or tomorrow night, and approximately where."

"What good is that? Do you know how many houses are just outside the city limits? There must be hundreds, maybe thousands."

"Not with windmills and circular driveways."

"There must be at least a few, and until we locate them, they're all in danger."

"We'll just have to warn them," Pope said. "If I have to go on the damn TV every hour on the hour."

She nodded thoughtfully. "That might do it. It certainly wouldn't hurt."

"If it comes to that, let's hope the bastards don't watch TV."

"We can beef up the patrols in those areas, get the county to do the same."

"We'll put everyone we have into cars, saturate the outlying areas. In the meantime, get out a call, see if any of the beat people can make that description. Even if it's out of town, somebody must have seen it at some time or other."

"The gray van, Ham. There's no doubt that they have access to it. That's something we need to check."

He nodded. "I already have. It's registered to the Free Animal Clinic. We'll need to get access information from the Burdock boys before we cut them loose." He pushed away from the table. "I may as well do that right now." He stopped in the doorway. "One thing you can do, Milly. Check with the Kellers, see if maybe Emily had a pet of some kind she got rid of. The others, too, except the Jacksons. We already know about them. Maybe that's the common denominator we've been looking for."

"I understand what you mean, Ham, but if the boys and Dr. Burdock are out of it, what—"

His crooked smile cut her off. "Did it ever occur to you that his name might not be Burdock?" The smile escalated into a grin at her expression. He turned and disappeared from the doorway.

"Daddy owns the building," Duke said. "He puts up the money to run it, along with four or five other people."

"Do you know their names?"

"Well, there's Dr. Webster, Daddy's partner. Mr. Lyle, who owns the wrecking yard next door. Mr. Slisz, who owns the lumberyard, and . . . let's see . . . Father Mumford, the priest at our church. I think there's maybe one or two more who contribute, but I don't remember their names right off."

"Who has keys to the gray van, Duke?"

"Us—me and Rocky. Daddy. That's all, as far as I know. Dr.

Webster has used it a couple of times to move some things, and so has Father Mumford, but I don't think they have keys."

"Does it stay at the clinic all the time? I mean, does it sit out there at night?"

"Yes. We used to take it home every night until gas got so high. We don't have anyplace else to leave it."

"You're not afraid of having it stolen?"

He shrugged. "We talked about that. We keep it locked up good, and Daddy says we have good insurance." He gave Pope an appealing "what the hell" smile.

"Then conceivably anyone could use it if they had a key?"

"Sure, I guess so."

"You've never noticed it being moved, gas level lower than you thought, more miles than you remembered on the odometer? In other words, have you ever had reason to believe someone was using it other than yourselves?"

"No, sir. I never have, at least."

"Where did you and Rocky get your nicknames?"

Duke looked startled. "Nicknames?"

"Yes. Duke and Rocky. Your names are Connie and Ronnie, right?"

"Oh, sure, yeah. We used to have fights, me particularly 'cause my name's Connie. You know, like a girl's name. I don't know. We've had them a long time. I came home with a bloody nose one day, and I remember Dad and Dr. Webster and some other men who were there playing cards saying we ought to have nicknames, that no guy should have to have a girl's name. They started suggesting names, and we picked Duke and Rocky. We made the kids at school call us that or we'd pound the shit out of them." He grinned cheerfully. "After Duke Wayne and Rocky Marciano maybe, huh?"

Pope studied the boy's chiseled features a moment longer. Then he got up and walked to the door. "I'll have someone run you boys back to the clinic. We appreciate your cooperation."

"Uh . . . Detective," Duke said. He wet his lips, his eyes shining. "Did you all really think me and Rocky's been killing them folks?"

Pope turned back to face him. "Whatever gave you that idea, Duke?"

He grinned. "All them dates you were asking about. That's when them people were killed, wasn't it? We may be a little slow, Mr. Detective, but we ain't stupid."

Pope answered the boy's grin with one of his own, cold and hard, without mirth. "Just don't be killing any more cats and dogs, Duke," he said softly. "Are you fast enough to understand that?" He walked away, suddenly realizing he didn't much like Milly's gorgeous twins.

Chapter Twenty-eight

"I hear you've been having a little excitement around here." Hack Wind pushed his hat back on his head and grinned. "Wish I'd come in this morning."

"You didn't miss anything important. How're you feeling?"

"Good. Headache's gone. Ribs are still a little sore. Still got my body all taped up, but I don't reckon it'll hurt the running of it none."

Pope sat down just as Milly Singer came through the conference room door at a mild lope. She was waving a slip of paper.

"You hit it, Ham! Every one of them, every last one of them except Emily Keller, turned in an animal to the Free Animal Clinic within the past two months." She flopped down beside him, breathing hard.

"Well, I'll be damned," Pope said. He rocked back in the chair, blinking slowly, his mind racing. A stab in the dark, a piece of make-work for Milly, and she had come up with a common denominator, the link between the victims they'd been hoping for. And it took them right back to those goddamned yellow-haired twins again—but that couldn't be! Milly had checked their alibis, cleared them. Nobody can be in two places at once. Could they? Of course they couldn't. The Free Animal Clinic was a link, all right, but a link in another chain entirely. All he had to do was find one end of it and pull.

He stared down at the list of names Duke had given him.

Dr. Phillip Burdock? Definitely linked with the clinic. Ostensibly cleared by Sally's background check . . . but people had been known to adopt other peoples' identities before. Particularly the identity of someone who had died at an early age. Check. Also check the good doctor's whereabouts on the nights of the murders. He made a notation beside the name.

Dr. James Webster? Also a link with the clinic, possible access to the van. Approximately the right age—but wait . . . Webster had given them their first clue to the Hamner link in Oldfield! And he had also been at the therapy session on the night of Keller's death. So had Dr. Burdock, for that matter. He snorted with disgust and went on to the remaining names on the list. Kyle, Slisz, and Father Mumford.

Kyle and Slisz were unknown quantities. Father Mumford? What did he know about Father Mumford? A contributor to the Free Animal Clinic, and a patient at Webster and Burdock's therapy clinic. About the right age and . . . what else? He had known Emily Keller, had possible access to the van, and had spent time in Chicago. What else? Nothing. Not enough, not nearly enough.

He picked up the phone and called Sally Minelli. He gave her the names of Kyle and Slisz and the information he had on Father Mumford. He hung up and lit a cigarette.

He stared at the wall behind Milly and Hack, who sat watching him silently, raptly, as if he had promised some amazing feat of legerdemain.

He closed his eyes and wearily retreated, forcing concentration through sheer strength of will, bringing a measure of order to the jumbled thoughts streaming chaotically through his mind.

Oldfield, Texas, and the Hamner murders. The Hamner twins —no, not Hamner—the John Doe twins, whatever.

Was there a direct connection to the Merriweather killings, other than as a blueprint for murder?

Yes, if the old man's last scribblings about his grandson Kerry could be believed.

Yes, if Maybelle's tape could be believed: Duke and Rocky discussing the planned atrocity.

On the other hand, the grandfather had said one of the twins was dead. Perry, nicknamed Duke, dead and buried in a windmill overflow tank in Oldfield.

So, who was the other man on Maybelle's tape?

And what about the Free Animal Clinic twins nicknamed Duke and Rocky? Coincidence?

Another thought struck him, and he stiffened. What if the tape was a phony? A gigantic hoax perpetrated by the Burdock twins as a ghoulish joke on Maybelle Norman? Maybe they had seen her plant the recorder and decided to have some fun. . . .

"No!" he muttered. He shook his head vehemently, oblivious to the two who watched him with astonishment. No, that didn't make any sense, either. There had been a chilling realism coming through in the voices on the tape, an unfeignable indifference at taking human life. And in addition, the lab's comparison of Maybelle's tape with the twins's interrogation tapes had proven negative.

He wrinkled his brow and ran what he could remember of Maybelle's tape through his mind again; something had bothered him from the first, something that had nothing to do with the content of the dialogue. What?

"Run the tape again, Milly."

"What?"

"Get Maybelle's tape back from the lab and run it again, please." He heard her chair scrape the floor and the quick patter of her shoes. He kept his eyes closed, hands pressed against the sides of his head. He lit a cigarette, and when she came back, he listened to it all the way through, motioned for her to run it again.

Halfway through the second run, he understood what it was and began listening to the words again, a tingling sensation tickling the back of his neck, his mouth suddenly dry.

He opened his eyes and met Milly's. "The voices. They're the same," he said hoarsely.

"They sound different to me," Hack said. "They're a lot alike, but wouldn't twins sound a lot alike, anyway?"

"I don't mean that," Pope said woodenly. "I'm talking about the volume."

"The volume?" Milly's brow creased. "I don't understand."

"The volume should be different," Pope said, a dreamy quality in his voice.

He knew why it wasn't. He knew it, but he had to force himself to believe it.

Pope closed his eyes again. He felt a faint shiver as images began to form; kaleidoscopic flashes of dim rooms and mutilated bodies, of ghastly grins and bulging eyes . . . another room, a slender compact figure . . . a newspaper . . . contact lens . . .

He got up and went to the phone and called Sally Minelli again. He talked in a muttering undertone that Milly and Hack strained in vain to hear.

He came back to the table and lit a cigarette. He began playing the tape again. He shook his head irritably at Hack and Milly's invitation to go have a sandwich and coffee with them. He sat staring at the wall. When they came back an hour later, he was playing the tape again and the phone was ringing.

They watched silently while he answered it.

He came back and sat down. Hack and Milly stared at him expectantly.

"That was Sally," he said, and played the tape through one more time.

He lit another cigarette and sucked smoke deep into his lungs, eyes lidded.

When, where, why, how, and who? You have to know them all, he thought.

How? We've always known that.

257

Why? We've known that for a while, too, only we didn't really believe it.

Who? We thought we knew that, also. And it turns out we were right all along.

He turned his heavy-lidded eyes to Hack Wind. "Didn't you recognize it?"

"Recognize what?" Hack glanced uneasily at Milly.

"Where's Wendy?" Pope asked gently.

"Wendy? Why, she's . . . Dr. Burdock wanted her to stay again tonight. Why, Ham?"

Pope sighed heavily. "On the tape. That house. They were talking about your house, Hack."

"Oh, my God," Milly breathed.

"My . . . house?" Hack's mouth formed incredulous words of denial, his dark skin gradually adopting the patina of milled steel. "How in hell do you know that?"

"The description: the little windmill, the pecans, the circular driveway, white rock—everything fits."

"There must be other windmills, dammit, other pecans—"

"I'm sure there are," Pope said softly. "But you're the only windmill owner I know whose wife is in the hands of the Trashman."

He watched with compassion as the young man's face crumpled and dissolved, reflecting his battle against rising terror.

And this time, he thought with bitter satisfaction, we know the when and where.

Politics, Maybelle fumed. All a bunch of damned politics! They let them little murdering sons of bitches go because their Daddy's an important man in this little shit of a town. Well, by gum, Maybelle Norman's not gonna let go. I'm gonna stick to them little bastards tighter than dried snot on a moustache.

She stopped at a fast-service grocery store and bought a quart bottle of Pepsi and a six-pack of Hershey candy bars. Thus fortified, she headed straight for the east side of town and the Free Animal Clinic.

She drove south on South Ruskin Street, gunned the little Ford around the last small curve, and straightened with shock. The van was gone, the clinic silent and dark in the gathering twilight.

"Well, I'll be a conservative son of a bitch!" she said explosively, spraying her windshield with a gummy mixture of Pepsi and chocolate.

Hack shook his head doggedly. "You can't ask me to do that, Ham. If it was just me. . . . I won't risk Wendy's life for you or anyone else."

Pope worried one of Roscoe's broken pencils in his fingers. He glanced at Milly, then back to the hard, set face of the deputy. "It's not for me, Hack. It's for the people he'll kill in the future if we don't stop him now."

"Then pick him up," Hack snarled. He slid to a halt across the table from Pope. "And what's this *he* shit? I heard two voices on that tape."

"You read the old man's notebook," Pope said mildly.

"Okay, so one of the twins is dead. So he's got a partner. So what? We don't even know for sure if he *is* the Hamner twin. And it don't matter a damn to me. I'm going down there and get my wife out of there. That's what matters to me."

"I'm not stopping you," Pope said.

"Aw, shit!" Hack threw up his hands and resumed pacing. He stopped again, his features working angrily. "Why in hell are you so sure it's him, anyway?"

"I put some things together," Pope said slowly. "Sally just found out, for instance, that there were fourteen murders in Chicago while he was there—couples, all similar, with some minor differences in some cases. The contact lens. He recently started wearing contact lenses. He was having trouble with them the day you and I were there. I thought it was a hangover or allergy.

259

The last time I saw him, he wore glasses. Why? Because he lost one contact lens at the Carlson murder scene. That's what I almost remembered at your place that day."

"That's it?" Hack towered over the burly detective, his expression incredulous.

Pope sighed and shook his head. "No, that's not all of it. He's the right age to be the surviving Hamner twin. And there's the Free Animal Clinic. He has access to that, access to the van. The clinic is where all the victims were chosen—with the possible exception of Emily Keller. He got her pregnant." He paused and smiled fleetingly. "One of them got her pregnant, anyway. The clinic files had names, addresses, and he picked them carefully according to his own criteria." He stopped and stared moodily at the broken pencil. "I know it's him, Hack. I just can't prove it yet. If we don't catch him moving, we don't catch him at all. After a while, he'll pack up and leave and start all over again somewhere else. He can't stop." His blue eyes sought out Hackmore Wind's. "He's in too much pain—or thinks he is—and that amounts to the same thing. Maybe all that pain stuff is a bunch of bullshit, but he believes it and that makes it real. On the other hand, maybe it is real. He went through a bad time as a kid, according to your man Slocum. He lost his brother to the same kind of sexual abuse he's perpetrating on others. He lost half of himself. I don't suppose anyone but another twin could understand the shock of that. If Slocum was right and he did kill his sister and brother and mother—well, even I can see what that might do to a little boy's mind, and I don't pretend to know anything about psychology." He pushed back from the table, stood up, and walked to the window. "But I know about hatred. I know what that can do. I've been dealing with its aftermath for a long time now." He lit a cigarette and stood looking out at the cold, windy day winding down to brooding penumbral twilight. "I think somewhere inside him, he wants us to stop him. I think he was leaving me a message when he wrote 'pain' on that bathroom mirror."

He watched Hack's reflection in the window as the young deputy paced up and down beside the long table.

"If it isn't him, Hack," he said, "if I'm wrong, then there's nothing to worry about, is there? Wendy's in no danger. If I'm right, and I believe I am, then he must bring her to you. You heard it on the tape. He needs you together." He turned away from the window and walked back to the table. He sat down and washed his face with both thick, muscular hands. He looked up and made eye contact with the younger man again.

"If you're going to be there," he said gently, "then you'd better be going. It'll be dark in a little while."

Hack glared down at him, dark eyes hot and seething. He opened his mouth to speak, then closed it and stalked to the door. He stopped and whirled.

"Ten o'clock, Ham. If he's not there by then, I'm going after her. If he hurts her . . . God help you if you're wrong." He stared at the silent detective for a moment longer, then turned and disappeared, his boot heels rapping sharply in the tiled corridor.

Pope sat silently for a while, aware of Milly's eyes. He reached for a cigarette and discovered his hand was trembling.

"Dammit, I'm right," he said finally, forcibly. "I know I am."

"I hope so," Milly said quietly.

Chapter Twenty-nine

∞∞∞∞∞∞∞∞∞∞

Following the map she'd bought in a drugstore, Maybelle Norman started as near the geographical center of Merriweather as she could get and began working outward in jagged circles. She had been driving for half an hour when she heard the first faint beep while crossing an intersection. She lost it on the other side, and despite the instant cacophony around her, bullied her way back into the intersection and swung left. A mile farther along, she lost it again, and in the middle of the block made a U-turn. She gunned the Ford and went through the corner light on late yellow, nodding with satisfaction as the intermittent beep of the homing device became a steady beat.

Three blocks south she had to make another U-turn maneuver as the sound diminished. She whipped right on McDowell Street. Five blocks west on McDowell she made another adjustment, and turned the corner on Pierre Boulevard in time to see the gray van pull away from the curb. She caught a fleeting glimpse of the van's occupants, enough to know that there were two.

She leaned back and smacked her lips in satisfaction. "Now, you little bastards. Let's see if you get away from Maybelle." She found a Hershey bar in her bag and happily stripped away the paper. She broke the bar in half, again in quarters, and crammed it into her mouth. Then she reached into the bag again and took out the .38.

Ham Pope could say what he wanted to, but she had heard the tape for herself and she had no doubt that she was following the murderers of Peter and Rochelle Jackson. She flipped out the cylinder and examined the loads, then tucked it back into the purse. It never hurt a body to be prepared.

"I'm terribly sorry about the mix-up," he said, glancing sideways at her with his warm, friendly smile. "Administrative errors. They will happen in spite of everything."

"Oh, that's quite all right," Wendy said. "No harm done at all. To be perfectly honest with you, I wasn't looking forward to another night in that room by myself."

"Well, quite possibly we can dispense with isolation in the future. Your progress has been quite remarkable." He eased the van around a pickup loaded with bricks and turned onto Flower Street. The briefcase slipped off the motor cover and landed in Wendy's lap.

"I'm sorry. Here, let me take that."

"No, no, it's fine. I'll just hold it until we get there. I appreciate you bringing me home. I could have called Hack easily enough."

"Not at all. It was our error. It's very little out of my way, at any rate."

"Well, he'll certainly be surprised." She laughed gaily. "And pleased, I hope."

"I'm sure he will. He should be a proud man. You're a very lovely young lady."

"Why, thank you. It's very nice of you to say so."

"Not at all," he said soberly. "That's one of the most critical problems in our society today. We don't tell each other what we think or feel. We're too afraid of ridicule or rejection. So we keep it inside and quietly warp."

Wendy laughed and lit a cigarette. "I like that: 'quietly warp.'"

"Thank you," he said solemnly.

"Jesus, it's cold." Milly wiggled her toes inside her fur-lined boots and shivered. "How much longer?"

"You heard the call. Bert said they were on Flower Street, and that was before we got out of the car. Another couple of minutes probably. I told you I should have brought Forbes or Cal—"

"Why?" she asked indignantly. "Don't you trust me to back you up?"

He chuckled softly. "I trust you. You shoot better than I do. If you don't shoot better than me, we're both in trouble."

"Why do you always give me the cruddy jobs, then? Keep me as far away from the action as you can?"

"I didn't do that with Hector Good, and look what happened."

"So I had to dump his ass, so what?" She shivered again.

He looked at her and grinned. "So you're a damned tough broad. I'm proud of you."

"Because I killed a man?"

"No, because you took it like a—"

"Like a man!"

"No, like a cop."

She raised on tiptoe and peered over the hedge. "Darn, what's keeping them?" She gave him a sidelong glance. "What if there's two of them after all, Ham? What if one of them is in there with Hack right now? He could have been dropped off earlier. . . ."

"Don't say that. Don't even think it. You heard Bert. There's only one man with her in the van." He hesitated a beat. "Only one that he could see, anyhow."

"Yes, but what if he came earlier, parked in those woods behind Hack's—"

"Hush, here they come." Pope crouched behind the hedge as lights swept across the long, sloping yard. "It's them. It's the van." He squatted on his heels and talked quietly into the walkie-talkie, then depressed the antenna and dropped it into his coat pocket. When he straightened he had the gun in his hand, cold and hard against his sweaty palm. His hand trembled with cold, excitement, or fear, he couldn't tell which.

*   *   *

264

"Well, here we are," Wendy said. "Thanks again for the lift." She popped up the latch on her door.

"You're quite welcome." He hesitated. "I wonder if I might trouble you for a glass of water. I'm afraid I've forgotten to take my heart medicine again."

"Of course you can," Wendy said. "No trouble at all." She opened the door and stepped out onto the gravel.

He picked up the briefcase, opened it, and fumbled around inside. "Now, where are those dratted pills? . . . Oh, well, I'll wait until we're inside where there's light." He snapped the case shut and smiled apologetically. "I'm afraid I'm not too well organized tonight."

"We all have those days," Wendy said sympathetically. "I hope Hack doesn't have the house in too much of a mess."

He chuckled. "I understand about that. My wife used to visit her mother in Chicago frequently, and I'm afraid I often heard the word 'pigsty' when she returned."

They reached the porch steps and Wendy tripped lightly up ahead of him. She tried the knob, then rapped smartly on the pane. She glanced at him and grimaced ruefully. "He never locks the door when I'm home." Her tone held a faint note of wifely suspicion.

The door rattled and opened. The porch light and a floodlight on a pole in the yard came on. Hack stepped into view from behind the door, his face curiously strained.

Wendy felt her guest come up behind her and she stepped inside. "Honey, I want you to meet someone." She half-turned toward the man behind her. "This is—"

She felt herself propelled headlong through the air, a sharp pain in the center of her shoulders. Her head snapped backward and she raised her arms frantically to break the impact of her fall.

Automatically Hack leaped to catch her. He realized his mistake as her thrashing arms closed around him, pinioning his own to his body. He watched helplessly as the gun in the smiling man's hand came up to center on his chest.

"I'm Duke," the man said. "We've already met."

Hack wrenched free of Wendy's arms and leaped backward. He felt his heel catch on a footstool, a sharp stab of pain as his ankle twisted. His arms windmilled and he crashed headlong toward the floor.

Like a big cat he twisted in midair, breaking his fall with his left hand. Tucking his left shoulder and rolling, he came to his knees at the end of the couch gripping the .357 that had been tucked in his belt at the small of his back. He froze.

Duke was still smiling. He tightened his grip around Wendy's chest and pressed the gun against her ear. "Put it down, hero. This thing has less than a pound pull. All I have to do is breathe too heavy and the lady has no more headache problems."

Hack's lips peeled back from his teeth. "No way, bastard. You're gonna kill us anyway. This way at least you go, too."

"Put it down, Mr. Wind," Duke said soothingly. "Let's talk it over."

Hack shook his head and tightened his grip on the gun. "*You* put it down, man. This house is surrounded. You got no place to go except down."

As if his words had been a signal, lights flashed across the room as a car turned into the lane. Duke flicked a glance out the open doorway, froze as his eyes came to rest on the stolid figure standing in the illumination cast by the pole light.

"Ah, Mr. Pope."

"Hello, Duke," Pope said. "Or am I talking to Rocky?"

"You got it right the first time, man. But Rocky's here with me. Tell him, Rock."

Even knowing, it was still a shock, and the facial transformation he hadn't counted on at all. He watched the cocky, sardonic face turn to spiteful petulance, drooping lips, and squinted eyes.

"You motherfuckers!" Rocky screamed. "Leave us alone or we'll blow open her head!" The hand with the gun jabbed spitefully at Wendy's ear and she stifled a scream.

"Duke!" Pope spoke sharply.

Duke chuckled, cocked eyebrows and tilted mouth back in place. "Old Rocky scare you a little, did he? He gets a bit nervous at times." He looked back at Hack and edged toward the door. "I'm coming out, Pope. I'm taking her with me. Just like in the movies, man. Only this time the bad guy wins." He wormed Wendy out ahead of him and pressed back against the wall. "Tell hero in there to stay the hell away. We don't much mind dying, man. I think you know that."

"There's no place for you to go, Duke. We know who you are now. We can help you if you'll let us."

Duke laughed. "Help us? I've been to the best there is, man. Not even he could help us. How in hell do you think anyone else can?"

"They got ways, Duke, things they can do now. New things." He moved a step forward, all the old feelings he'd thought he had left behind in Houston flooding through him. He tried to catch the dark sardonic eyes with his blue ones, sought to communicate without words: *I understand you, Kerry. I understand your fear, your overwhelming need to hurt, your desire for vengeance. Goddammit, I understand! Let me help you!*

Duke gazed back at him, a mocking smile curling his lips. "Get out of our way, Sergeant Pope. You can't kill us without killing him—Kerry. You won't do that. He has nothing to do with this." He paused, the smile twisting. "You can't help us, either."

"Let me try," Pope said earnestly, hoarsely, feeling an unwilling kinship with this evil essence of a madman, this distillation of pain and degradation. He felt his own skin crawling with memories of knotted fists and steel-capped boots, of nights spent shivering in anticipatory terror, his mind alive with images of the harrowing pit, fire and brimstone, demons with great red eyes and forked tongues.

"Here," Duke said suddenly. He flicked his left arm, sent the briefcase flying onto the gravel. He changed his grip to Wendy's waist. "Put that in the van for me."

Pope motioned to Milly, his eyes still fixed on Duke's. *Look at me.* He waited until he heard the van door close and Milly's footsteps come up behind him and stop. He started to speak, then stopped to listen again.

More footsteps. He glanced over his shoulder. Maybelle Norman was standing to his left, near the edge of the windmill garden.

"Who's she?" Duke demanded.

"I'm her aunt, young man. What do you think you're doing here?"

"Better go home, old lady."

"Stay out of this, Maybelle," Pope said, breathing deeply, seeking stability. He turned back to Duke. "Look, we don't want to hurt you. What if we put down our guns? Will you . . ." He hesitated, unsure of himself. "Will you let me talk to Kerry?"

"No!" Duke spat. "This is our time! He's got no place in this."

"Why not?" Pope asked reasonably. "He's the—" He broke off again, searching for the right word. "Isn't he the leader . . . the dominant one?"

"Not anymore," Duke said savagely. "I'm as strong as he is now. Pretty soon . . ." He trailed off as Pope walked to Wendy's car and laid his gun on the hood. He motioned for Milly to do the same. She stepped forward, then stopped and shook her head.

"No, Ham. I'm not giving up my gun."

"Do it," Pope commanded coldly. "That's a goddamned order."

She shook her head mutely. Pope snorted and took the gun out of her hand. He laid it beside his and escorted her back to their original position.

"All right, now. Good faith. I want to talk to Kerry." He took a step forward. "Kerry! Kerry, talk to me!"

"No, goddammit!" Duke slid farther along the wall, his face

twisted with fury . . . and something else, something Pope inter-
preted as fear.

"Kerry!" Pope yelled, winging it, playing it by ear. "Are you in
goddamned charge here or not?"

"Stop it!" The face had dissolved into Rocky's, ashen and
contorted, the hand with the gun shaking, the barrel digging into
Wendy's jaw. She gasped and moved her head. He changed
position; he jabbed the gun into her pubic region. "Stop it! Stop,
or I'll blow out her hole! So help me, I'll do it!"

"Rocky, Rocky," Pope said softly, soothingly. "We just want to
talk to Kerry a moment. That's all. Is that so bad?"

"He won't . . . he'll . . . I can't—" He broke off, his teeth
suddenly chattering. "I—I can't. . . . Duke won't like—"

"Hey, man, you're in charge now. Duke's not here. Come on,
Rocky, just for a second. . . ." He saw Hack edging forward just
inside the doorway, but was afraid to make a motion. Jesus H.
Christ, man, not now, he thought desperately. "Come on, Rocky,
just one second. Okay?"

"I don't know . . . maybe . . . a second . . ." He was abruptly
still, his face half-shadowed by Wendy's hair, his features
smoothing slowly, like cold liquid, assuming scope and dimension
that the others had not possessed.

"Kerry?" Pope asked tentatively, his breath hanging in his
throat, his soft voice an invasion into the eerie stillness that
cloaked them all.

"Yes." It was a soft sigh. His arm dropped from Wendy's waist,
raised and hovered fleetingly over her hair, then dropped limply to
his side. He looked at the gun in his hand and grimaced. He tossed
it out onto the rocks of the driveway. "I'm sorry," he told her.

She was gone through the doorway in an instant, wrapped
securely in Hack's long arms. He moved to go around her, but she
clung to him, pressed him back. "No, no," she murmured. "Leave
him to them."

They gazed at each other for a long ten seconds: the killers and the cop who had finally run them to ground. Quiet dark eyes locked with twinkling blue ones, and Milly, watching, wondered vaguely if the relief was all that one-sided.

Pope cleared his throat finally. "I think you'd better come on down now, Dr. Webster."

James Kerry Webster nodded silently, the bright porch light haloing his head, flashing from his bald pate. He spread his hands slowly. "I'm ready, Sergeant Pope. I think I have been for a long time now."

A muttering sound to his left, and Pope whirled to see Maybelle Norman's hand come out of the big straw bag. She spread her stubby legs and held the gun in both hands, steady as stone, random strands of gray hair dangling down puffy cheeks, lips drawn in an unwitting grimace.

"Rochelle Jackson was my granddaughter, you son of a bitch!" The gun thundered.

"My only granddaughter!" she screamed again, and the gun thundered a second time.

Pope's yell was lost in the crashing sound, his leap too late by seconds. He swatted the gun out of her hand and turned to see Webster dancing on his toes, hands pressed against his chest. A graceful pirouette, and he pitched headfirst into the gravel. Pope wondered later if the smile he had seen on the dying face had been from relief or the rictus of approaching death.

"Goddammit!" He touched the neck of the fallen man, felt the last fluttering pulse of life tremble and die. He glared up at Maybelle.

"Cuff her!" he yelled to Milly.

Milly came up to Maybelle and put her arms around the sobbing woman, her own chin beginning a telltale quiver.

"Cuff her, Milly, goddammit!"

"Cuff her yourself!" Milly yelled.

"She just killed a man! You know the damned law as well as I do."

"She killed an animal!" Milly gulped back a sob, her face streaked with angry tears. "A damned, stinking animal, and you know it, Ham Pope!"

"Makes no difference," he said gruffly. "Ain't no way we can explain shooting down an unarmed man." He snapped the cuffs on Maybelle's pudgy wrists. He looked up as tires squealed out on the highway. "Here come the guys," he said placatingly.

"Let her go, Ham." Hack Wind stood on the porch steps looking down at Webster, Wendy nestled under his arm.

"Can't do it, man," Pope said plaintively. "How're we gonna explain this?"

Hack left the steps in a flying leap. He picked up the gun Webster had tossed aside. He stalked to where Maybelle's handbag sat on the grass and fired twice. The heavy bag hardly moved. He wiped the gun on the way to Webster's body. He knelt and pressed the limp fingers around the gun-butt. He dropped it beside the body. He looked up at Hamilton Pope and smiled thinly.

"Easy," he said.

He was still smiling when Milly helped Maybelle into her car, when the rest of the Trashman task force came boiling out of cars to stand admiring their fallen quarry.

Milly scooted across the car seat and looped her arm through Pope's. She stretched and kissed his cheek, then reached across with her free hand and patted him on the chest.

"In spite of what you want everyone to believe, you've got a big heart in there."

"A lot bigger'n my damn brain," he grumbled.

"It's better this way," she said. "We still didn't have much of a case."

He sighed heavily. "Yeah, I guess you're right."

"Poor Maybelle," Milly murmured.

"I wonder why she didn't turn up in the background check of the Jacksons?"

"Like she told us, Ham, Maybelle is a bachelor lady. She gave up Rochelle Jackson's mother for adoption when she was nineteen. She later worked as a nurse at the hospital where the adoption was handled, and she managed to get the people's names. All these years she's been watching her daughter and then her granddaughter grow up. She never married. They were her family. They just didn't know it." She leaned forward and peered at his face. "What I want to know is how you knew we were dealing with multiple personalities?"

He shrugged. "The tape—Maybelle's tape. The voices were exactly the same volume. Since the mike was under the driver's seat, the passenger's voice should have been more indistinct, muffled. It wasn't." He sighed and shook his head, his face morose. "I should have known, or suspected, before that. Webster talked about splits, and so did Burdock. I wasn't listening. I was so certain it was one man trying to make it look like two."

She squeezed his arm again. "Well, you were right."

"Yeah," he said slowly. "More or less."

They rode in silence for a while, Milly's head on his shoulder. She hummed while she lit them each a cigarette. She made a happy, exuberant sound and kissed his cheek.

"We won, Ham."

"No," he said after a while. "We didn't win. Kerry lost."

She shrugged and lifted his arm around her shoulders. She brought his hand up to her breast and cupped it there. "Somebody wins, somebody loses. That's a universal truth."

He cut his twinkling eyes down at her. "There's only one universal truth."

"What's that?"

His hand molded her small breast. "If they're big, they sag."

Chapter Thirty

He was old. In his late seventies, Pope estimated, a lean, almost cadaverous figure with wispy white hair and rimless spectacles. He had a large, straight nose emphasized by sunken cheeks and a convoluted mouth, the quick bright eyes of a squirrel.

"Dr. Severenson." Pope shook the dry, horny palm and resisted an impulse to put out a steadying hand as the old man swayed.

"Sergeant Pope." The sharp eyes flicked over him and away. He chuckled dryly. "You picked a fine time to visit our fair city. Biggest snowfall Chicago's had in thirty years. I'm surprised you found a cab at the airport."

Pope smiled. "I didn't, sir. I hooked a ride with a patrol car part of the way. They passed me on to another, and another, and here I am. Professional courtesy. Being a policeman does have some advantages."

Dr. Severenson bobbed his head perfunctorily. He folded into the swivel chair behind his desk and rested one clawed hand on a manila folder in the center. His fingers drummed idly. "Kerry Hamner. So he was your Merriweather Trashman, was he?"

"Yes, sir. As I explained to you on the phone, we found your name in his effects. His real name, though, was James Kerry Webster."

"Yes, yes," the old man said testily. "I understand that. What was it you wanted to know, Sergeant? What possible difference does it make now that he's dead?"

273

"Not much, sir," Pope said stolidly. "Not officially. It's mostly for me, unresolved questions in my own mind. Even though I saw him with my own eyes, I'm having trouble with this multiple personality thing. Unfortunately, he was killed during the arrest and I can't ask . . ."

"It is essentially an altered ego state brought on by dissociative reaction," Severenson said, his eyes on the ceiling. "In forty-two years of practice, I've only had three cases. Only one with multiple personalities: Kerry Hamner. I was bitterly disappointed when he abruptly terminated his treatment. I've wondered many times what happened to them."

"Them?"

"What? Yes, of course. Them. Three distinctly different personalities occupying the same organism at the same time. A rare occurrence, regardless of what you may read or see in the movies." His fingers touched the file folder lovingly. "An unprecedented opportunity . . ." His voice faded.

"Did Kerry tell you about his childhood, Doctor?"

He nodded slowly. "Yes, of course. And a sad one it was indeed. Unfortunately, such abuse is all too common in our society."

"You know he killed his mother and sister and brother in Oldfield, Texas?"

"I didn't know that until I read the newspaper accounts. He failed to tell me about that during therapy—understandably enough."

"I've done some reading, Doctor, and I understand, or think I do, why a personality splits. I believe I understand about the Rocky character. Did he not create Rocky as a substitute whipping boy during the periods of abuse? Rocky was already his nickname. It seems logical to me. . . ."

"You are essentially correct, Sergeant Pope. Rocky as an alter personality was created precisely for that purpose—to bear the brunt of the elder sister and brother's sadism. Duke, on the other hand, was created out of love and a necessary desire to keep the organism whole. You must understand there was a deep-seated identity crisis at work also. Both Kerry and Perry in all likelihood considered themselves to be one person. I know that Kerry did. Quite possibly due to the manner in which they were treated by the other family members, the singular designation of 'little man,' their apparent interchangeability as the objects of abuse by their brother and sister. At work also was a naturally deep devotion one for the other." He got up and shuffled to the window and stared across the snow-capped rooftops of Chicago. "So when Perry was killed, it was a catastrophe of unbearable proportions to a timid six-year-old. Duke told me he was born at the moment Kerry saw them put Perry into the black water and mud of the pond. Kerry created him intact, his more aggressive nature, his own set of character traits as Kerry remembered them." He came back and sat down. He picked up the folder and touched its ruffled edges with one finger.

Pope cleared his throat harshly and asked the question he had come to ask. "Do you think Kerry knew what was happening, Dr. Severenson?"

Severenson tugged at his nose, bright eyes touching Pope's briefly, then flicking away. He shook his head slowly. "On a conscious level, I don't believe so, not at that point in time. On the subconscious level, he, of course, knew.

"Duke told me that up until their late teens, Kerry was definitely aware that he and Rocky existed. They were all good friends. Kerry allowed them to come out almost at will. Then something happened during their junior year in high school. Something to do with a young girl on a date with Kerry. Duke evidently came out while they were petting and insisted on having anal intercourse with the girl. She resisted. He raped her, sodomized her. I don't know what happened after that. Rocky was telling me the story, and Duke came out and interrupted him, called him a liar

275

—among other things. But from what I gathered during subsequent meetings, Kerry began blocking them out, allowing them out less and less until finally he consciously denied their existence."

"Kerry never mentioned the other two at all?"

Dr. Severenson wagged his head fretfully. "No. Not as they existed at that time. He made vague references to the 'other two' who were always getting in trouble with the older boy and girl, being punished by the mother. They were named Duke and Rocky. Obviously alter-ego personalities created to take the abuse the two small, defenseless boys could no longer tolerate. Duke and Rocky were tough and defiant. They could handle it. The twins could not."

"So when Perry was killed, Kerry already had the Rocky personality? Why would he create Duke?"

"Companionship, I suppose. To replace Perry. Rocky wasn't a particularly lovable sort, and Duke was fashioned more or less in Perry's image with the toughness and resiliency added in. I'm sure it wasn't all that precise and clear-cut, but that is the general idea."

Pope shook his head. "It's confusing. What was he doing during the time he was coming to you?"

Dr. Severenson leaned back in his swivel chair and crossed long skinny legs, bony hands cupped at his concave chest. "All he told me about his current background back then was that he was a last-year medical student. There were killings occurring here in Chicago at that very time. Much like yours in Merriweather. I believe Kerry used Duke and Rocky as cyclic release valves. When the pressure, the tension became too great, he summoned them out of his subconscious and let them run amok. Possibly guided them. They were, after all, an integral part of his id. I talked to them both under hypnosis. Rocky not so much. He was more timid, sullen to a degree. Duke, on the other hand, was a rather cheerful person, carefree, devil-may-care. Certainly more aggressive. There was, of course, no hint of violence." He shrugged hollow shoulders. "Perhaps I should have suspected and moved at a more rapid pace. Perhaps I should have questioned more thoroughly the need for Duke and Rocky. I'm afraid I was too enthralled with the reality of their existence to delve too deeply too fast."

There was nothing Pope could say to that. He busied himself lighting a cigarette.

"I did have a suspicion at that time that Duke was intent on becoming the dominant personality, was in fact slowly moving in that direction." Severenson steepled his fingers and gazed at Pope through the triangle. "Since Kerry tended more toward shyness, timidity, I didn't particularly think that would be such a bad thing if indeed it were possible. Duke was a likable sort."

"A real prince," Pope muttered.

Dr. Severenson cackled dryly. "In cases of irresistible compulsion, Mr. Pope, it's difficult to assign blame."

Pope heaved himself to his feet and buttoned his light topcoat. "It wasn't irresistible compulsion in the Emily Keller killing, Doctor. He—one of them—got her pregnant. One of them tied her up in one of their isolation rooms when she came to the therapy session that night. He tied a bag over her head and left her to suffocate while he carried on his routine upstairs. We finally came across her car in the wrecking yard next door to the animal clinic. Webster's prints were inside the car. He took her out after the therapy session was over and dumped her in a ditch." He took a deep breath. "That wasn't irresistible compulsion. That was premeditated murder with a deeply personal motive. How could Webster not have known about that?"

Severenson's keen eyes scanned the big man's stolid face. His thin lips formed into an austere smile.

"Tell me, Detective Pope, did you come here looking for answers or did you come here looking for absolution?"

"No," Pope said slowly, "I didn't kill him." He crossed the room to the door. "I'll give him this much, Doctor. I think he wanted to be stopped. He gave me the first clue, the first real clue we had. Oldfield and the twins. It eventually led us in the right direction. I've never fully understood why he did that unless he wanted to be caught. And he was Kerry when he died . . . and he was smiling, I think."

Dr. Severenson pursed thin lips. "Of course he wanted to be caught. To be stopped. It's the guilt factor in our nature, Pope. Psychotics most of all. They want to be caught—need to be caught. They have an overwhelming compulsion to explain, to make the world understand why they did what they did, the rationale behind what they perceive to be justifiable behavior."

Pope nodded as if it all made perfect sense. He shook the old man's hand again, thanked him for his time and courtesy, then took his leave.

Outside the snow had stopped, but the wind had picked up, a screaming scimitar that sliced through to his thin southern blood. Thankful that he had had sense enough to wear his boots, he slogged through freezing slush toward the police station a few blocks away. He tucked the inadequate coat around his throat and shivered.

Maybe he's right, he thought glumly, maybe my coming here was a kind of atonement, a search for something beyond the questions I knew the answers to already, an expiation of an indefinable guilt at being part of a society that spawned a Kerry Webster, a society that continually and loudly proclaims that the future of mankind lies with its children, and spends millions in support of their education and nutrition and virtually nothing toward their mental well-being.

He glanced around him at the furred and booted figures scampering through the ice and snow, bent and twisted against the bitter fury of the wind, teary-eyed and miserable.

278

He felt his lips crack when he tried to grin. Absolution? Well, maybe. Why else would anyone in his right mind leave seventy-degree weather in Texas to come to this godforsaken land in the dead of winter?